KNOT QUITE READY

CABRIA SHIFTER FALLS

RUBY SMOKE

To my Fated-Mate.
Julian, you are the very reason that writing a love story comes second-nature to me—you prove to me every damn day that soulmates are real.
You are also that reason writing the smut scenes are...well... you get it. ;-)

To those who are hoping to meet their destined love...I promise you they are out there. Love is real. Love is amazing. & FUCK it is absolutely worth it.

BLURB

When fur, claws, and fate collide, this omega's heart won't be easily tamed...

After escaping her old pack, Aneira discovers Cabria Falls, a Mixed Shifter Community that feels like home.
But just when she's enjoying her newfound peace and hard-earned freedom, a wolf pack snarls into town. And with it? An Alpha who smells like the stuff of nightmares and wet dreams combined. Furrr-ccckkkk.

Casimir is hell-bent on claiming Aneira as his fated Omega, but she's insisting that she's not about to be another notch on the rollercoaster of wolf-fanged destiny. Aneira can fight it all she wants but Casimir will chase her no matter where her paws take her.
Will Aneira resist Casimir's magnetic pull, or will she succumb to her desires and embrace her...reluctant... fate as his mate?

Wolves, and Horses and Bear...Shifters. Oh, My!!!
Welcome to the First Stand-alone Book within Cabria
Shifter Falls Series
...Scratch Your Shifter Itch...

ANEIRA

The heavy bass thrums through my body, in tune with my rapid heartbeat, as I move to the music, letting it wash over me like a wave of pure energy— the beat somehow feeding the emptiness in my soul. As bodies gyrate around me, I let my body sway and twist with the crowd, realizing that for the first time in a few months, I didn't have a single fuck to give. In fact, I feel free, and as my hair bounces around my face, I can feel my grey eyes glow as my wolf agrees with me. With a smile, I mentally thank my best friend, Storm, for dragging me out of my self-created bubble of worry, work, and responsibilities.

I lean over to her, the three inches I got on her 5'3 frame seeming to dwarf her as our bodies bob and weave. "I'm so glad we came here," I yell in her ear, and she throws her head back with a throaty laugh, the dark ringlets of her hair pasted to her face with sweat as her hazel eyes shine with the ever-present joy that was just...Storm. As the tinkle of her laugh floats into the air, one of the guys around us turns towards us, pupils dilating at the sight of her exposed neck. I bite back a growl, careful to keep my wolf under control as I casually, not so casually, observe him. I take a deep breath and pick up the scent of fresh air and feathers. Not wolf, I think gratefully. Although not that I truly expected it, there was no established wolf pack in Cabria Falls, it was part of the appeal.

M y nose twitches bird shifter, Osprey, to be exact. Regardless, his look of *interest* can kick rocks. And as he moved closer, his body somehow grew two inches taller as he readied himself to go in for the kill. I roll my eyes. You know those alpha man displays? The stand-taller, puff out your chest, wet your lips, and try to look intimidating type of displays? Yeah, don't do that. It wasn't sexy and tweety bird over there can fuck all the way off. I stare until his gaze meets mine, and I bare my teeth. He nods in respect, understanding flowing between them, and thankfully, he turns away.

I expel a sigh of relief. Tonight is supposed to be a night off, and I would rather not have to eat a bird. Feathers are a pain in the ass to clean out of your teeth. There aren't a lot of humans in Cabria Falls, or Cabria Shifter Falls as the shifters called it, by typical small-town standards, just a few hundred, but this particular human is my best friend and off-limits. I love it here, though, the comradery between the mixed shifter community, with a few witches thrown in, being the greatest surprise and a much-needed reprieve from where I came from. Still, having a human best friend can make me a tad more protective when we are out. She may know all about me and the community around us, one of the only humans that did, in fact, but knowledge can only protect you so much.

She smiles brightly at me, "I'm glad you came too. You've been a little snarly recently. I mean, I know it's part of the entire ahh-ooo thing you got going on, but sometimes you just need to pull yourself out of your hole and get stuff put in your holes...If you know what I mean." I roll my eyes as she waggles her eyebrows and bumps and grinds into the air.

"I'm serious! Don't you roll those eyes at me, Wolfarella, you can't find your prince charming at work! I mean, take me for example, I go out twice a week with the girls, who have been asking for your ass, by the way. I don't think you're supposed to say no to witches, they hex you and shit," she grins, and I buckle myself in for the ADHD-inspired rant that was coming my way. Being neurodivergent was a fucking superpower, and Storm? Well, she was as powerful as her name implied.

"Witches are terrifying. Thank god they love us. Anyways, like I was saying. Take me, for example. I go out, I have fun. I am always chipper, and this body," she runs her hands down her athletic, yet ridiculously curvy, body clad in a tight dress. "This body gets a workout. Dancing endorphins. You need to find yourself a boy toy, like in all of those romance books, so you can go howl at the moon and share a bone under the stars."

I laugh as she mimics eating a bone, and I shake my head. Storm is the only one who could get away with borderline insulting my wolf. Okay, at this point, she's beyond the border, but there's something about her that exudes 'genuine.' Any feelings a shifter might have about being spoken to in a remotely disrespectful way seem to just melt away.

"I would like to point out that you don't have a boy toy either," I say, and she scoffs.

"I don't need penis energy to ruin my awesomeness. But I am not the one in need here, anyway. And you know it," her gaze narrows as she points at me.

It's not her fault that she can't understand the situation I'm in, as Storm is deliciously human— even though she is a total badass who can bring down a man three times her size and is constantly underestimated by those around her. No, what destroyed my life is something to do with back home and with my old pack. I know that my wolf craved to be mated to her true mate, hell, it was a biological need and drive, especially at the age I am now. But I don't want it.

I sigh internally and shake off the melancholy thoughts while I beat back my internal demons using a bat laced with mental holy water and jagged nails. *Night off, night off,* I chant to myself. That includes a night off from my persistent memories. Even when I keep them chained down tight, they still try to escape. But, Storm is right, I've been indoors for too long with my men, Ben and Jerry, and other than Storm and my employees, human interaction has been at a bare minimum. Tonight I will forget all about the shit of the past and think about the present…hopefully.

"Hey asshole, stop thinking. You're doing that weird squinty face thing you do," she tries to mimic my face, and I scowl at her. I know what she's doing. She's trying to take my mind off the past by antagonizing me, and it's working.

"Fuck off, you Cloudy fuck." My lips curl into a grin as she stops her mocking and gives me a pout, hating being called that —Granted, she had no problem being the mock-er, vs. the mock-y— I've seen what she's done to others who have mocked her name, but because it's me she just flicks her hair back and points to the empty glass in her hand.

"Fuck off, Lady Wolfington." I roll my eyes. See? "Anyways, let's get some more drinks. I need a couple of shots." She doesn't wait for an answer but blazes a trail through all the other partygoers who part like the red sea, completely oblivious to the power she wields in the sassy shake of her hips. For the millionth time in our relationship, I stop to consider if maybe Storm is otherworldly; her strength would indicate yes, and her sheer magnetism is potent enough to make me second guess my wolf senses, but I can't pick up anything other than human. I follow her and take note of the few men that stop in their tracks to gaze at her ass, one even reaches out to grab it, but I intercept him and squeeze his fingers harder than necessary as I bare my teeth, and I hear the grinding of bones even through the din of the club.

"Bitch," he hisses at me while his friend tries to hold in laughter.

If only he knew how much of a bitch I can really be—Ah,

Oo. Internally, I shrug off the insult, men are so unimaginative when getting shut down. I take a breath, and I roll my eyes as I catch the scent of a human. Unlike shifters, most humans have no sense of self-preservation when drinking. At least shifters, for the most part, will back off. Still, I stare him down in silence, watching as his sneer drops right off his face, his most basic senses alerting him to the danger he is in. He falls back with a barely audible gasp, grabbing his friend and taking a step back, retreating. My wolf surges forward at the show of fear, making my eyes glow. He yelps and scrambles away. My wolf growls in satisfaction.

I close my eyes briefly, regaining control and making my wolf pout. *Tough, Agatha, we are supposed to be low-key tonight. It's a night off. Especially when we are close to our heat and even more so in a mixed club, most of the shifters and humans here may know me, but it's summer, the town has a shit-ton more visitors, and we need to be cautious. We don't need to be scented after being free for so long.* Her low growl echoed through my head, discontent at my words as well as her nickname. In my defense, she did act like a grumpy ass old lady most of the time if old ladies were perpetually volatile and horny. Agatha sounded like a good name for that. She gives me one last internal scowl as she settles back down.

I sighed internally, good ol' Agatha is getting more restless, and we are approaching the point of our basic nature over-riding the 'human' part of me. It isn't her fault, even though we are technically the same being, my wolf still needs to be let out and to be perfectly fair, I would be going crazy too if I was locked away in *her*, unable to stretch my legs. However, with the summer months hitting, Cabria Falls was a tourist's dream vacation, with beautiful scenery with a hometown feel. Well, actually, it was the Cumbria Lake District that was the tourist trap, but our little town situated within it reaped the benefits.

Still, all of that meant she can't get out to run as much as we would both like to. Some of the other shifters in our town had the advantage of not looking like a vicious beasts when in their animal forms, however, Agatha is a bit little larger than your standard small wolf that one could overlook. Think Jacob in Twilight or a science experiment that went horribly wrong, regardless, our wolf form is not for the faint of heart.

Then, consider that she, or rather we, are getting closer to the end of the standard mating age in my old pack—our peak time of fertility to breed the strongest wolves. Admittedly, every pack handles this differently. In the Ceartas Pack, that could be anywhere from 16, *fucking gross*, to 26, and after that time, we were lucky if we were allowed to mate. Only families with clout had the ability, or rather permission, to mate after that time, and that was really rare. In effect, older she-wolves are considered spoiled goods, made to work within our village in shops, kept away from social events, and living in a commune rather than in the nicer pack houses, at least those who were sane enough for it anyway.

The outdated beliefs and practices of my old pack not only harmed our wolves, but they often pushed our omegas into depression after years of suppressing their true natures. In some cases, our wolves would even become feral, and omegas would be put down. Despite the knowledge that we could still find mates and have pups after that period, the ingrained mindset left Agatha feeling uneasy. Biologically, she yearned for a mate and the chance to have pups of her own.

According to the pack, wolves have a duty to the moon goddess: to stay hidden and increase their numbers. Crazy, right? Growing our numbers while murdering omegas or preventing them from mating at all. And don't even get me started on the irony of needing growth and secrecy. But, some-how, these two basic principles kept us going as a whole. We managed to survive through wars with other supernatural beings like vampires and witches and even the not-so-magical but equally dangerous humans who just couldn't keep their noses out of our business. But let's be honest, survival isn't the same as thriving. Survival is just getting by, doing the bare minimum to keep our heads above water. And our souls were still taking on water.

Despite how the Alpha had wanted the communes to be some sort of punishment, the 'communes' were not as terrible as they were made to seem, far from it. For the rare few wolves who grew up in one, it was more of a pack within a pack, a true family. I was one of them, my mother having given birth to me at 31 after having run away a few years prior and finding her true mate outside of the "acceptable packs."

What made it worse was that my mother, Esmeralda, was the daughter of the Alpha, and for all intents and purposes, she should have been one of the strongest voices advocating for tradition. Instead, despite punishment, she rebelled against it. Going as far as barging into meetings and demanding they change the breeding age guidelines to allow children to actually *be* children. I smiled at the thought. I heard she was a force to be reckoned with, even as a young omega.

Still, despite her beliefs, or maybe because of those beliefs, the Alpha, her father, still tried to mate her to one of the allied packs when she was only 16. On the eve of the ritual, much to the everlasting embarrassment of the Alpha, my mother chose to run away instead. She survived 15 years in the outside world before she was caught, and they brought her back kicking and screaming. Then much to the distress of the Alpha – who I guess was also my Grandfather, not that I ever called him that– I was born. Despite my mother committing the unthinkable, not only shunning her duty but the Alpha family too, she was allowed to live. However, from the date of her return, instead of living within the Alpha's home or even the other pack homes in the village, she was regulated to communes.

Her homecoming spurred talk within the pack, especially the Omegas because the truth was, it wasn't too clear in the end as to what the punishment was truly for. Was it for running away, or was it for proving that you cannot only breed *and* have a healthy pup after the age of 26 but that an Omega, if given even a modicum of freedom, could also find their true fated mate? Then there was a pack-wide gag order put in place, and that simply served to stir more talk, which resulted in severe punishment. Each doled-out punishment converted the curious to the fearful, and soon, my mother was soon seen in an unfavorable light instead of being a beacon of hope. I'm sure the Alpha and his top advisors regretted their decision to bring her back. Then again, they probably enjoyed the chance to teach Omegas' their place—under their paws.

I like to believe that we still won, as the commune took us in with love and understanding, and I grew up surrounded by more affection than most wolves ever received growing up. That is, until I had no choice but to follow in my mother's footsteps and leave her and my true family behind for my sanity as well as my happiness.

Shaking off my intrusive thoughts, I continue to the bar where Storm has already ordered the drinks. She raises an eyebrow in question, a small smirk on her face. "Get his number?"

It took me a second to realize she meant the human whose hand I almost, probably, crushed. I scoff, "Sure if his number is 911 and his bitch ass can use his fingers enough to dial home for help." Rolling my eyes at her burst of laughter, I reach for one of the drinks in front of me, chugging without bothering to ask what is in it. It didn't matter, my wolf would burn through the alcohol in minutes. There was no 'getting drunk' for a wolf, but fuck me if most days I wouldn't at least settle for a buzz.

"One fucking day, you will have to have a steady guy to fuck senseless instead of your five-minute get-the-heat-edge-off quickies. It will help with whatever you got going on locked deep inside your vault of secrets," she waves her up and down my body, taking a drink at a much more moderate pace than me.

I snort back a laugh, "I don't want anything serious, and steady dick turns into serious dick. Then he will expect me to wash his socks, and I'll have to kill him, and then you'll have to help me hide the body. You'll become an accomplice and will end up in jail. You're too pretty for jail, so in all honesty, I'm looking out for *you*. You're welcome." I sigh dramatically and reach over the bar to signal the bartender for another round of drinks, his attention caught almost immediately as my breasts spill out of my too-small top. *If it works, it works,* I shrug internally.

"Gee, you're such a gem," Storm says dryly.

"Aren't I, though?" I laugh and glance at my watch, cursing the time. We had to open up the bookstore in just a few short hours, and despite living right above the shop, there is still a full day of work ahead of us as we are getting a shipment first thing.

I look regretfully at Storm, who looks like she is ready for another round on the dance floor, "We have to get going, Storm. It's already 2 am."

Instead, she reaches for another drink, chugging it in one go and turning around, to run into the crush of people, screaming, "One more dance!" Scowling, I punch her in the face in my head, and I rush after her knowing damn well it was never just one more dance. I attempt to frown as she seizes my hand and whirls us in a lively spin, yet her infectious grin causes my lips to curve upward involuntarily. I feel my body start to move as the beat picks up, trapping me just as effectively as Storm, and I sigh as I feel my stress and worries melt away again, replaced by a feeling of pure joy and freedom.

Fuck it, I think to myself, *what's a bit longer?* At that, I close my eyes and surrender to the music, and as it moves through me, I move with it, a force of nature that can't be tamed or held back. Because right now? I am free. But…for how long?

CHAPTER 2
ANEIRA

It was 5:30 in the morning when we finally dragged our asses through the front door making enough noise to wake the dead. I had just enough time to peel off my sweaty club outfit, shower, and throw on fresh clothes before making my way back downstairs to open up the shop for the book delivery set for this morning.

I curse Storm, who's passed out on the couch, her long, curly hair framing her face. My body feels like it's made of lead as I stumble through the bookstore, desperately trying to shake off the remnants of last night's non-stop dancing at the club. The pulsating beats that once invigorated me now echo in my head, only amplifying the exhaustion that weighs me down.

We are too old to be going out without proper naps and sustenance. You must eat if we are to breed strong pups.

Although she can't see my reaction, I narrow my eyes, knowing she will get the gist as I respond to the growly, tired voice in my head.

My voice is pitched low, a stark contrast to the vivacious chatter that had filled the club just hours ago. "We are 26 years old, Agatha. And sure," I walk behind the counter, each step feeling like a Herculean effort, and I can't help but notice how my once energetic, shifter limbs now feel like limp noodles. I flick on my expensive coffee maker, the one and only love of my life, and then prop myself against the counter while it gets to work and begins to create the most delectable source of power. A power that transcends species. Transcends the very Veil that separates us from the Gods... Bean soup... okay, coffee. But as much coffee as I have, if I call it soup. It's healthier.

I continue as I feel Aggy Agatha poke me internally for some attention—dramatic ass giant puppy. "Stop nagging me, Grandma! Sure, I could have had myself a rare steak or wild rabbit before going out with Storm. And sure, maybe my sleep cycle needs a little bit of help, but you got out, didn't you? Got a little bit of extra energy out? No longer want to rip out a few throats?"

She huffs in my head. *You can huff and puff all you want, wolf-lady.* She knows I'm right. It's tourist season, a summer holiday, and we are very close to our heat. Grandma Agatha knows damn well if we go gallivanting into the forest to hunt a wild rabbit, even in the dark, even with the witches working over-time for concealment charms, considering the amount of boy scout camping trips in the area, we will attract attention.

I thrum my fingers against the countertop in an attempt to

shake the cloudy sensations in my head. But my eyelids hang heavy, stubbornly resisting every attempt to stay open, and the world around me appears hazy as if seen through a foggy lens. And yet...the coffee machine takes its damn time, Gordan Ramseying these bitch beans. I look at the watch on my wrist and sigh...Delivery would be here any second.

*I have lived several lifetimes...*Agatha starts, but her repetitive speech about the rebirth of her soul throughout time gets cut off...thankfully...as the clock hits six am.

The shrill sound of the doorbell pierces through the book-shop, an assault on my eardrums, and I wince. I give the door a vicious glare before taking a regretful look at the still-brewing coffee I feel my chin tip back, my long ponytail ticking my lower back as I say a quick prayer to the moon goddess that this goes quickly, as I simultaneously wish the delivery men could come back later. But...books. With that thought, I straighten my shoulders and walk around the counter, *away* from my caffeine.

With a low growl, I open the door. "Morning, right on time. As usual." I manage to get out, but instead of my normally sweet, husky voice, the greeting comes out as a combination of a feeble croak and a pterodactyl going into labor.

"Delivery! Sultry Reads with a Dash of Clit-erature and Lust! Here comes the latest supply of literature love potions, bound to make hearts race and cheeks blush! Handle with care, for their enchantment is irresistible!" Jasper, a short, portly man in overalls, cheerfully sing-songs with a chuckle, far too perky at this ungodly time in the morning, looking at his clip-board instead of at my face, luckily missing my pitiful attempt at a welcome.

As I usually do when Jasper makes me deliveries, I quirk my head and take him in, a sweet old man who started the book delivery company with his wife, Kate. But what always hits me over the head is how just how much he reminds me a bit of a sweet Disney character with his small stature, greying bushy beard, and happy demeanor. When I first met him, I instantly took a liking to him, half of me fighting with the urge to want to call him grandpa, the other half wanting to ask him to sing me a Disney song. I held back...barely...

Or... we need to give him a red cloak and chase him through the forest. Humans are gamey, but it gives us something to do.

Internally, I bite my a sigh. Clearly, team-no-sleep-no-meat Agatha has other plans, and I wrestle with her to back down.

You cannot eat our delivery men. You're going to need to take several wolf tranquilizers. What happened to the 'many lives' bull-shit? Shouldn't you have more control at this point? I mean, really, Aggie.

Jasper is still blissfully unaware of the cranky wolf that is desperate for a bite of innocent cherub grandpa while I finally gain control. *I am going to put your furry ass on time out. This is ridiculous.*

The energy it takes to settle her down is due less to the pervasive exhaustion in my very bones and more to the arrival of my heat. My wolf is cranky and volatile on a good day but during my heat? She was downright feral and ridiculously strong. Instincts...*ammiright?*

I force a chuckle at his usual greeting, "Hey, Jasper. thank you. Please put them over there." I gesture to the wall closest to the entrance of the shop. Jasper, the sweet little clipboard cherub, finally looks up, his eyes meeting mine and widening.

"Woah. I mean su...sure..." he sputters, a flush going from his face to his neck before he scrambles back and clears his throat. I bite back a sigh, my eyes must have been slightly glowing, and Jasper isn't privy to shifters. He turns quickly and starts to direct the hulking guys behind him. I prop open the door, letting them do their thing as the scent of freshly brewed coffee teases my nostrils, a cruel reminder of the much-needed rest I was denied. Before stepping back and heading back to the counter, I glance longingly at the plush chairs at the front of the store, envisioning them instead as a plush bed that could cradle my weary body, if only for a moment. But as the sound of cardboard rubbing against the floor reaches my sensitive ears, the reality is harsher, as my duties demand my attention, leaving me no choice but to muster every last ounce of energy and soldier on.

I pour myself a cup of coffee as I lean against the counter, ignoring the lingering looks from the delivery men. The closer to my heat, the more alluring I become, even to humans. I know what they saw, as even under the soft lighting of the store, with no rest under my belt, my bronze skin glows, and my grey eyes are heavy with suggestion. With every movement, my body leaks sensuality, my hips swaying gently even while I simply drink my bean soup.

I drain my cup with a sigh, a little more energy bursting through my veins. I move back around the counter to help, needing them gone. I catch the faintest whiff of candy around the men and wrinkle my nose. One of these men has diabetes, I thought to myself. Our noses were sensitive to human diseases, and since humans were always sick and dying, it made working with and around them all the more difficult.

One of the delivery guy moves around Jasper and hauls a box over towards me, the apple of his cheeks pinkening as I smell a rush of lust coming from him. He pauses briefly, looking me over as the other team members call out box numbers from behind him. With a quick shake of his head and a slight glaze over his eyes, he drops the box where he stands and goes back to the truck. I frown. While I don't mind the looks of appreciation, I do mind that he couldn't at least multi-task. Mental porn and literary porn. Simple.

I take a deep breath and try to avoid snapping, then heave the box off the floor myself because physical activity is better than pre-mediated murder. For a very brief second, I almost forget to pretend to struggle with the weight of the box, and start to huff as I move the box against the wall, so it's out of the way.

I straighten up and wipe my palms over my pants as I hear a delicate cough. I turn as another guy comes in with his own box.

I smile, "Sorry, I was just adjusting it to be out of the way," I say tiredly to him, and I pause to look up at him, eyes roaming over his large arms and tattoos. *Very nice. Human, though. Lame.*

He smiles tightly as he places the box he has down against the wall turning back to glare at the fuckup, "So sorry about that, he's new. Won't happen again." He nods before he heads back to do his job.

My wolf stirs faintly within me, stirred by the sight of his retreating form. *Human,* she growls in mild annoyance before reclining lazily. I can't help but sigh. True, he's human, but in this small town, my options are limited. It wasn't as if I had a buffet...Well, technically... never mind.

Don't get me wrong, when I'm not in heat, some humans can scratch the itch, and then some. But after a brief tryst, they always want more—like my phone number, for example. I don't do that. Besides, Omega females can't mate with human males, anyway, for many reasons. Firstly, we're not genetically compatible to produce offspring. Even if we were, human relationships typically lead to marriage and children, and I can't commit to any of that. I wouldn't. Secondly, my wolf and I would be forced to live a life of perpetual hiding, unable to change when needed and constantly making excuses to disappear when my heat inevitably strikes. During heat, wolves are simultaneously feral and desperate for contact.

Can you picture it? Honey, come fuck me, and when he does, I take a bite out of his throat before his reflexes can catch up. Yeah, No. More laundry. Heat sex can be dangerous to anyone that *wasn't* a wolf. I would eat a human alive. Figuratively speaking. Well, maybe. Thirdly and most importantly? My wolf, as restless as she is, will never settle for anyone that is not her mate. I don't blame her. A true mate was a blessing. But in the case of that particular blessing, call me an atheist.

Sure, I can have a nice romp with other shifters, but there was something about fucking a bunny shifter that turned me all the way off. I mean, silly rabbit, *you* are for dinner…and lunch. Okay, maybe breakfast, too, depending on my mood.

Still, I think to myself, it would be nice to have some pussy pounding consistency…and Storm off my back about a real booty call instead of quick hookups.

I snap out of my thoughts as the last box is brought in, and the tattooed man comes and passes me the clipboard, "just sign here, and we will be on our way," his gruff voice and demeanor perking me up more than I care to admit. I quickly sign the forms, and he takes back the clipboard and hands me a piece of paper with a number on it.

I look at it, and the confusion must be evident on my face because he chuckles. "That's my number. Call me," he winks at me and turns to walk out the door.

"Wait," I call, and glances back at me, "what's your name?"

He looks me up and down and licks his lips, "Call me, and you'll find out when you're screaming my name." He walks out, closing the door behind me, and I'm left standing there, staring at the door holding the paper lamely in my hand. My wolf practically preens at the appreciation, and I admit he played his card well.

I nod appreciatively at his confidence and tuck the paper into my pocket. If he were a wolf, the sheer possibilities would be endless, but he wasn't, and I had to consider that he would be someone who I could potentially run into again while he was delivering my smutty books to the shop.

I move to take another sip of my coffee, but the cup is empty. *Fuck*, I scowl and move to the door, locking it before walking back to pour myself more. But I opt to drink from the coffee pot instead. Convenience. I expressly ignore the vast pile of boxes that are going to take me hours to unpack while I sip, okay chug, my coffee.

I close my eyes for a brief moment in appreciation of the drug that was bean cuisine and drum my fingers on the counter before I take a second to admire the beautiful wood-work under my fingers. This counter was one of my favorite things in the shop, the books non-withstanding. Pure oak and carved directly from the source, not built with small pieces and hundreds of bolts and screws in instructions that not even a fucking vampire could understand with their vast years of bloodsucking shit…and not sparkling. Anyways, it was the one piece in the shop that made me feel at home and centered.

My shop, "Flip My Pages," is a gem, and everything I could have dreamed of, decorated semi-lavishly with plush reading chairs and couches and gorgeous dark wood desks with matching chairs that are placed along a wall of glass that provide a perfect view to the edge of the forest that lines the back of my shop. It is situated perfectly in the town Main Street, and despite the town being nestled within the semi-mountainous area near the Lake District of Cumbria, you would never guess it by the look of the main street.

The town itself, considering I am the only wolf here, is perfect for my need for anonymity, and it provides a place for my wolf to breathe. When I went to view the property, I did so without expectations. But when I discovered that the shop had direct access to the forest and lakes from the back, I jumped at the opportunity to buy it from the retiring owners and started renovating the shop from the ground up. I mean, paired with the above apartment as well as access to the surrounding national park, it was a no-brainer for me. Even more so because although other shifters may be able to settle in a national park comfortably, hence the Cabria Fall Shifter

Community, wolf packs wouldn't be able to for fear of discovery. Everyone jumped at the sight of gigantic wolves, not so much for foxes, lynxes, and the various other shifters that made their home here. And after the other shifter packs made themselves known to me and I explained why I was here, they left me to my own devices, so no one would guess to look for me in Cabria. It is a pretty tight-knit community, and I love it.

I lift my coffee pot for another sip, only to find it drained. "Ugh," I groan, dragging out the sound while I plop the empty pot into the tiny sink behind me. I stretch my arms up high, trying to work out the knots in my back, cursing Storm for her sleep while I turn to face the piles of literacy porn. I grumble drowsily, "Welp, time to get to fucking work."

CHAPTER 3
ANEIRA

"What in the actual fuck is howl-ing on here?"
Storm's voice startles me, and I have to peel an
open book off my face as I blink up at her with
one eye.

"Did you fall asleep while sorting the books out?" She giggle
snorts, "damn, I left my phone upstairs or I would have taken a
picture of you in your little wolf nest."

Bitch. I wipe the sleep from my eyes, uncurl myself and look
around in a daze—the hell. I wasn't sure exactly when I did
this, but I am surrounded by stacks of books of various sizes
and colors, arranged in a haphazard yet still orderly fashion, a

mix of my preferred fiction, non-fiction, classics, and modern works. Then, I look down and realize that I'm not only in just my bra and panties but I am lying on various plush cushions and blankets. *Jesus, Agatha. Go big or go home, huh?*

I clear my throat, "firstly, this isn't a nest. This is a highly organized structure that I'm making so that I can accurately arrange my books." I fastidiously ignore her knowing smirk at the fact that I somehow built a mini nest that was my ideal haven; warm, secure, perfect for curling up in, and filled with my go-to happy books…a book haven of sorts.

I resist a groan. "Errm, uh, secondly, I arrange better while napping, without clothes on. Thirdly, if you dare take a picture, I will shave your eyebrows while you sleep. Think carefully." She continues to laugh as she walks around my nest and I stand up and attempt to stretch out the kink in my back from sleeping in a bunch of blankets instead of my nice warm bed.

I look back at the nest and breathe out in resignation, if I was indeed building a nest without being consciously aware— and clearly I was unless there was a bookstore poltergeist I wasn't aware of—my heat is close as fuck. At least Agatha had enough sense to lay out blankets because, I mean, can you imagine the paper cuts in questionable places if she hadn't? I shuddered.

Omegas make nests for a few reasons, and the nests are *always* a reflection of that particular Omega's personality and interests, as that is what will give us the maximum comfort and distractions as needed. Because while Wolves, in general, are social creatures needing a sense of community and belonging, Omega's are different than our male counterparts. For one, we are typically, more sensitive to our surroundings and more empathetic to others. So pretty much, we build nests to retreat when we are overstimulated and for our heat. Sex and safety… best of all worlds.

Still, despite Agatha longing for a mate that could handle all of her needs, I have been lucky that she has let me hole up in my room with snacks, a tent full of blankets, and several vibrators and chargers to ease the ache. It may be because she doesn't sense any wolf around, but whatever it was, I was glad for small miracles. All in all, it looks like I running out of time to replenish my room fridge and charge up my toys.

Briefly, I wonder how amazing my heat could be if I had a mate to take care of my needs not just any mate, but a true mate. Like my mother was lucky enough to find. Someone who loves me for me and not for the political alliances our mating would bring. *No. Do not go there, Aneira.* I quickly stifle the thoughts and squash them into the 'do not touch' category of my brain with barbed wire and steel to encase it.

I've learned that living in the moment makes life easier for Aggy and me. Back when I was with my pack, I was always scared about the future, stressing over what they expected from me or if I'd be pushed into some political marriage like my mom. My grandpa's plans for me weighed heavy on my mind, and I was sick of feeling paralyzed by those fears.

Once Aggy and I were free from his grip, we decided we'd had enough. It was time to focus on the present, on the choices we could make, and the life we could live for ourselves, not just for the pack. That's when we started finding joy in the little things—the sun's warmth, the beauty of nature, and making new friends.

So fuck Grandpa and his outdated and abusive rules. The new Aneira can handle her fresh reality and build a life where she's accepted and loved for who she is. Right now, I am free, and that is all that matters.

"Hey. Annie. You okay, babe?" Storm delicately steps around my books and nestles into my side, placing her head on my shoulder. I sigh in contentment, leaning my head toward hers. Wolves are naturally tactile, and constant touches and reassurance were a few of the things I missed the most since leaving. Storm and her penchant to snuggle definitely makes up for it.

"Yeah." I blow out a breath. "Just thinking about some shit, nothing to worry about. I think it's just the exhaustion catching up to me. Anyway, what time is it?" I have no idea how long I've been asleep.

She checks her watch. "A little past two. Do you need a hand with these books?"

I look around the room and wince. It's still carnage around me, and I had to keep the shop closed while I restocked, but I know we have to get things ready for tonight, so I nod, gratefully accepting her help.

We get to it, after I throw on my clothes, an easy conversation flows between us, and I tell her about the hot delivery guy and his salacious offer. I then have to physically restrain her from running upstairs and grabbing my phone to call him on my behalf.

Squealing in excitement, she jumps up and down, forgetting the stack of books in front of her, "You gotta wear that turquoise dress, you know, the one that hugs all your curves. That is a sexy as-shit outfit." She huffs at the look on my face and hauls a stack of books closer to place them in alphabetical order.

"I think you're more invested in my sex life than I am," I start, and she cuts me off.

"No, I am more invested in your *consistent* sex life. I mean, seriously, quickies are fun and all, but they are *quickies*. Wham bam, and those fuckers *never* say 'thank you, ma'am.' Although if they did, I'd take back the pussy and erase it from their minds. But yeah, " she waves her hands in the air, " no passion, no sexy words. Just grunting and nutting," she wrinkles her face in distaste, and I roll my eyes.

"I don't want passion," I lie. "I just need to get the edge off, you know I cannot get involved with anyone seriously. Besides, grunting is sexy." It's not. "It is very caveman. You Tarzan, Me Jane."

Storm narrows her eyes, and I feel the daggers of disapproval carving into my skin. "You stop right fucking there, Aneira. Tarzan was a sexy, gentlemanly beast. All because of a certain fellow gentleman named Phil Collins. If you diminish Tarzan, you take away the power of our Patron Saint Collins, and I will not have you take the name of Phil Collins in vain. Not in this bookshop."

"But the movie was written by…" I start, and she jumps to cover my mouth with the palm of her hand.

She looks around the shop, her eyes wide before turning back to meet my gaze, her fiery look shooting a shiver of apprehension down my spine, "without the dulcet tones of his voice, Tarzan may have taken longer to become one with his inner beast. If you ask me and fellow followers of the Collins Revolution, Phil Collins is the only reason Tarzan didn't become some British pansy who ate crumpets without a good cup of tea. I mean, who even are those guys? Some kind of fucking unevolved savages? No. No." She breathes deeply, her chest heaving. "Phil Collins is sacred."

She is a terrifying little thing; she doesn't even have teeth. I am proud. Agatha's voice thrums through my head, and I roll my eyes.

"Besides," Storm continues in her normal voice, turning away as if she didn't just have a breakdown. "Tarzan had that loin cloth thing going for him. A sweaty club romp could neva! I mean, take these horny bitches, for example," she waves dramatically at the books on the wall with a spin, almost falling over the pile of books in front of her, and I giggle. She scowls at me, "Like I was saying. Take these horny bitches. They all get thoroughly fucked in their stories. No grunting, none of that 'oh that pussy is tight' shit," she deepens her voice, mimicking a good 90 percent of my bathroom lovers, pretty spot on. "You need more than that. At least call this guy and get a consistent, passionate fuck every once in a while. In a bed, couch, or on top of the kitchen counter. At least you already know he can lift your tall ass. Munch on that pussy while holding you in the air, Lion King style. Hell, let him eat that pussy for sunrise and sunset while you stare at the shadowy place. Having a regular booty call is better than the shit you've been doing."

With a laugh, I shake my head at her first passionate speech of the morning. She was just getting started. Expecting quite a few more, I turn back to finish up my stack of books, and I don't reply, choosing to walk around filling up the empty spots on the shelves, ignoring her pointed stares. And for a while, I think she's let it go until she opens her mouth again. "Call him, you Lucious Lupine. *Now* is the only time that you are ever going to experience. Fuck your past. Don't let it fuck you. The dick is limp, anyway. Don't let limp dick win." She says pointedly, finishing her stack and heading toward the back. "I'm going downstairs to make sure we have everything we need for tonight, call him you wolf-tastic whore." She disappears, and I sit and walk to one of the many comfortable chairs.

I bite back a sigh, she isn't wrong. Having something consistent, especially with the high sex drive of shifters, would be useful, but it wasn't possible. I admit her tangents are part of the reason I would ever consider, barely, something like it. Maybe a regular rotation or something with a strong shifter who also had the same itch to scratch.

I smile as I hear her singing as she makes her way to the lower levels. Storm always seemed to connect the dots of life before I do. She is a special one, for sure. We met when I was new in town and overly cautious about everything. Despite all of my precautions, I was so sure that the enforcers would come and drag me back to the commune, and I would have to face their wrath, but then along came Storm. Her personality is just like her name, all-encompassing and intense. She was working in the Bed and Breakfast I was staying in, and after looking at me, decided then and there that we would be friends. Eventually, after several tangents, I gave in to her demands for friendship, she's not someone you really say no to. Ultimately, it's been almost 8 years, and my old pack still hasn't found me. That, or the shame, finally killed my grandfather socially and he didn't bother setting up a search party.

My friendship with a human caught me off guard, but Agatha didn't see an issue with it, seeing something in Storm to trust, and slowly, I did too. One day, she scared the shit out of me in a shop, and I whirled around with my wolf peeking out my eyes, ready to react. That was it for me, I was ready to pack my shit up and leave, but all she said was, "cool." Since then, my wolf and I agreed to keep her forever. And after a drunken night of a full-blown confession and rant, she knew the majority of the bullshit of my past, swore secrecy and fealty to me, and offered a secret assassination mission. I knew she would protect me with her life... or rather...the lives of the people she would surely stab—blood-thirsty little thing.

Storm is the reason I snagged this bookshop before it even hit the market. After venting one too many times at the B&B about needing my own space and dreaming of a bookstore close to where I could roam freely at night, she whipped out her phone in a heartbeat. Calling her grandparents, who happened to know the store's owners wanting to retire, I managed to secure this heavenly spot.

During the complete makeover of the place and the addition of a few extras, Storm didn't hesitate when I asked for her help with my other venture. The one that operated beneath the shop after hours, letting me unleash my pent-up frustrations in a way that surpassed any physical pleasure.

Blood and fury.

CASIMIR

My teeth grind together in an attempt to keep my temper under control. To the world, I am a civilized gentleman, my old-world money going into local charities and schools wherever I roamed. Little do they know that it's all a front to keep them quiet, just look the other way, ignore my furry tail, and no harm will come to them. Granted, they couldn't see my tail, but that was beside the point. Covers saved lives, mine and my packs'.

Accidents still happen, though. For example, we had an unfortunate incident a few months ago down in Norfolk where one of my younger pack members hit it off with the wrong girl, a human, and it got a little too heated. She freaked out when his knot appeared, and I had to spend a fortune getting everyone's mind wiped so we could leave the town without consequences.

Unfortunately for Michael, he's currently working as a personal security guard for a witch enrolled in University a couple of towns over and wishing he was dead. Some Alphas make an example out of their pack members when they fuck up, but I preferred for punishments to match the crime. In Michael's case, the Witch, Samantha, was a rage witch, specializing in bringing out and controlling the worst emotion in all beings; anger. I smiled as I thought of the young witch, smart as a whip but impulsive and hot-headed. Just the type of 'punishment' Michael, with his usual easy-going nature, needed.

As an Alpha, there have been instances where I could have strung someone up by their balls, but I always found that packs work better when they respect their Alpha instead of living in fear, like now. One of my trusted advisors—well, the son of one of my trusted advisors, who was trying his hand at his father's position—Greg, is currently droning on and on about budgets and where they should go now that we've found a new place to live. It's a risky area, about an hour from the national park, but we're hoping the risk pays off. It's not going to be forever, maybe a few years. Although, in all honesty, that is not entirely truthful. Something drew us here, and even though it wasn't intentional, not too far from our settlement was Cabria Falls, a rare mixed shifter community that was downright incredible. However, I do expect a visit from whatever councilman headed this area. It is inevitable because, although we hoped with our progressive way of living, we could skate under the radar, a wolf pack so close to a shifter settlement would have to be a formally recognized pack, and we aren't...yet. And that was another headache in the making.

I lean forward, resting my arms on the table before me, and

rub the sides of my head in small circles. Under the radar. Under the radar. The stuff I have to listen to and repeat as Alpha sometimes is a freaking joke, I think to myself. I understand his excitement; this land feels more like home than any place we've been. While packs are supposed to be a source of stability, security, and protection, both physically and emotionally, having established pack lands is just as important and necessary to nurture that. So while I understand it, expansions, including building homes, medical facilities, a schoolhouse, and renovations, have to be a priority. Especially when we still have to contend with the visit from a councilman. We have to show that we're a good, strong pack, and as it is, we'll all be working around the clock to help facilitate the basics, not a Taj Mahal of pack facilities.

As it is, the way Greg is droning on about having a spa and even a fucking cinema area, not only is he trotting way beyond the 'under radar' sign, but he is rapidly approaching the 'hey look at us' billboard.

My yawn is so wide that my jaw cracks, and when I dart my eyes to the side, they latch onto my closest friend, second-in-command, and fellow Alpha, Tristan, who's barely suppressing his smirk.

As my enforcer, he was probably one of the most vicious fuckers I've met, his temper, control over his wolf, and skill were nearly unmatched.

Nearly. Because when compared to me, Tristan is an explosive kind of guy, that kind that will react first and then think about the consequences, whereas I'm a simmer. Slowly bubbling, taking it on, until my rage is a striking cobra. Swift, calculated, precise, and fucking lethal. So while Tristan commanded respect, I wielded it, owned it.

I bite back a sigh as Greg's mouth moves animatedly; I don't know what part of staying under the radar he doesn't understand, at least until we are ready to rejoin werewolf shifter politics. Which if I were lucky, I would never have to because even though every wolf pack ran things a little differently, a whole lot of wolf politics were outdated. The idea of a pack reaching out to us for the chance of mating our Omegas for alliances doesn't sit well with me. Omegas should be able to choose when, where, and how they mated. More importantly, their wolves should be able to find their true mate.

Tristan leans back in his seat, arms crossed, and I bite back a sigh, knowing he's close to baiting Greg. And sure enough, he doesn't disappoint.

"So, pup," he starts, and I bite back a smile at the low blow. Greg may be young, but in his twenties, being called a pup was an insult.

Tristan stands up from his seat, opting to lean against the desk, looking down at Greg reproachfully, "What I understand is that you want to cut down how much our pack pays towards charities, keeping us in the good graces of various human political groups to, instead, keep yourself in a nice, heated pool? Did I get that right?" He lets his wolf peek out of his eyes, the usual green now glowing amber, as he bares his teeth in a feral grin, which stretches even further at the slight perspiration dotting Greg's brow.

"Well, I, uh…uh…" he shifts in his seat, making himself slightly smaller. The slight smell of fear and trepidation permeates the room. Having Tristan sit in on all meetings could be both a blessing and a curse and, in this case, a slight curse. Still, Tristan was right. Greg might be learning, but he needs to align his priorities with the pack's vision. I understand the thrill he feels—discovering a place where our wolves can finally find peace instead of being constantly on the run. But the fact that we've made it this far against all odds didn't excuse incompetence. Money and abilities alone don't guarantee success, but shared purpose? Unity? That is what *is* crucial to a pack's growth and progression.

I take a deep breath and school my face. Clearing my throat, I bring Greg's attention to me rather than Tristan, who, I now notice, is sheathing and unsheathing his claws.

Cut that the fuck out, I growl out mentally to him, and he sends me back a mental chuckle but sheaths his claws and crosses his arms.

"Thank you, Greg. Our purpose here is to establish ourselves *before* we start to allocate any funds toward extensive and *expensive* renovations. However, in the meantime, if you would like to *personally* fund building a cinema and spa in the future, then maybe I'll reconsider it. Though, I think that helping sick children, staying in the good graces of various groups of humans, shifters, witches, and so on while still ensuring that our pack continues to thrive, with basic needs, is higher on my priority list." My sarcasm, although tampered down, isn't missed, and Greg goes an interesting shade of grey.

I pause, meeting his gaze wordlessly. Catching the hint, Greg hurriedly stands up from his seat and murmurs his goodbyes. The minute he scurries away, Tristan is up and pacing the room, an office space in the rustic cottage in the middle of nowhere that we had bought for peanuts as it was pretty much condemned, large enough to house my inner circle and have room for my office. We then purchased the several acres of land surrounding the cabin, labeling it a sanctuary to cut the red tape. Then with a bit of magic from the witches to seal the deal with the humans, we were all set.

I understand Tristan's pacing, and to be honest, I would join him if I didn't have to show a semblance of control. Moreover? I'm bored. Bored and fucking annoyed by the constant repetition some of the pack wolves needed recently. But I must keep reminding myself that their baser natures are practically skipping with joy.

My wolf prowls restlessly under my skin, and it becomes a burning itch. One that indicates that I need to get out and run sooner rather than later.

"Hey Cas, can we kill these entitled pricks and start fresh? Go on, please say yes." He bats his eyelashes, poking out his bottom lip. *Moon help me, this wolf thinks murder is akin to begging for candy.*

I can't help but laugh, "No, I can't be fucked with rebuilding yet another pack."

I lean back with a sigh, "They might need a lesson in humility and control, though, so I'll leave that particular punishment to you." In every pack, even if the dynamics were amazing, there are going to be a few members with less control over their wolves. Usually, as long as they respect the pack hierarchy, there isn't a problem, but in this case, it's more of them…needing a reminder to reign it in.

"Already on it," He smiles ferally, unsheathing his claws. I roll my eyes, and he chuckles, his hands back to normal before he walks over to the opposite side of the room and leans against the window to watch the pack as they hustle around, completing their designated tasks. "So, boss man, I can't help but notice you're a little agitated, and I have the perfect solution for you." Tristan's eyes gleam as he rubs his hands together in a way that indicates that whatever is going to come out of his mouth next may be either the worst plan or the best. I'm thinking it's more than likely the latter. "I've found a place about an hour away that hosts an underground fight club once a month. It's called Shifter Wars, and anything goes. You have to get an invitation to it, and luckily I have. The next fight is tonight. Fancy going?"

Hmm. So maybe not the worst plan. I lean my head back on my chair. The thought is so tempting. More than tempting, actually, especially with my wolf battering against his restraints. I pause to consider my wolf, and while he's more than eager to go and take a pound of flesh, he isn't at the point where he would pose anyone imminent danger. Fuck it. What's the worst that can happen?

"Yeah, fuck it, I'm in," I nod.

CHAPTER 5
CASIMIR

We stroll out to his car, one of those fancy SUV types that the companies boast can handle going off-road but, in reality, can't handle more than a deep puddle. "I have no idea why the hell you still have this damn truck. Trade this petrol guzzler out for an electric SUV," I grumble, jumping into the passenger seat. Tristan scoffs, "No way, and I told you, my Range Rover is a *Hybrid*."

Now it's my turn to scoff. He insists his truck is better than my Electric Rivian R1T. He fucking wishes. At least my car won't cause forest fires. I hold back my eye roll as Tristan jumps into the driver's seat, taking us out of the rural forest and towards civilization.

My shoulders tense, and I force them to relax. It makes me somewhat uncomfortable getting closer to humanity. In our old pack, we weren't allowed to fraternize with humans in almost any capacity, so despite how I strive for progression within the pack, I have to fight the learned behavior every day. I didn't care much for frivolity. I care about the comforts of my packs and ensuring they had everything we needed to survive, be happy, and still be off the map.

Traditionally, many of our wolves attain their degrees online, and because of those degrees, we can have schools for the younger pups. For higher education that required more of a tactile approach like our doctors, Tristan being one of them, we send those wolves out with enforcers for the duration of their degree. It is a bit much, but the last thing anyone needs is discovery *and* no way to fight themselves out. I preferred attaining my various law and economic degrees quietly, from the comfort of my pack grounds, less unnecessary interactions with humans, and less stressful when avoiding the condescending attitude of the more traditional wolves, my father included.

By the time an hour passes and we pull into a quaint village, my nerves are shot to shit, and I'm desperate to get out of this car and into a fight. The place to get into the fight is down an alleyway past a few quaint shops, including a little bookstore, a charity shop, and an independent coffee shop.

I take a deep breath as we step out of the car and smell a mishmash of shifters. "The fight club is in Cabria Shifter Falls?" I arch my eyebrow.

Tristan shrugs, "Even the well-established Cabria Falls would need a place for shifters just to be…feral every once in a while. You can't expect a Disney movie. We are still animals by nature."

I ponder his words as we walk. He is right, of course. Although, I wonder how they stayed under the radar from whoever headed up this area. Chances are they didn't, but rather the councilman understood the need for a place for shifters to release tension. Not my problem, though.

We turn into an alley, where about halfway down, there's a small door cleverly disguised to appear abandoned and covered in graffiti. The only giveaway was the very slight scent of shifters in the air that was only detectable by other shifters.

I don't ask how Tristan found exactly where to go for this fight club, but he always seems to know things, and I never question it. It was his job as my enforcer to know everything. Like now, when he raps a strange pattern on the battered door. He tosses back a smirk as the door swings open to reveal a surly man, trying to appear intimidating, which might work with humans, but I can't see how this works with any of the shifters.

My wolf agrees because he manages to slip through my careful restraints to come to the forefront, wanting to play with this... I take a deep breath picking up his scent, rabbit shifter. I roll my eyes internally and wrestle my wolf back down as the guy rears back, casting his eyes downward in submission. *Good,* my wolf whispers, appreciating the small mark of respect—as if a rabbit shifter could do much anyway. *Monti, was that entirely necessary?* I feel his scowl at the nickname before he shrugs mentally and settles back down. After 32 years, my wolf, Montgomery, is still a surly show-off. Although, according to him, he has lived several lives and deserves more fun.

I manage a smile as we pass the rabbit, head inside, and follow the twisty corridor, down, down, and even further down until, about five minutes of walking later, we get to a large, dimly lit room with a large steel door and silver handle. *No shifter was breaking in here unannounced. Smart.* I look around briefly, taking note of the blinking cameras in the corners of the room as well as several directly in front of the door, spaced at different heights and, upon further inspection, encased in shatterproof glass. Well, damn.

Another quick beat on the door blocking our entrance, and the door swings open, letting out deep pulsing music. *Sound-proof doors,* I note. I step in, and Tristan and I whistle apprecia-tively, taking in the currently empty dance cages on the side of the immense room and raised daises where, presumably, dancers danced outside of the cages. The walls are painted a deep green, and along the walls are booths, tables, and plush lounge chairs, all currently occupied with laughing shifters and the occasional witch group. At that, I smiled.

Witches and shifters usually work in a transactional fashion —shifters handle the muscle part, and witches put up magical protection for packs and shifter homes. But they don't really hang out together in public places. Instead, many older super-natural folks stick with their own crowd, going with what they know instead of trying something new.

I get that traditions matter, but holding on to those snobby, old-fashioned attitudes can make someone a prime target for human experiments. I've always pushed back against that kind of thinking in my own pack, and eventually, I left because of it. Among other reasons, I decided to start my own pack of like-minded wolves so that we can lead shifters into a new age of growth and change.

My dad, Alpha Casemiro, who I was named after, and the pack Council were shocked when a bunch of younger wolves—and even some older ones—decided to follow me. Now, typi-cally, this would be seen as a declaration of war, but my dad chalked it up to a rebellious phase and let us go without a fuss. That was pretty surprising, given his violent nature and crazy mating rules. But, of course, he had to promise some harsh punishment when we'd all come crawling back—that part wasn't shocking at all. In truth, it was easier for him to act like he was giving permission instead of facing the real challenge to his position in the pack. But I didn't want his pack; I wanted to create my own.

After two years of 'roughing' it, roaming from place to place, and dealing with a few skirmishes with other packs, we managed to thrive. We even picked up random like-minded wolf shifters along the way; omegas, betas, and some mated wolves with wolf pups. While we made due with ensuring everyone had what they needed, pups were educated, and our wolves could attain their own education as well; we were all itching for our own pack-lands. But our last discovery near Lincolnshire Wolds, as we made our way from our Norfolk slip-up, was deciding factor in ensuring we quickly found a more permanent settlement for our pack.

We tried to travel mostly at night, keeping to our wolf forms as much as possible, using pendants provided by witches around our necks to avoid detection. We stumbled across a broken group of Omega females, some with small children, who had run away from their pack. Bruised, delirious from hunger, eyes sunken in from lack of sleep, and scared out of their minds, they still stood defiantly and said they would rather die than return. It took everything in my power to stop myself from finding their own pack and unleashing a hell storm. The other members of our pack felt the same. After much convincing from Tristan and me and, later, the other wolves in our pack, we assured them that we were not there to bring them to their old pack and meant no harm. After a couple of weeks of careful treatment, hunting for them and finding them all proper clothes, *and* after much deliberation, they decided they wanted to join us. After some research, we headed towards the lake district, understanding that while the actual National Park was not a place for wolves to settle safely, we would aim for about an hour away, west, from the main areas. We hoped that with some assistance from like-minded witches, we met along our journey, we would be able to settle and avoid detection for years to come. Call it luck or fate, but it looks like we finally chose the right place to make that happen.

My thoughts reeling, I continue to observe the room. In the center of the room was a large sunken area in the shape of a circle, with blood splattered on the surrounding floor; the fighting ring. While there were no seats directly in front of the fighting area, people milled around, angling for a good view of the next set of fights. The room seems to go on, from the raised dancing area for the patrons to the back, which appears to lead to the restrooms and probably an office or two. From the outside, one would have never suspected that directly under their feet was a vast shifter club and fight scene. In fact, despite it being underground, I wonder how the owner managed to conceal such a space from humans. Shifters can be resourceful and convincing, but whoever owned this space was especially so, considering blueprints for buildings were public records.

It's busy in here but not overly packed yet. A few feet away, directly in the view of whoever walks through the door, sits a long bar with an oak top and racks of shelving behind it full of various liquors. We shifters like the taste of alcohol, and it takes a lot to get us feeling the effects, so the owner here has all the top-shelf goods that those watching the fights can savor. Tristan and I make our way there, feeling the stares from the shifters in the room. Being the only wolves here, I can understand the confusion. From our information, there weren't wolf shifters in the area. Although for a good reason. Our forms are more significant in size than most, and a wolf was already considered person-non-grata to most humans.

My curiosity more than peaked; I keep my face carefully blank as I observe the room, trying to figure out who owned this place. A secret club, a fight club, and top-shelf booze? I mean, shifters usually pool their resources, and some clans can be wealthy, but this kind of wealth—the kind that's tough to keep under wraps—takes some serious smarts to build and maintain.

Looking around the room, I further observe the fight zone, which I now notice is accompanied by a cage suspended from the ceiling which would then come down and enclose those in the ring — more than likely so they can beat the everlasting shit out of each other and the damage would stay inside. *It doesn't do much to keep the blood inside, though,* I think to myself, noticing that the initial splatters were a lot more than just a few drops.

Tristan whistles, his eyes following my gaze. "That cage is top of the range. It's a highly specialized material that takes over a year to forge. After, the metal is warded to absorb the impact from a hit and then released back into the circle as a low-pitched sonic boom to the one pinned, rendering them useless." He shakes his head in awe. "That's not cheap. The witches who ward that metal don't take cash payment—They deal in favors. It makes me more than curious to find out who owns this place. We need to make sure our pack is on their good side," his face takes on a look of determination. The look that meant he would find out who owned this underground club and force them into a submission of friendship, much like he did to me years ago. They were goners.

I chuckled, "Down, boy, you cannot bring home any more strays. We just got new carpets." I tsked, and he throws a punch that lands softly on my shoulder. "You're no fun, Dad," he pouts, turning around to signal the bartender for a drink.

As he orders, a weedy-looking man sidles up to us, holding a glass of scotch, the smell of rat wafting from his direction. *A rat shifter, the lowest of the lows.* I resist the urge to curl my lip as he opens his mouth, his yellowing teeth on display, "Are you boys in a fight tonight?" He asks, licking his think lips, "You both look like the, uh, discerning types and I... uh...placed a lot of money in the next few rounds of the shifter wars. I bet you're a strong one judging by all that muscle," he leans closer to me, a crazed gleam in his eyes. My second breath came with the perversive smell of addiction, and I felt nothing but disgust for the shifter before me. Drug addiction, in general, did not end well. But mix drugs and the magic of being a shifter? The shifters became unhinged, dangerous and were often put down. The fact that his addiction seems further along indicates that this rat didn't belong to a pack; the closest shifter council would decide his judgment before he became a danger to humans and shifters.

My lips curl into a sneer, and it takes everything in me to paste on a benign smile. "We're just scoping out the competition at the moment."

The rat nods. "Okay, fine. But if you want to know who to beat, I'm your guy."

Tristan leans across me. "We don't want to cheat if that's what you're saying. We don't need underhand tactics to beat anyone in here. So go on, little rat, fuck off." He flicks his fingers at the shifter, who gives us a scandalized look and scurries off like a....well...rat. "Seriously. What a twat. Are you going to fight tonight, though, Cas? I recognize that look in your eyes. Your wolf is riding you hard."

I shove the little rat into the dark recesses of my mind and consider Tristan's words. He doesn't need to remind me that I'm itching for blood and need a good fight to exhaust my wolf and me. Since moving, we've been reluctant to change, needing to settle in and not alarm the wildlife and any locals too much. So maybe tonight would be a good relief for me.

"Yeah, I think I am going to fight tonight. Go and put me on the list." Tristan nods at my words and slinks off to find out who the organizer is.

I cast a critical eye over the current shifters in the club, sizing up the potential: leopards, lithe bird shifters, and even a bear shifter whose imposing frame could intimidate most. As I catalog their features, I start to break down what I know about their species and consider their strengths and weaknesses, wondering which one can give me a real challenge in the ring. Not that appearances mean much. Experience has taught me that even the 'tamest' of shifter species can surprise you.

I watch a couple of men step into the circle, and the low buzz of noise increases until cheers ring out. They peel their tops off as the cage lowers and closes, the wards letting off a slight pulse of magic, effectively trapping them in there.

A woman's voice blasts from the speakers, sultry and smooth. "Welcome to The Cavern! And most importantly... Shifter Wars, motherfuckers! Round two of our fights are about to begin, and while you should all know the drill, we noticed a few newcomers joining. So, if you're new, here's the lowdown. One. Once that cage comes down, you're in there until the buzzer sounds, or one of you is nearly dead. Apart from that, anything goes. Two. What happens on the floor stays on the floor. Be paired with another combatant on the signup list at random and work out all our anger, or Challenge a combatant and work out whatever the fuck you got going on with each other, but you will shake at the end and part on amicable terms. This is not a breeding ground for feuds. Three. No drugs allowed on site, violators will be banned, and mind scrubbed. Four. Consent. No explanation is needed there. Five. The Cavern is soundproof for your safety and the integrity of the club and Shifter Wars. Six. We are a secret club, and it will stay that way. The minute you stepped into The Cavern, you may not have felt it, but you are now bound to keep it a secret from those seeking to do us harm. If, for some reason, magic or otherwise, you find a way around this ward and we find out any humans hear about this, then you will be executed. Okay? Cool." There are a few anxious chuckles around me like they don't know if she's joking. However, with a club of this scale, there is no doubt that she is absolutely not joking.

Soon, there's a sharp ring of a bell, and within seconds, the two fighters are on each other. I shift my head slightly to catch their scents, *osprey*. For bird shifters, I have to admit that I am impressed. They're fighting with a lot more savagery than I thought possible, and as their attacks increase, I have to wonder if their anger is a combination of pack politics and youthful hormones or, in fact, just friendly shifter rivalry.

They dance around each other and take vicious jabs with as much force as possible. A tooth flies out, causing a woman near it to shriek and recoil in disgust. A man next to her reaches out to hold her and rub her back in comfort.

Tristan is suddenly back at my side, his presence announced by the disgusted scoff at the actions of the shrieking woman. His nose twitches as he shakes his head. "I couldn't be with someone so sensitive to blood and gore. It goes against my nature."

I hum in agreement but don't respond, concentrating on the two fighters. They're pretty evenly matched and take turns getting the upper hand for the next few minutes until the buzzer sounds and the cage lifts, letting the two battle-weary men emerge. They give each other a huge grin, shake hands, and walk away with their arm slug around each other's shoulders. Friendly rivalry it is. Understandable. Shifters are built differently; emotions flare high, but with quick healing abilities and level heads, we calm down as fast as those tempers flare.

"I got you in for the next fight with a little sweet talking, so let's make our way to the front of the cage. They should be announcing you in…." His voice trails off as the mic cuts back on, and we turn our attention to the sound.

"That one was a tie, ladies and gents. So stay tuned for their round two and the deciding match," the same, deep sensuous voice comes out of the well-placed speakers placed in various locations of the club, followed by a low thrum of music. "Coming up, we have a new fighter tonight, but while he makes his way up to the cage, just a quick overview. The cage will dampen powers just enough to ensure there is no cat-tastrophe if some of your furry little asses decide to shift. "

There is a collective groan at the pun.

"What? Can't have you leaving here bear-ly surviving," the voice chuckles.

Tristan huffs a laugh, "She's funny."

I nod with a small smile, "and well-loved, or feared if she can say jokes like that to a bunch of shifters."

Shifters are notoriously touchy about insults to their nature, so I am interested to know who the announcer is if only to keep her far the fuck away from Tristan's ass. I can't imagine having two versions of him.

He spins on his heel and moves toward the ring with me on his heels. I tug off my shirt as the voice over the speaker changes to someone more lively, "Storm had to pop out, so I'll be taking over for a few. Right now, we have ...Pierce and Sir Snarls-a-Lot." She chokes on a laugh, and I glare at Tristan, who shrugs a sly grin on his face.

"Just giving the people what they want, Alpha. Comedy with their daily dose of blood," he says with a quick salute, snagging my shirt as he moves back to watch with the rest of the crowd. Fucking asshole.

I turn my attention back to the ring as the announcer starts running down a list of rules that fade into the background; I understand the basics. Don't kill and make friends after. Fine.

As I step into the ring, I take a deep breath as I face my opponent, Pierce: Leopard and an Alpha. I observe him with new respect, but as the cage starts to come down and I immediately feel the dampening effect of my powers, Pierce briefly fades to the background as I test my connection to Monti. There, but just barely. It is...uncomfortable, to say the least.

"First time in the cage can be a mind-fuck. My Leopard doesn't like it either," Pierce says, his arms crossed against his heavily tattooed and scarred chest.

"Yeah, I can see why," I nod as I meet his gaze, a striking golden hue that is so like his leopard counterpart; even if I hadn't just scented him, it would be difficult for anyone to mistake him for anything other than a leopard. Just slightly shorter than my 6'3, he cut an impressive figure, and I wonder how my eyes looked him over when we first walked into the club. As it is, with the way his muscled rippled beneath his skin and his eyes followed every slight movement, it was clear that he would be precisely what I needed to satisfy my blood lust.

"You're a wolf, huh?" Pierce smirked. "Didn't think there were any wolves in Cabria Falls, aside from the owner...of course."

I raise an eyebrow, intrigued by the mention of another wolf in town, even more so by the casual way he said it as if he knew that I wasn't aware of the owners' status. "Really? Well, it looks like Cabria Falls just got more interesting," I reply dryly, although I admit my curiosity is certainly piqued. A lone wolf allowed *within* a mixed shifter community? Very interesting.

Pierce grins, reaching his arms up to tie his hair away from his face. "I think you're right about that. I'm interested in seeing how quickly I can take down an Alpha Wolf."

The bell dings as I huff a laugh at the teasing note in his voice, laced with a hint of excitement as he moves around the ring. Following his movement, I let my arms fall to my sides and let my need to destroy come to the forefront.

In seconds, our bodies move towards each other, a fluid dance of power and agility. My shoulders shift as I throw a powerful punch at Pierce, who twists his torso to dodge it effortlessly before retaliating with a quick jab to my ribs. I manage to lean back just in time, avoiding the blow.

Moving back from each other, I see a note of respect in his eyes that I have to mirror.

"C'mon Casimir, stop playing with your damn food. I just made a bet, and I swear if you cost me more than your worth, I will tie you up, steal your blood, and feed your blood to a vampire clan. I hear Kibbles and Alpha-Bits are in high demand for the Coven of Capillary Connoisseurs!" Tristan shouts from outside the cage, and I roll my eyes.

"Your second in command?" Pierce laughs.

I nod, " how can you tell?" I respond with a dry voice.

"Don't listen to him, Casimir, lose so that I can make my money back. Pierce, get your whisker-licious ass back in there and stop having tea with your victim!" A voice shouts from next to Tristan.

Pierce winces and points toward the imposing figure, adorned in tattoos and shirtless, standing next to Tristan, waving his fists. "That's Ramiro, my second-in-command...."

Another voice cuts him off, this time feminine but no less bloodthirsty, that slices through the din of the crowd, "Hey, Pierce! Did you come to fight, or should I grab you two furry-fuck faces, some beauty masks, and cheap wine while you chat about the fucking weather? Get to the heart-ripping already! Or let me in there!"

Pierce rolls his eyes with a heavy sigh, "And that's my grandmother, Imelda."

I can't help but laugh as I spot the petite older woman. I can feel her commanding presence and a powerful aura from here. Her long, silver hair is styled elegantly on top of her head, giving her a regal appearance that is in total contrast to the savage words spewing from her mouth. She shows off her fangs with a wild, gleeful laugh as she and Ramiro playfully shove each other around.

We grin, and with a nod, we move toward each other again, ignoring our family as we focus on each other's small movements as our muscles ripple under our skin, trying to gauge one another's next moves.

Suddenly a predatory smile comes over Pierce's face as he explodes into action, his body fluid as he launches into the air, his body almost contorting as his torso twists and he rakes his claws down my chest, landing a hit. Relishing in the sting of pain, I use his momentum against him and rain a flurry of powerful blows into his side that reverb up my arms and cause him to grunt.

While we may not be able to shift entirely, our ability to bring out our claws was possible.

He grins as he dances back, his eyes glowing. His leopard becomes more than interested in the fight. I feel my wolf respond in kind.

You are evenly matched with this cat. He is strong, a worthy opponent and ally. This town is unique. Montgomery's voice echoes my thoughts. This town was indeed quite remarkable.

"Come on, wolf boy, is that all you've got?" Pierce taunts me as he sweeps a leg at my ankles. I jump over his leg with a chuckle, landing gracefully on my feet before launching a powerful kick aimed at his chest. He bends backward, narrowly avoiding my foot as it whistles past his face.

This continues for several minutes as we draw blood, and our bodies vibrate from violence pouring through our veins. Finally, a particularly heavy punch from Pierce leaves a small cut on my cheek while I land a solid hit on his jaw. The cage's wards amplify the impact of each hit, causing sonic booms to ripple through the air.

I relish the ache starting in my muscles as we push each other to our limits. Then, as our bodies drip with sweat, our muscles straining, Pierce spins and delivers a roundhouse kick that I narrowly avoid by ducking low. In response, I lunge forward with a powerful uppercut, but he shifts his head to the side, evading the blow.

A ring of the bells and the mic cutting back on has us both stop short, "Well, then. I may have missed the majority of that, but from what I *was* able to watch from the cam, that just made my lady dick hard as fuck. So we can most certainly call that— and by *that*, I mean what I am here-by dubbing The Fur-ious Feline Fiasco: A Paws-itively Wild Showdown…— a tie."

The crowd collectively cheers, groans, and laughs at the pun as the cage starts to come up. Pierce and I shake hands with a laugh as Tristan, Ramiro, and his grandmother come closer.

"This was a very enlightening night. If you ever need anything, My name is Pierce; ask around, and you'll find me," he nods in respect.

"Same here. My name is Casimir," I look at Tristan.

"Ah, so not Sir Snarls-A-Lot, got it," Pierce teases, and I huff out a laugh.

With another nod, he turns and walks away.

"Well, at least I didn't lose any money," Tristan grumbles as he passes me my shirt, and I start to shrug it on.

As I'm about to reply, the most intoxicating scent hits me like a tidal wave. My eyes widen, and my wolf springs to attention. The aroma - a blend of rose, lavender, and vanilla - sets my heart racing and ignites a fire within me. My wolf strains against me, desperate to break free, but I fight for control, beads of sweat forming on my forehead, flames coursing through my veins. I draw deep breaths, the overwhelming urge, unlike anything I've experienced. My blood rushes from my head to my groin, leaving me with a throbbing headache. The scent envelops me like a tender embrace, and I know I must find the one it belongs to. Now.

Mine. My wolf growls. *Mate.*

My world grinds to a halt, time standing still. Tristan's voice reaches me, muffled, as if from a great distance. All my senses blur, with only my sense of smell remaining sharp. My pulse pounds, my arousal throbs, and my wolf claws at me, desperate to escape. This isn't just about finding my mate, my Omega. No, she's going into heat.

*

EVERY INSTINCT IS on high alert as my senses come rushing back to me.

"Cas, boss man," Tristan yells, on alert and looking for any potential threats. My eyes snap up to meet his, and he takes a step back, my wolf at the forefront, taking any close wolf as a threat to his mate. His eyes widen in alarm, and he holds up his hands and bends his neck in a show of submission. I feel my wolf pull back a little as he observes the room.

"Cas, I can smell her too," Tristan says softly, and I snarl in anger. "Boss, listen to me, she is all yours, man, but this is not the place to wolf out right now. You let go of your wolf now, you won't be able to bring him back in. Not after that fight. We are going to have to leave. Now."

"I. Must. Have. Her," my wolf snarls, and I feel my control slipping, something that hasn't happened since I had my first shift. This is something completely unprecedented. I never wanted a female as badly as I do now. But not any female, my mate. My Omega. And by her scent, she needs me too. I have to find her.

"We will come back tomorrow, boss. We will track her down, but right now, I'm doing this for you and for the pack," Tristan says in an angry whisper, trying not to draw attention to himself. A part of me wonders why, but then my whole world goes dark as I pass out. *My Mate.*

CHAPTER 6
ANEIRA

S torm and I watch the fight from one of the elevated booths, drinks in our hands. "We have a good turnout tonight," Storm shouts in my ear. She forgets that my hearing is so much better than hers, and I wince. "Oops, sorry," she adds, lifting the beer to her lips and taking a deep pull. "Full roster of fights tonight. Just the way we like it."

She says it like it's a surprise, but it's usually a full night of fights every time we do shifter wars. It started out as a passion project—my love for teaching self-defense to those who may need it—and when remodeling, I found this... cavern... under the bookstore basement, and it ran deep underground. In fact, when I was mapping it, part of it was under the lake and ran quite a long ways into the forest. The crew I hired did an amazing job making this space comfortable, insulated, and most importantly, soundproof; all exits and entrances reinforced with steel doors and beyond the sunken fighting circle floor, luxurious seating, and bars—the works. The reconstruction in this particular underground chamber was done after hours, and while the crew had no recollection of their extra work, they were compensated generously. I also paid a pretty penny for memory charms, and after all, was said and done, I had been down to the last few thousand of the 'nest egg' my mother provided me with. If you could even call a few million a nest egg. But it came in handy with my move, identity change, and complete renovation of this place.

During our walkthrough of the secret basement, Storm and I realized there was an entrance in an alleyway not far from the bookstore. It provided the perfect anonymity and a double layer of protection. Of course, I still had to do a lot of work to ensure the humans didn't stumble across it, but once warded properly, we were in business.

Soon after, we put out feelers to the shifter community, and what started as self-defense classes morphed into fight nights. After a few short months, it all paid for itself ten times over, and that was just from the income of the lovingly dubbed "Shifter Wars." On weekends, we operated as a shifter dance club; a steel trap covered the sunken fight floor, and the surrounding area was scrubbed so well you would never notice that anything other than bumping and grinding was happening here. I made the Lake District my home, and despite all the bullshit I had to run away from, I was happy and all the better for it.

"We always do," I take a sip of my drink as the two fighters go at it furiously. To anyone observing, these two osprey shifters, Lance and Onyx, have a real issue with one another. In truth, despite their large stature, they're teen twin brothers who, despite being birds of prey, have a human step-mom trying to get them to convert to veganism. They're so worked up from the lack of meat in their house and having to sneak out to eat what they wanted, even when their packmates sneak them meat, that they have a lot of pent-up rage. The Osprey pack is one of the few packs that allow human-shifter relationships, especially after a mate passes away. Their frustrations, although hilarious, are understandable.

Their story, despite being a tad strange, is adorable, and it brings a smile to my lips every time I think about it. When a shifter loses their mate, they can go a bit crazy. Some even go feral and have to be put down or locked up for safety. It's truly heartbreaking, especially for those who have younger children. In the twins' case, they were fortunate; their father Luke took off into the forest and grieved in solitude. Their step-mom, Cassandra, stumbled across Luke, literally, while he was in shifted form.

Feeling terrible, Cassandra took him home and nursed him back to health. It was a shock to her when one day, he shifted back to human form, and the rest was history. Their story convinced their pack that relationships with humans were possible, and I was glad. Cassandra was honestly one of the sweetest and kindest people I have ever met, making it her business to stop into the bookshop to load up on new releases every two weeks, have a chat, and drink a cup or six of tea. I could see why their father fell in love with her; everyone did.

So, the twins, not wanting to upset her but so worked up from the lack of meat in their home, took out their frustrations elsewhere, like Shifter Wars, and a few times a week showed up at our apartment for dinner.

"The twins look extra on edge today. I think Onyx just punched Lance's eye shut!" Storm shakes her head and laughs.

"Yeah, Cassandra made them vegan meatballs out of some

new corn mix that just hit the vegan stores, and they were not pleased," we chuckle as their fight comes to an end and the cage goes up, Storm grabbing the mic to make her after-fight announcements.

I watch as she leans over the railing and nods at one of our closest friends, Lynsday, a persuasion witch who works at the club with us, usually behind the bar. She looks behind Lynsday with a scowl before nodding. Lynsday takes the mic from her hand, stepping onto the platform in Storm's stead.

I frown as Storm walks over to me, fire in her eyes.

"You know that little rat-fucker, Larry, that we graced with a warning for coming in high but not actually having drugs on him?"

I nod, "What about him?" I immediately let my senses sharpen as I look around the club and, within seconds, pinpoint said rat shifter toward the back of the club, near the restrooms, twitching.

I feel my claws dig into the soft skin of my palms and bite back a growl. He's definitely tweaking on something, which is dangerous enough, but to do it out in the open? The last time he just came in high, and not only did we give him a very gracious warning, but I also paid for one of the top rehab facilities for him when his mate reached out to me shortly after he was kicked out of the club. We had a hard rule, one backed by the Council in every territory.

Shifters don't do well with drugs; they damage a shifter's senses and mess with a shifter's mind. Since we have a stronger connection to our animal side, it makes it impossible to control our shifts. Picture a honey badger, that's rabid, and asking for the manager because their coffee is cold. Yeah. Dangerous.

With him back doing this shit, not only were we running the risk of coming under heat for the suspicion of selling, but I also had strict rules in place. Looking weak in any shifter community, despite the camaraderie Cabria Falls has cultivated, wasn't ideal. Especially as a predator shifter. Fucking shit.

"Well, not only is his greasy ass high again, but he also just snorted something that has his body fighting to shift. The wards won't let his body complete the shift, but..." her voice trails off as she looks back with a curse. He's starting to draw attention.

I stand up with a growl and weave my way through the bodies excited for the next fight. He won't be able to shift in the club; I'm the only one who could. A shifter would have to be exceptionally strong to bypass the wards our witches put around the club. Which means that his body will either shut down and knock him out, or the combination of magic and unnatural substance will make his heart stop.

Unfortunately for him, he broke the rules of my club and the council, and by my rules, his life was forfeit. And since he was in my "territory" since I owned the establishment, it was my job to dole out the punishment.

Reaching his twitching body, I wrinkle my nose in disgust as the smell wafting from his unwashed body assaults my sensitive nose. Without hesitation, I easily grab him by the back of his greasy shirt, and everyone clears the way with a sad shake of their head as I drag him toward the back rooms to my office. Whether the sadness was for Larry's current state or his limited future, I don't know, but what I do know is that there was no love lost between my regulars and Larry. He was a sneaky little bastard. Rats were already considered lowly shifters, but his penchant for lying and trying to convince newcomers that he could guarantee them a win with tips made him less than low.

How he ended up mated to the one decent rat shifter I have ever met was beyond me. But fate works in fucked-up ways. I would have to let his mate know, but she knew the rules of the shifter world. There was no way around this.

With a sigh, I touch the two-way pager on my chest, "Colette, can you come to my office, please?"

"10-4, boss, on my way," Colette responds immediately.

Colette was a godsend; well, all of the witches in my employ were. Even more so, over the years, we had all become close friends. While shifters and witches tended to have a symbiotic relationship, we had moved beyond that. Witches tended to get a bad rap, especially when those with particular specialties caused some to become uncomfortable. It was a new age, and Cabria Falls was a place that accepted that. At the end of the day, there were good and bad in every magical and non-magical community, same with shifter communities. The bad would weed themselves out; nature worked out a balance.

Colette, in particular, was a medical witch, handy to have when people were often getting bloody and injured during fight nights, especially for those wounds that even our abilities took longer than normal to heal, like a missing arm. While we don't encourage predator shifters to fight with non-predators, it happened a few times in the past. Those injuries were always a tad more gruesome.

While my decision wouldn't be swayed, I was hoping Colette could clear Larry's mind enough for me to talk directly to his animal counter-part, since the human side was dead set on self-destruct mode.

I turn my head to look behind me, "Storm, can you text his mate and tell her the score?" I ask, and Storm nods.

"Oh, Aneira! Fancy meeting you here," Larry gives a high-pitched laugh tinged with hysteria as we arrive at my office and close the door behind us. I shake my head and drop him to the floor as his twitches become more pronounced.

Moments later, Colette knocks softly and walks in.

She wrinkles her nose in disgust as the smell coming from Larry assaults her. "I figured this is why you needed me. Need to talk to the shifter part?" She guesses accurately and at my nod, moves closer to Larry and murmurs a few words that have Larry calm immediately.

She moves back, and I kneel at Larry's side. "You know the rules of my club, Larry. I gave you a chance before, but you disrespected me by coming into my territory and blatantly breaking the rules. You know what happens next?"

His eyes flash from brown and start to glow slightly, his animal counterpart coming to the forefront. "I have warned him of the consequences of his actions. But he has fallen too deeply. Today, he has hurt our mate..." he trails off, his voice roughening with anger and sadness.

I look back at Storm, who nods sadly at the phone in her hand. I breathe through my anger and make a mental note to reach out to his mate.

"Wolf, I'd rather our lives end here than cause further harm to my mate. Or anyone else. I pray to the gods that if my life cycle does not end here, my next one is with a human who is worthy. Do what you must. I understand the laws. I just ask you for one thing..."

I nod for him to continue, and he takes a rattling breath, his voice shaking. "Rat shifters are not well respected... most of the smaller shifters aren't. However, having us on your side can be incredibly useful. My mate... she is everything good and pure in the world. Look after her; I know what you have provided for the shifters here. A place to let out our frustrations but still maintain our community strong. She will survive my loss; she is strong, and I know you will give my Stacey purpose. She deserves it."

A tear streams out of his eye at his words, and my throat tightens as my heart starts to ache. I close my eyes briefly in sadness. Our animal counterparts were a part of us, but the damage that can be done when acting selfishly is heartbreaking. Losing your fated mate could have dangerous aftereffects, but if he has faith, then so would I.

"I promise," I say, letting my hand shift and my claws emerge.

He nods, his body going slack as his features soften, and with a quick swipe, I rip out his throat, making his death quick. I lean back on my heels, "May the shifter gods give you peace."

I stand up, and Storm passes me a towel for my hand, her gaze fixed on the security monitors as she watches the fight, not interested in what's going on in the room. Storm is a bit different; this is simply a side effect of duty, but I know that the cogs in her head are turning as she processes the next thing that needs to happen, like the rest of the fight night and how she would help Stacey now that Larry is gone.

I sigh and turn my attention to Colette, who shakes her head sadly, her lavender eyes swimming with emotion. Medical witches, by trade, are more connected to those around them. As such, any death isn't easy for her.

"Absolutely heartbreaking. I'll take care of the body," she says, and I watch as she closes her eyes and murmurs a few words. Larry's lifeless body starts to glow brightly. I wince at the intensity, shielding my eyes. Within seconds, Larry's prone figure is gone, and in its place is a container with his ashes. Colette leans over to pick it up. "I will get this to Stacey and check on her, make sure she can get through the night." She gives a small smile and strides out of the office, urn clutched tightly in her hands, her fingers white.

"We are going to have to check on Colette later," Storm murmurs, her eyes still fixed on the screens.

I sigh as I walk toward the bathroom in my office to wash my hands. "I know."

It was your duty. It doesn't make it any easier, but that was a mercy killing. Every moment on this earth, you prove yourself worthy of my spirit, Aneira. Take solace in that. Your heart is what separates you from those who abuse their power. You are greater than your past. You are stronger.

I don't respond to Agatha, but I nod in agreement. Taking a life is more straightforward when it's driven by anger or hunger, whether for honor or protection, or a meal. Those reasons are easier for my shifter nature to process. But when his shifter side begged me to end his life, to bring peace to his mate, it struck a different chord. I became more than just a judge and executioner, and it was... uncomfortable. But Agatha is right. If I shied away from what makes me a better shifter than my grandfather, I would be turning away from embracing what these eight years have given me: the ability to rise above my past and become who I was meant to be. And, fuck that.

That's something no one will ever make me do again.

CHAPTER 7
ANEIRA

Aneira

We make our way out of the office just as the current fight has ended, and Storm grabs the mic from Lynsday. My body goes limp as I sit down at our booth, and my eyes flutter closed, feeling heavier than normal. The last twenty minutes sapped my energy more than a run through the forest. I hear Storm cut across the speakers, and a chuckle escapes my lips as she makes another terrible pun. At this point, everyone who knows Storm realizes that whatever comes out of her mouth is done good-naturedly. Well, that and she has no problem bringing even the fiercest of shifters down to size. She would talk in circles around them until they forgot why they were upset in the first place. It's a very effective skill.

Suddenly, my mouth goes dry, and my nerves feel electrified; every hair on my body stands on edge. My eyes fly open as I lean forward and look at my hands, my black claws emerging and retracting of their own volition. *What the fuck?* My chest goes tight as I try and fail to fill my lungs with air. Shaking my head, I go to stand as a wave of heat overcomes my entire body, and I shudder, my core tightening and my head whooshing as sounds dampen around me.

A groan escapes my lips as I clutch the table before me. I feel Agatha restlessly pacing inside of me, and I shove myself back down into my seat, in an attempt to catch my breath. This is more than just my heat about to come on. The influx of sensations flowing through me—my skin tightening and my scalp burning as if the weight of my hair is too much for it to bear—are stronger than anything I've ever felt before.

I breathe deeply, picking through the room's various scents: blood, leopard, bird, bear, alcohol, sweat. Until one, in particular, stops me in my tracks: heady, masculine with hints of cinnamon.

Agatha pushes against me. *Mate.*

Ah, fuck. No. Nope.

Barely holding her back, I force myself up and out of the booth, creeping along the walls until I get to the doors that lead back into my office. I quickly put in the code, my claws detracting and retracting, my jaw aching as I fight the change.

Agatha, you need to calm down. But like any female when you tell her to calm down, she does the opposite. She snarls and throws herself against her cage, rattling the very fiber of my being. I gasp and struggle to maintain any semblance of control as my emotions war with one another. Excitement, fear, dread, joy, and anger threaten to suffocate me and overwhelm my senses as I wrestle with the doorknob.

I almost cry in relief as I burst through the doors, desperation fueling my movements, and lock them behind me. The change swiftly overtakes me, transforming me from two feet to four paws in seconds, thick silver and white coat, peppered with dark black fur instead of skin and a wolf that is throwing herself against the door in desperation instead of me crying in the middle of the room in fear.

After several minutes, a keening cry escapes my muzzle in defeat, the sound raw and achingly painful as Agatha finally tires and rubs herself against my desk and chairs in an attempt to alleviate the emptiness in her heart.

My mate. We must go to him. Her voice is raw, filled with the tears she's unable to shed, longing for our mate with a palpable force that threatens to tear me apart. And even though I don't have the heart to say it, I know she feels my stance on the matter...I don't *want* to go to him. I don't want a mate at all.

WHAT SEEMS LIKE HOURS LATER, I catch the smell of candy apples moments before the door beeps as Storm lets herself into the office. With one look, Storm tsks and strides over. "Oh, my sweet, beautiful, ridiculously giant claw-some companion."

Agatha lifts her head with a low whimper as Storm settles on the floor and lays her giant head on Storm's lap. Storm is pack, wolf or not, and Agatha loves her.

She strokes us softly between the ears hugging our giant head close to her heart. "You still have another couple of days until you are supposed to go into a full-blown heat. What's going on Aggie? I know you know that I can't speak she-wolf, so let's make a deal. I will get you some prime raw treats, and you give back the reigns to your human side so we can talk a bit. I'll even order some chocolate!" Storm gently cajoles my wolf, who huffs but wearily gives back control, and I lay naked on the floor, completely wiped out, my head on Storm's arms.

I sit up slowly, trying to ease the churning in my stomach as I fight the wave of dizziness trying to knock me back on my ass. A combination of the violent change, Agatha's needs, and my warring emotions.

"Let me grab you a robe."

I sigh as she walks over to the closet behind my desk, grabs one of the various robes off a hanger, and strides over to drop it over my shoulders. "Let's cover those lupi-titties, and you can tell Storm all about your hairy hurdles of life."

"But first..." She doubles back to grab an uncracked bottle of whiskey off my desk before she settles herself on the floor next to me, legs crossed.

I tug the robe closer, pulling it around myself, then grab the now-open whiskey out of her hand, hands trembling as I take a drink, trying to rid myself of the sour taste of dread in my mouth before I start.

"I smelled my mate out there. I barely made it back into the office before I shifted."

She hums and grabs the bottle from my hand to take a drink.

After a few moments, she sighs and shifts her body to face me directly, her hazel eyes almost piercing through my very soul. "Okay. So now we have a mate to contend with. That's not all bad in the grand scheme of things. You're going into your heat, and you have found the one person in this world, other than me, of course, that you are supposed to be with. You won't have to hide out in your lonely self-pleasure nest this time around. Also, isn't this a better alternative than a forced arrangement? All of the running, hiding, and bullshit has brought you right to the place where you can give your grandfather a clawed middle finger because you technically won."

Her face splits into a mischievous smile, "Now... did you see who it was? Was he gorgeous? Or was he so ugly that that's why you ran away? I'll have, you know, ugly guys have something to prove in the sack."

I can't help the laugh that bursts from my lips, and with a grin, she grabs hold of my hands and yanks me to my feet before she wrinkles her nose. "Ew, paw hands. Go shower. You smell like sweat, fur, and sexual ungratification. It's a very unappealing combination. I didn't sign up for the gross best friend package, so I'm going to have to ask for a refund. By water." She drags me towards the bathroom and walk-in-shower on the opposite side of my office. Quickly turning on the water, she shoves me in and closes the shower door behind me, humming contentedly.

After a few moments of hot water beating down on my sore body, I groan, "I don't want a mate. You know that. I'm over shifter politics and the bullshit that comes with it, I just want to be free from it all," I say for the thousandth time, although this time, my mantra sounds weak as fuck even to my own ears.

"You don't even sound convincing. We are going to have to work on your shitty acting. Also, look at the bigger picture Aneira. You see what you've created here. Times are changing, shifters are changing, and the younger generation is bringing about change. Whose to say your wolf-in-shining fur isn't the exact opposite of the stuffy fuckers from your old pack?" She had a point. "Also, didn't you say," she continues, "that finding a true mate was every shifter's dream? You used to be worried about being set up by your old pack and being tied down to some asshole but also because that forced bond would stop you from forming a true bond. But you beat that entire fucked up system. This is a huge deal."

She opens the shower door to look at me closely while I lather myself in soap, "I will help find you the booty of all booty calls to help ease your loneliness. I will shove chocolate and meat down your throat. But I won't help you lie to yourself. I am not qualified to be a shitty friend."

She moves in closer, inches away from my loofah, "Also did your boobs get bigger?"

I roll my eyes, used to the lack of privacy.

"No, they didn't. What if he is NOT up to date on the times and then I fall in love with a wolf who wants to make sure our future kids won't have a voice in the pack and they have to run away too? I just can't." A thought occurs to me, "Also, when the fuck did a wolf pack come into town?"

"Don't change the subject, furball," Storm scowls at me and reaches over to turn off the water, leaving me naked and soapy. The bitch.

She points a finger at me and comes closer, "Listen up, Aneira. If your mate is an asshole, we will shove his furry ass in a kennel and feed him only Cassandra's vegan meals. But you won't know that until you stop being a fucking punk and take the chance. You also cannot deny Agatha the chance at her mate, or you'll both go crazy and then fuck up the nice couches in the apartment. Also, your wolf is about to be supercharged with your heat. In the meantime, take advantage of a shifter's stamina and care of your vaginal insertion needs. After all of that, You can hide all you want, I will help your ass hide if that's what you want. But right now? Woman, the fuck up."

She turns the shower back on and glares at me while closing the door, " The club is cleared out. I'm going to help our witch bitches clean it up. Then we will review the fucking cameras, ask Dale the Guard Rabbit— which still sounds hilarious to me, by the way— and find out who this fated furry fucker is. Now finish up in the shower and get back out there. You have a club to help me clean. You Love-averse Lupine," she adds the last and growls menacingly, turning around to march out of the bathroom and office, her hips swaying with every step.

I stare after her for a moment, genuinely and suitably chastised and not in all surprised by my wolf's lack of reaction since I felt her nodding her furry head in agreement with everything Storm said. *Two against one... bitches.*

I turn re-lather myself as the hot water beats against my muscles, but instead, I sit on the shower bench.

"Fuck, me." I may not have wanted a mate, but it looks like after all these years, just when I started feeling safe, fate wasn't quite finished with their rousing game of "How to Fuck Aneira's Life."

CHAPTER 8
ANEIRA

I lock the door of the bookstore with a sigh of relief as the last customer pays for their purchase. Striding over to the till, I start to count down the register, trying to stop myself from checking the clock on the wall for what seems like the thousandth time that day.

Four days. Four days have passed since I scented my mate, and all we know, after having Dave review the security tapes with us and then reaching out to the established Leopard Pack, is that my mate's name is Casimir, his Second in Command is named Tristan, and that Casimir fought Pierce, the Leopard

Alpha, in the ring. He was absolutely lethal and downright fucking gorgeous.

Unfortunately, Pierce didn't know much more than their names, either that or he wouldn't share much, seeing as how our reception kept cutting in and out when I was finally able to reach him on the phone. The video showed Casimir being carried out by his second, which is the last time he showed up on any security cameras nearby. And since there was no established pack in the area, we couldn't risk asking too many questions. The witches had already scrubbed the floors clean by the time I made my way back into the club, and any clear trace of his scent on the floors was gone.

We did, however, happen to find a cup that he used before the barkeep was able to wash it out. I snuck it into my nest—not that I would admit it. Unfortunately, since it was a cup used in a club with so many different shifters and magical wards, there were too many scents for me to really discern his specific scent.

However, just the slightest whiff was enough for Agatha to demand that we keep it. She was having a tough time accepting that we couldn't actually track him down. But we weren't bonded, so there wasn't a way for me to figure out his location. Which, I suppose, is a good thing? It is what I wanted...want.

I growl in frustration, shoving the till closed and turning to flip the switches off before heading upstairs to the apartment. I'm flipping back and forth between wanting to find him and wanting to run far away. Agatha won't hear of it, though, and for the first time, I feel like I'm losing control of my shifter side. So I lock her down tight, and I try and fail to put his identity to the back of my mind and just focus on getting through the next several days.

Luckily, although it was close, my heat hasn't started yet. The waves are coming, though, and they're damn uncomfortable—more so than usual—and I know it has to be because of

Casimir. At least with the waves, I'm able to take the edge off with the furious use of all my vibrators, enough to stop me from feeling like my skin is going to melt off with lust. My favorite one, Sir Howler, even mimics an alpha's cock, knot, and all. Although I'm positive the real thing is a lot better. The shit I have to do to avoid a mate is ridiculous.

You should stop this nonsense; our heat is coming closer. I cannot stave it off any longer while you come to your senses. Find my mate.

I scowl as I make my way to the apartment. "You do realize that I am not a tracker. Most wolves wouldn't be able to weave through that cocktail of scents to properly hunt someone down. Besides, we have a date tonight, so stave it off just a bit longer, and we may be able to take a break from the toys tonight."

She grumbles in annoyance, and I ignore her as I strip and jump into the shower to start the motions of getting ready for tonight. Because, on the pain of death, as much as I want to stay in my nest, I'm going to have to go. Even with Storm avoiding my crabby ass for the last couple of nights, she hasn't stopped in her quest for me to find at least a good, consistent fuck. And last night, after hitting a popular shifter club, she found an alpha for me to go on a date with. Granted, she did let it slip that he was a cougar alpha, but even though our species didn't mix well, cougars were notoriously good in bed. That fact, coupled with her assurance that this guy is sexy as sin and unattached, is why I promised to at least entertain the idea. Then she told me to get my head out of my ass, picked out an outfit, and laid it out before heading out to check on the Bed and Breakfast for the day.

I would deny it until my dying breath, but that woman scares me. But, as Agatha pointed out, a best friend should always be a little terrifying; otherwise, they're boring.

I look at my phone as it buzzes on my way out the door.

Storm: Hairy the fuck up.

I roll my eyes as I put my phone in my back, not bothering to respond to her ass; I would see her in a few minutes anyway. Everything in town was a few minutes away, another plus for Cabria Falls, not that it needed more.

We are going to be meeting in one local restaurant that is popular with tourists and locals alike, A Pounce of Flavor. Pierce's grandmother owned it, and the pack ran it and everything there was mouth-watering, so even if the date goes tits up, then at least I'll have enjoyed the food.

Pulling up to the restaurant, I take one last look at my reflection in the car mirror and deem myself acceptable. More than acceptable, actually, with my long hair tumbling over my shoulder, the light, subtle makeup, and the turquoise dress that compliments the golden glow of my skin, I'm sure Storm would approve.

As soon as the thought crosses my mind, the car door opens with Storm on the other side.

She lets out a low whistle and nods in approval. "You are so getting laid tonight."

I laugh as I jump out of the car and smooth my hands down my dress, which Storm hikes back up.

I roll my eyes at her.

"You look fucking stunning. I know this isn't your mate—he's dropped off the face of the earth, but in the meantime, you will have some fun tonight. His name is Ralph. He will be the one that smells like a cougar," she cackles.

"Got it. What does he look like?" I ask.

She shrugs, "Hot. Anyways, I love you dearly. Get your ass inside. I'll be a few shops over with the girls. If you need me, text me, and I'll be here ready to shank someone and hide the body."

I manage to get out an 'I love you' before she shoves me inside and strides down the street.

❦

As I walk into the restaurant, I'm instantly hit in the face by the aromas wafting from the open kitchen, where I can see the chefs preparing the meals. Half of me wants to jump into the kitchen and eat straight from the pots. But I didn't think Imelda would appreciate that.

"Hey, Aneira, Storm just texted me." I wipe up the mental slobber as Paige, Imelda's granddaughter, calls my attention to where she is standing at the reception desk.

I roll my eyes, "of course she did. That little busybody."

She laughs, the throaty chuckle making heads turn our way. I could have told them all to a. Pay attention to their date and b, Paige was far from interested in anyone other than finding her true mate, and c, Pierce would rip the head off of anyone who looked at his younger sister. But I couldn't fault them for looking; with her bright green eyes and lush curves, Paige was a knockout. She would also knock you out. The appeal was double-fold.

"She just wants what's best for you. Even if she has to tie you down and beat you into submission to make sure you get it. It's what makes her so damn loveable," Paige smiles warmly.

She isn't wrong. Storm has a choke-you-but-love-you thing going on for her that makes everyone adore her.

"Yeah, yeah. Now, where am I going?" I look around the cozy restaurant, passing the many diners as I try to sniff out a cougar, but the scent isn't coming through. I frown.

"No worries, I'll take you to your seat. He's in the back."

I give a nod of thanks and follow her through the crowd towards the back, where a man sits with his back to us. His head turns as he senses us, and he stands in a smooth motion, turning to greet us with a smile on his handsome face as he buttons up his suit jacket.

I fight the urge to stare, but just barely, because he is something to behold. Imposingly tall, his gorgeous mocha skin glows under the light, and his obsidian eyes glint with some emotion that I can't fathom through my mounting confusion because *this* guy in front of me, with a panty-melting smile, is not a cougar shifter. He's a horse shifter.

I've never met one in person before. They're notoriously territorial bout letting people into or near their herd. I knew there was a herd in Cabria Falls, the Swiftwater Herd, but seeing as how they didn't work in town, only on their lands, I didn't meet any. I know of one horse shifter, Calian Swiftwater, who is the head of the Council in this area, but I had never met him either, so I had no idea what he looked like. Although, it is a good thing I haven't met him, seeing as how the council rarely looks for you until you get on their radar, and I was okay with not being anywhere near their radar.

Paige inclines her head with respect which he mimics before giving me a wink and spinning on her heel to walk back towards the front of the restaurant—another move that makes my confusion ramp up several notches; a predator showing deference to a non-predator.

He steps closer to grab my hand, bringing it to his lip to place a chaste kiss, "you must be Aneira. Lovely to meet you."

I pull my hand back and pause momentarily to admire his rich, posh accent, something out of a Bridgerton episode.

"Hmm, you must not be Ralph, seeing as you are not a cougar shifter, and I don't think Storm would have mixed that up. So, you know who I am, but who are you? Other than a viscount who apparently still kisses hands in greeting?"

His warm laugh envelops me, although it does nothing to perk up Agatha, who I feel hovering, watching this shifter with extreme interest. Although why her curiosity is peaked, she wouldn't tell me—*moody ass wolf.*

He pulls out my chair without responding, draping a napkin over my lap before settling opposite me and pouring us each a glass of red wine. I'm still waiting for his response as he eases back into his chair and pins me with a look that feels soul-deep, as if he knows all of my secrets and is ready to lay them out on the table to dissect them further in a weird, satanic, demonic horse shifter ritual.

I feel Agatha push to the forefront, her gaze meeting his over the rim of his wine glass, and I take that second to look at him—really look at him. Hair longer than my own, straight and tied at the base of his neck, his soft yet hard features accentuated by his thick lips. As handsome as he is, his face looks like it hasn't seen a smile in a while, as if he was rarely one for unnecessary laughter. Yet... I think to myself with a slight turn of my head, he feels warm, safe. His eyes flash as his shifter counterpart comes forward just enough for me to fall into his gaze, into a bottomless pit of untold stories that span several lifetimes.

He is indeed safe. His shifter soul is very old, very powerful. But he is good.

I almost respond out loud to Agatha when I'm suddenly hit with a wave of power so profound it almost knocks me out of my chair. Storm was right about one thing; he was most certainly an Alpha. However, he wasn't just any Alpha... No, with power this deep, he could only be...

"Allow me to introduce myself. I am Alpha Calian Swiftwater. You may call me Calian," he bows his head ever so gently, and I almost swallow my tongue. Of course, Agatha would recognize a shifter of his strength before I could register it. And, of course, she would keep it from me since she was still cranky about Casimir.

"Well, that explains why I didn't recognize you. It is a pleasure to meet you, Council..."

"Calian, call me Calian. And yes, I may know of you as is my duty, but we have not had the pleasure of meeting. So I'm glad it is on peaceful terms," he smiles.

I'm temporarily blinded by his beauty. But, wow. That smile could knock the panties off of geriatric grandmas with broken hips.

I register what he says and am glad it was on peaceful terms too. Anyone on the Council of Shifters, no matter where their jurisdiction was, is not someone to take lightly. As much as I hated shifter politics, we still had to adhere to certain universal laws, even if we weren't directly associated with a pack. And technically, you weren't supposed to ever be without a pack association. So the fact that he knew of me, and yet I was still left to my own devices, made it clear that at least he wasn't a Council asshole.

The Swiftwaters, though? I had to hold back a whistle of admiration. The Swiftwater pack was notorious for their secrecy but more so because their breed, The Shire, was dying out. So they were *the last pack* in the entire United Kingdom. I couldn't even imagine how that must feel for them as a whole, but as the Alpha, it must be even more heart-wrenching. Alpha Swiftwater was a hell of an Alpha, making a name for himself even after taking the mantle from his late father. He was a brutal fighter, ruthless with his protection, but widely respected as a loving Alpha to his people. His family had held a place in shifter politics for hundreds of years. So... yeah...fuck...

Still...

I clear my throat and reach to take a sip...okay, chug of my wine, "Hmm... me too. Although, I am curious why you are here tonight. I was supposed to be meeting someone else, and forgive me, but it's pretty damn rare to see a horse shifter let alone a Swiftwater Alpha, out in the wild, or should I say field?"

I almost laugh at his expression, and he shakes his head and sighs. By his reaction, he has most definitely met Storm and had prepared for an onslaught of the mere possibility of verbal vomit. But the question was valid because, despite their ongoing position in the shifter council, the Swiftwater Alphas didn't make their presence known often in public, choosing, instead, to stick behind the scenes and tend to the needs of their pack. So the fact that he decided to come out here made me more than curious.

"Yes, you were supposed to be meeting Ralph, my enforcer. However, I came in his stead because we have something in common. A shared interest, if you will."

My eyebrows shoot up, " Oh? And what might that interest be?"

He takes a moment to reply, and I'm partially expecting him to say he is also going into heat and wants to grace me with his horse cock, but the sane part is expecting a formal decree of death for running shifter wars. But what came out wasn't either of those things, and color me shocked when the words fall from his sinfully shaped lips.

"Your bestfriend, Storm. She is my mate."

My hand spasms on my wine, causing the ruby liquid to spill onto the white tablecloth.

Placing the cup down, I don't attempt to hold back the growl that forces itself from my throat. "Excuse me? Have you lost your ever-loving sea-biscuit shifter mind? Storm is *human;* beyond that, she is like 5 feet, barely anything; you would split her in half with a horsedick. Councilman or no, I swear, if you so much as look at her the wrong way, I'll kick your trotting ass up and down Cabria Fal—"

He holds his hands up to soothe me, and I realize that my

hands are braced on the table, spilled wine forgotten, as I find myself seconds away from lunging at him.

"Calm down, Aneira," he says lightly, though his tone is laced with power.

I narrow my eyes...you can throw your power around you, Galloping Powerhouse, but I'll put your ass to pasture, I think to myself as he runs a hand through his hair and the sleeve of his suit jacket drops down to expose his diamond-encrusted watch. I correct my previous thought...*Filthy Rich Galloping Powerhouse.*

It takes a second for me to remember where I am and instead force my shoulders to drop to listen to everything Calian has to say. I give him a nod.

"I met her last night at my club, The Stallion. It was not my intention to walk in and claim a human as my mate, but Storm is not human; she can't be," he shakes his head. "My stallion immediately sensed her; something about her that drew me in, like she was the sun and I was in her orbit. Or rather, she was gravity, and I was a meteor crashing head-first into her furious tangent as she pretty much offered you up on a platter to Ralph." I roll my eyes at that; it certainly sounds like Storm.

He shakes his head and chuckles as if recalling the moment they met. "The entire time, her focus was single-mindedly on him, while mine was on her."

My head tilts as I look at him, taking note of his absolute confidence. He's poetic. I'll give him that. As for Storm? She is a force of gravity for anyone who comes into contact with her so that part is pretty damn accurate.

I sigh internally as a server runs up to clean the table, fill our wine glasses, and leave a basket of breadsticks, which I rabidly descend on. Double-fisting two breadsticks, I take a bite and chew thoughtfully, okay ferociously, as I try to ignore the ache building between my eyes as my mind whirls a million miles a second.

Only Storm would go out to a club, try to hook *me* up with a Cougar, and end up finding someone as powerful as Calian to claim her as a mate. Figures. Storm loves a good romance book, and this was a recipe for a great one. Lone Stallion finds a mate within a crowd of people. It was gold. And, she could do worse…I suppose that someone legitimately 'hung like a horse' wouldn't necessarily be a bad choice. If he was right, that is.

I swallow the mouth full of bread in my mouth and point my half-chewed bread stick at him, "She isn't a shifter…I would have scented it ages ago…."

"Ahh, well. Horse shifters come into their change later than most others. Have you ever asked her about her family history?" He looks at me, a knowing smile playing on his lips that I want to smack off as he sits back comfortably.

I open my mouth to respond, but instead stuff more bread in my mouth because while I want to say, 'Of course, we discussed her family,' we hadn't. Not really. But I think she would have told me if she had a shifter background unless she didn't know. Her grandparents raised her, and they definitely were not shifters. Doesn't mean much, though, in this world. They could have had recessive genes somewhere down their line. Storm also didn't mention her parents much either, both of them having passed away when she was young.

I slump back in my chair while he continues to look at me curiously as if I have the answers. Unfortunately, I don't have shit but an unwanted, missing mate and an upcoming heat that is going to knock me on my ass. Especially now that I am certainly not leaving here with a hookup.

This was a lot to digest. And I'm not just talking about the bread I was inhaling. Because *if* Storm is due to emerge as a horse shifter, which, I begrudgingly admit, was likely if Calian could sense her at all, then she needed to know, and I needed to be there for her. First shifts were painful enough when you knew they were coming, but a random ass shift into a horse?

Moon Goddess take the wheel.

"Okay," I lean forward, placing my elbows on the table. "Let's say you were right, and to be very clear, I still don't think you are; why not go to her? How do I know this isn't an elaborate plan for you to get your Spirit on with my best friend," he glares at me, and I chuckle. "Calm down, you Galloping Gigolo." I snort with laughter at his darkening look, and I temporarily forget where I am going with my rant as he glares at me and takes a deep drink of his wine.

"Well, I certainly wouldn't find the time to come into town to meet with her best friend at a well-known shifter restaurant for a hook-up. Even you know that is quite a far-fetched assumption," He tsks at me disapprovingly.

"Fair point," I admit. "Hmm, here I was, thinking tonight I would stop the abuse of my vibrators," I say with a deep sigh.

"Sorry, I can't be of service with that," he says wryly. Not sorry at all, I bet.

I bite back a smile and wave my empty hands as I reach for more bread. "Regardless. How sure can you be? I mean, think about it...How do you know she didn't decide to go prairie that day and then accidentally rubbed across your *real* mate and brought her scent along with her," I say this with a straight face, maintaining my eye contact even when his gaze sharpens with a glint of anger, that makes me want to squirm in my seat. If he is Storm's mate, he will have to get used to more than just my quips. Storm's arsenal of word vomit is impressive.

He leans forward on the table, bracing his thick arms, "How do you know a quick trip to the dog pound won't take the edge off your heat?" I stare at him for a beat and then burst out laughing, tears streaming out of my eyes.

After a beat, he joins in, and the shock on his face at his own laughter sends me into another fit of giggles, and we start to laugh even harder as I feel the stares from the people in the restaurant. Then, wiping my eyes, I catch my breath and smile brightly at him, "Touche, Calian. Touche," I say breathlessly.

He glances at his watch before speaking again, his voice under control. "I can understand your hesitation Aneira, but I wouldn't have wasted your time or mine if I wasn't sure. So all I ask for is a chance to court your friend and, if I am right, which I know I am, offer her a place in my heart and my herd," he holds his hands up in supplication, and the earnest look on my face tugs at my 'I-don't-want-a-mate heartstrings.

I clear my throat and resist the urge to rub my chest as it twinges with a pain that I am growing too familiar with these past few days. *Want.*

"Fine, but I still have to know; why use your friend to get to me? Why not just ask Storm out yourself?"

"Well, the Swiftwater pack are a formal people. We respect and honor the old ways of courtship, and despite who she may be to me, Storm, from what I was able to find, has no family other than you. And for the past several years, you two have been very close. Your wolf has deemed her as 'pack,' it is only right to come to you to ask for your advice, guidance, and permission," he says softly, looking into my eyes with respect. *Damnit, he's smooth.*

I point a breadstick at him and say as much, "You are smooth as fuck. I'll give you that."

"Thank you," he chuckles.

I smile, "I approve of you," and Moon help me, I did. I hope Storm approved of him as well; she needed love just as much as my hussy vagina did. Although if she was his true mate, it wouldn't matter. Storm doesn't like casual boyfriends; she hates the idea of wasting time on relationships that won't mean anything. But a true, fated mate? Yeah, she would fall hard and fast. Even while I ran far and long, she wouldn't do the same.

Because Storm understands that you cannot fight against the lure of a fated mate, if only you would see the same, Agatha growls at me. I ignore her.

I take in Calians pleased expression and add, "You are going to have to get to her yourself. You know where to find her. Court her, do all the flowery shit she deserves, and if she accepts, then I won't stand in your way. But hurt her…." I don't finish my sentence, taking the butter knife from my place setting, reach for a breadstick from the basket on the table, and cut the tip off with a smile.

He shakes his head, "duly noted." His eyes go from my face to a point behind me, and a slow smile melts across his face. Suddenly I feel pinpricks of awareness on the back of my neck, and heat flares through my body. Before I can turn around, Calian stands up from his chair and gives me a slight bow before coming around to drop a kiss on my cheek, "It looks like your batteries may catch a break after-all little wolf. Don't fight destiny," with those parting words he straightens up to his full height, six feet WTF inches, and strides away and out of the restaurant.

I cock my head at his words, and abrupt departure and my confusion temporarily dampens the heat coursing through my body. That is, until a body hits the vacated seat in front of me, and the delicious scent haunting my dreams hits me like a runaway truck. Then, my eyes snap up to meet the eyes of the wolf that has been plaguing my every moment for four days.

"Hello, Little Wolf," Casimir says with a smirk, his glowing eyes and clenching hands belying his calm, cool words. I feel Agatha perk up furiously, throwing herself across the bars of my mental cage. *Mate.* Fuck.

Fuck.

CHAPTER 9
CASIMIR

My heart pounds against my ribs as I drive into Cabria Falls, the wolf within me rising like an inferno, demanding its mate and threatening to consume me in a blaze of unbearable agony.

My eyesight shifts from one sight to another as unearthly growls rumble from deep inside my throat and razor-sharp claws emerge from my fingertips. Inhaling deeply, I try to quell the tidal wave of emotions crashing over me, but patience is wearing thin.

After waking up three days ago from Tristan's blow to the back of my head, who, despite shifter healing, was still limping after I beat the shit out of him, I've been fighting every instinct roaring within me to get back to my mate. Not out of choice, if it were up to me, I would have rushed back the moment I woke up, but in the middle of beating Tristan's ass, I found out that Michael was having an issue with a rogue Leopard pack.

After reaching out to Pierce and visiting the University, we were finally getting back. While I could have sent Tristan in my stead, he needed to heal, and there was too much going on with the pack. We were in the middle of building the pack homes and the schoolhouse and were getting shipments of wood and materials every second, it seemed. With our shields in place, thanks to our witch alliances, we are able to have human help knowing that they won't remember anything other than taking a job for a wealthy businessman who decided to build a wilderness retreat. Between the humans and wolves working together, we were making a hell of a headway. I just had to quiet the voice saying that we were doing all of this for naught. Considering we weren't a formal pack yet.

But that was a concern for another day. After returning, I stopped long enough to shower and change before jumping back into my car and driving into town. My intention was to sniff around the entire town like a feral savage, but within moments of parking on Main Street, I picked up the hints of rose and lavender in the air weaved in with... a rump roast?

Frowning, I shove my keys in my jean pocket and follow the scent until I'm standing in front of a small restaurant bustling with shifters and humans alike.

"Casimir, I thought you found your mate. You're going to have to stop seeking me out like this. I'm not into wolves, man," Ramiro slaps my shoulder in greeting, and I roll my eyes. We had gotten to know each other while dealing with the rogue pack, and every moment I was grateful Tristan wasn't with us. Both of them together would probably do me in.

I turn to see Pierce chuckling. "I do have a mate, asshole," I direct to Ramiro, my voice deep and more wolf than man. "I scented her, and it's coming from here," I wave at the restaurant.

Ramiro smiles brightly, "Good taste then. This is our family restaurant. Get your mate, man. And try the roast. Shit is amazing!"

I shake my head as he enters the restaurant with a loud 'whoop.'

"Go get your mate, Cas. If you need anything, you know how to reach me," Pierce slaps my shoulder with a knowing smile before striding after Ramiro.

For a second, I close my eyes as my wolf slams against me. *Do you wish to terrify her? You need to control yourself, Monti.* I've seen too many Omegas be treated as if the only thing they were suitable for is to be bedded and bred. An Omega is special, a mate even more so. She would be mine, of that I have no doubt. But I will not rush in like a savage.

With a grumble, he settles, barely, and once I feel more in control, I stride into the restaurant. Her scent grows stronger with every step forward, and as if being tugged by an invisible thread, my eyes immediately hone in on a table in the back.

The carefree sounds of her laughter hit me like a runaway squirrel dashing through a forest rave. The scent gets heavier, and once again, I wrestle for control, my wolf raking at my insides, wanting to get out and kill whoever is making my mate laugh.

My eyes flash, and the horse shifter she's with looks in my direction and stands with a knowing smile. He kisses her cheek and whispers something in her ear that, even with my shifter hearing, I cannot make out with the din of the restaurant and the blood rushing through my ears.

He walks in my direction and pauses briefly when he reaches me. "Alpha to Alpha, her best friend is my mate, and by your reaction and the pheromones you're giving off right now,

Aneira is yours. Good luck," he says the last with a deep chuckle and a slight shake of his head and strides out of the restaurant.

I scoff internally as I make my way to where she sits, confusion marring her features. I didn't need luck. She is *my* mate. I spent the past few days working this out and had a simple plan. I would stake my claim, letting her know I was her forever, take care of her heat and live happily ever after— the end. Taking advantage of her confusion, I sit across from her.

"Hello, Little wolf," I growl out softly. Her gaze snaps to mine, her wolf pushing for supremacy as she scents mine, and her eyes start to glow softly. My wolf surges to the surface in response, and I take several seconds to undress her fully with my eyes, peeling off that turquoise dress that is so lovingly caressing her curves and holding in her full breasts, knowing that soon I'll be following every dip and curve on her body with my tongue. She is a fucking vision. All golden skin and defined muscle that spoke to her training, and yet she was undeniably feminine.

"Holy hotness," she stutters, and I laugh, pulled out of my fantasy by her words paired with the most delectable deep, yet feminine, throaty voice that all wet- dreams should be made of.

"I usually prefer Alpha, but holy hotness works too," I smile, but the corners of my mouth quickly turn down as her expression shutters. "Hello, Aneira," I add, testing the name on my tongue, and I find that it suits the wolf in front of me well. It gives me a little thrill of satisfaction that she jerks back in her chair, her eyes narrowing.

Her nostrils flare, and despite the sweet, pervasive scent of her arousal, she glares at me angrily.

"So, *Casimir,* you do know who I am, then. Which means your ass was what? Hiding after you scented me?"

My eyebrows shoot up. I quite liked my name on her tongue.

She scoffs, squirming in her seat, "Oh, yeah. I did some research after I told my hussy-ass wolf to calm down when we scented you at the club. We couldn't find you, though. Which is fine because I'll have you know I am not about to be another notch on the rollercoaster of wolf-fanged destiny. I may be a little blind-sighted by all of this," she points at herself and then back at me, and I bite back a smirk.

"But itches can be scratched, and then you're going to have to leave me alone. I don't want a mate," she huffs angrily.

Internally I rear back as my wolf growls at her attempt at rejection. Outwardly, I lean forward and watch as the pink of her cheeks deepen, and her eyes darken with lust as I cut off her tirade by placing my hand on top of hers.

"Breathe, little omega. I know your name because that delightful horse shifter told me. Unfortunately, you couldn't find me because my asshole of a second thought that I would lose it at the club and knocked me out, and then I had a pack emergency, or else I would have been in your arms and your bed that same night."

She rolls her eyes, "you seem quite sure of yourself there, Cas." She shortens my name like a curse, her eyes flaring, and it takes everything in me not to whisk her out of this restaurant and see how far I can push that defiance until she submits to me. I lick my lips at the thought and watch her eyes as they track the movement, and she visibly swallows.

I chuckle and meet her gray eyes with mine, "Yes, little wolf. I am very sure. You're my mate, and now that I've found you, there isn't anything that can keep me from your side. We belong together."

Her eyes lose some of the anger she is trying to hold on to, for moon knows what reason, and lighten with another emotion. Her eyes remind me of tempered steel. Strong. And if her words didn't already prove her inner fire, her eyes are a dead giveaway that she isn't going to be the docile creature that I had once imagined my Omega to be once I met her.

But I don't need or want docile; the pack needs fire, and I need fire. I want her.

She grabs the two last breadsticks in the basket and frowns at the empty basket before taking a bite from both of them and chewing slowly. Now that I am in her orbit, I can be patient. My wolf is settled, despite still being peeved at her lack of desire for wanting to have a mate. I had to briefly consider if my mate was broken. Most omegas, while balking at the idea of arranged unions, justifiably so, wanted their fated mate. Luckily, a little duct tape and Windex fixed everything. Or so pop culture said so. Regardless, her recalcitrance won't change anything. She doesn't have a choice. I'm not going anywhere.

"Listen, you're coming on a bit strong here. Let's say I acknowledge that you are my mate. That doesn't mean much..."

I cut her off, "You are wrong. It means absolutely everything."

She scowls, "Listen up, you Lupine Lothario, keep all that mystical flirty shit to yourself; I can barely think past my vagina right now. You have me at a disadvantage here. I am not exactly sane of mind and spirit here, and you know it. What I was going to say, before I was rudely flirted with, is that I propose we make this into a business arrangement of sorts. You scratch my itch, we tame our wolves, and we go about our business. No need for moon-ly matrimony."

I raise an eyebrow, "firstly, Lothario? I don't need to run around and seduce women. I only care about the one in front of me. Secondly, technically marriage is a business arrangement; being my mate is a fated arrangement. But if you want to make it business, I will consider marriage. But let me make this very clear, you are not a notch on the bedpost of fate or whatever other nonsense you have been spewing or..." I hold up a hand as she tries to interrupt, " or will, apparently, continue to spew. You are my mate. Period. And there is running from fate, and then there is running from me. I will chase your furry ass no matter where you go. And if you run, when I catch you, I will turn you over my knee and spank that ass until you can't do anything other than beg me for more."

Her eyes flare, and her lips part, letting out an almost inaudible moan as I'm rewarded with the sweetest perfume of her slick, dampening underwear, and she shifts to cross her legs. Yeah, she can deny it, but she wants me as much as I want to bury my face between her legs and lap up all the sweetness going to waste between her thighs.

She pinches the bridge of her nose and starts to mutter to herself, and I sit back and watch her war with her wolf. Outloud.

"This is not happening. I was supposed to escape shifter politics. Oh, shut the fuck up with the she-wolf shenanigans, you snarling show-off. I didn't want this. Okay, fine, we are one person and all of that, but I refuse to believe that the inner Aneira wants a mate. I don't care if that doesn't make sense. You shut your mouth when you're talking to me. I will go vegan if you betray me like this, Agatha," she runs her hands through her hair, tugging at the long strands as she wages her not-so-internal battle.

I bite back the urge to laugh at her threats to her wolf but fail to hide my growing smile.

Her eyes flick to mine, and she groans, "You see? I'm unhinged and horny. You should run for the hills while you can. Find a nice lake to sit by and howl at the moon."

I shrug and shoot her a smile, "I happen to like unhinged, and I *definitely* like horny. So the two together should make for quite a bit of fun, no? Think of all the possibilities. We can even experiment with some rope and handcuffs, maybe a gag while I fuck you so deeply that my knot..."

She grips the table and visibly shakes," Nope, nope. I am KNOT quite ready for that."

Ignoring the flush of her skin and the scent of her heat becoming stronger, I opt for a shrug, knowing that in minutes she would lose the battle, her wolf won't take no for an answer. But she knew that in the end, she and her wolf were the same, no matter how much she tried to fight it. "You are ready. We can discuss this more later, but I think we should get you out of here; you are very close to losing control. I don't think you'll want that to happen here."

"I'll have you know I am in perfect control." She takes a deep breath between each word as sweat starts to bead on her forehead.

By the Moon, she is stubborn. She is testing me in the best and worst way possible. I need to get her out of here and get her into a comfortable place so she can nest and go crazy. I'm amazed at the restraint she's showing so far, but her DIY effort at keeping the heat at bay has come to an end because her time was officially out. Standing up, I tug her chair out and gently grip her under the elbow so I'm supporting her as she stands. As she turns, her now golden eyes latch onto mine, fully dilated; I'm hit with the full blast of her heat.

I groan as I harden instantly. I breathe deeply as we start to make our way through the restaurant. It is time for her to let go and hand me the reins. There is a deep-seated need for her to trust me, and her wolf recognizes me as her mate. Any minute now, she will be completely lost in the heating haze, and her comfort is paramount.

On my way out, I slip a couple of bills to the hostess to cover anything outstanding on the table.

"Oh, Calian paid for the table," she smiles brightly.

I shrug lightly," Consider it my condolences for putting up with that," I nod towards Ramiro, who is currently juggling two squashes while Imelda swats at him.

She laughs and takes the bills from my hand, "Well, in that case. This will go a long way toward the adoption fees. I'm sure we will have to pay someone to take him off our hands."

I laugh and shoot her a wink as we make our way out of the restaurant and into the cool air.

A sour tang filters into my nose, and I have to stop myself from saying something stupid. My mate is jealous. Logically it's the haze from her heat, and she probably isn't fully aware, but it doesn't make me any less smug.

"Rude," She mutters. "Sharing that sex-dripping laugh with another female right in front of me." Hmm, maybe she is fully aware of it then, yet still denies the fact that she wants me for more than the ludicrous 'business arrangement.' Not that I would ever entertain the idea, but the sheer cheek to even mention it? If it wasn't evident already by the fact that she was a lone wolf in a shifter community, her past must be as traumatic as it was for the Omegas I took into my pack.

My jaw ticks, and I ground my teeth as I tamp down the rage that shoots through my body at the mere thought of her coming to any harm. I push my thoughts toward the present. There will be a chance for retribution if needed.

"Jealous, little wolf?" I taunt her. "The only woman I will ever have eyes for is standing beside me. You'll realize that soon enough."

She scoffs at me but adds no more scathing remarks as her body shudders.

"I need…uh…" She pauses with a deep moan that goes straight to my dick and grips my forearm, her claws leaving scratches as her slick gushes down her legs.

"Fuck. Get me home. I need…"

I groan as her scent envelopes me, and she unconsciously steps closer, rubbing her body against me as she pants.

"Where do you live?" I grab my keys from my jeans as we approach the car and usher her into the front seat. Her dress is damp with sweat, her nipples on full display, and it is taking everything in me not to peel her dress off right here.

She's so fucking beautiful, and in a few moments, she will be completely mine, and all thoughts of not wanting a mate will be erased entirely. I will be making sure of that.

Fated
Means Forever

CHAPTER 10
CASIMIR/ANEIRA

Casimir

"Flip My Pages, book store. Park there. Down the road." She groans, her voice husky with hints of a growl as she rubs her hands down her body.

Doing my best to stay in control, I follow as Aneira points and waves, unable to speak as she directs me to somewhere close to where the shifter wars are held. Finally, I pull up outside the quaint bookshop, and she jumps out of the car, trying to pull her keys out of her purse. When she fails for the third time, I take the bag off her and fish around for the keys.

She doesn't protest when I let myself in and guide her up the stairs and into her immaculately clean apartment. "Do you have a nest, Aneira?" I ask her gently while she not so subtly grinds against my leg to get friction. "I'll help you however you need; just direct me to the right place."

"Second door on the right. Nest." She staggers to the door, trying to pull the dress over her head and cursing when it gets stuck. Then, with a growl that echoes off the walls, she yanks the fabric to shreds, sending pieces of cloth flying around her like confetti.

I want to be offended because it's my job to rip clothes off her, but instead, I'm momentarily stunned by the sight of her lacy bra and panties. Until she tears them off with one swift motion, exposing her golden skin.

Fuck.

My throat goes dry as she pushes past me and stumbles into the room, and I wait at the doorway to be invited, in-knowing better than to barge into an omega's nest. Instead, I watch as she throws blankets around haphazardly, making her nest perfect in only the way she knows how.

It's a beautiful space in soft, muted colors. The mattress on the floor is covered with soft blankets and cushions, and the room is fully equipt with enough food and water to last through her heat. And that is saying something considering a heat can sometimes stretch on for several days and are incredibly intense, and the entire time she would be insane with lust and need. It takes an incredible level of control to force your Omega to eat and drink so that you can do the same. Otherwise, you would be fucking each other to death.

But fuck, what a way to die, I think to myself as I watch her body move around.

I'm snapped out of my lust-filled thoughts as she rises in

one smooth motion from her frenzy and stalks towards me, yanking on my arm to enter her safe space. The wolf seems to have taken over as she shoves me onto the floor next to the nest and tries yanking my clothes off.

My wolf growls, eyes flashing as he rises closer to the surface, balking at the loss of control. Now that we were invited into the nest, all formalities are off the table.

"No, "I growl out and pull her away from me, pushing her onto the mattress, pinning her feverish body with mine so she can't move. Then, reaching over, I wrap my hand around her throat and pull her up slightly so her perfect ass is pressed against my dick. I curse at the fact that I'm still clothed, but all in good time.

"You led an Alpha into your den, Little Wolf. Heat or no, your pleasure is mine to give. Do you understand, Aneira?"

She lets out a whimper, pushing back against me as her slick gushes down her thighs, her body saying what she couldn't vocalize.

"Good," I feel my claws lengthen, and I lightly draw them down her back, causing her to moan, before I sheath them and push two fingers into her tight channel, still holding her firmly by the neck with my other hand. She shudders, a keening cry escaping her mouth as I plunge my fingers into her, savoring the look of her perfect ass in the air as I fuck her with my hand. I bite back a curse at the feel of her, so hot, wet, and ready for me to take her in all the ways I planned to use her body.

As her sounds become more desperate, I pull my fingers out of her and suck my fingers into my mouth. Fuck.

"So fucking sweet. So, responsive. Mine."

I withdraw my hand from her neck, wrapping it around the silky length of her hair, giving her a sharp tug.

"You hear that? Mine. Say you understand, Aneira, because you are never going to leave me. You want to run? You'll be running into my arms, into my bed. You'll be running to suck my cock in between those perfect lips."

She whimpers, "Please."

I frown and place a hard smack on her plump ass, making it shake. The scent of her arousal gets impossibly stronger as she gives a sharp yell.

"I believe I gave you a command. Say you understand Aneira right now." I lean forward, drawing her ear lobe into my mouth, "Your body knows it belongs to me. Do you? By the end of your heat, you're going to be begging me to take you wherever the fuck you want. So, say it. Now. Say you understand."

"I...I understand," she breathes out, and I smile in satisfaction and give her ear lobe a small bite before soothing the sting with my tongue.

"Good," I step back from her body, and she growls lightly at the loss of contact.

"On your back, little wolf, I spread your legs for me and play with your Alpha's pussy. Eyes on me," I command as she crawls forward, falling onto her back, her legs spreading wide, her pussy glistening.

My cock twitches and strains against the zipper of my jeans as my nostrils flare, and I groan at the sight of her pussy, sweetly pink and smooth.

She doesn't hesitate to run one hand to the apex of her thighs to play with her clit as the other hand grabs one of her full breasts, tugging on her nipple, her eyes on me as her lips part on a moan.

I shed my clothes until my cock is jutting out, swollen and weeping, as the cool air gives me a modicum of relief.

The energy in the room crackles as her eyes fall on my dick, and she moans softly.

"Such a good little wolf; I think you've earned a little relief," I smirk as I settle between her thighs, grabbing her waist firmly, lifting her ass off the bed slightly to angle her hips to take my size comfortably. Wasting no time, I push inside her body, my head falling back as I flex my hips, my size stretching her impossibly tight pussy.

"Fuck," I grunt as she screams out in pleasure, her back arching and her breast now jutting into the air.

Leaning forward, I continue to work myself inside of her while I draw one of her nipples into my mouth, biting down gently, rolling it with my tongue.

She pants, her hands finding my head and drawing me closer," yes, Cas."

I pull back, pushing myself deeper, her body almost taking all of me. Alpha's were notoriously bigger than average, but our Omega's were made to take our thick, long cocks and our knots so sweetly inside of them. Still, it was a struggle for a few of my previous partners, but Aneira, as my mate, is made for me. She won't have a problem with my girth or length.

Rocking my hips, I'm almost halfway inside of her, and she will still need a few orgasms to get her ready for my knot, and I can't wait to feel her milking me like the good girl she is.

Fiery and mouthy but putty in my hands and on my dick. The way she should be.

Still... "You're to call me Alpha when I'm claiming your body for my own." I reach down between us to roll her clit between my thumb and forefinger, working myself inside another inch.

Her body clamps down on me in response, and her head falls back as her first orgasm rips out of her, making her body shake.

"Yes, Alpha," she cries out, and I slide in deeper as she coats me with her juices.

"Fuck yes, Aneira. Cum all over your Alpha's dick," I grit out as I look down between us and watch her pussy convulses and pulls me in deeper as it contracts, stretched to the limit. Almost.

Greedy little thing. I push the rest of my thick length into her, still caressing her swollen clit, drawing another orgasm out of her heated body, her head tossing side to side as she pulls and tugs on her nipples, the sweet sounds of 'Alpha' tumbling from her lips.

Unable to resist a taste of those lips, I draw out all the way before driving myself to the hilt, her legs instinctively wrapping around my waist as I lean forward and capture her mouth with mine as she screams out.

I slip my tongue into her mouth, tasting her sweet moans as the sounds of our bodies fill the room.

I fuck her fast, stopping short of my knot, knowing she isn't ready for it yet.

But soon, she will be. I feel my balls tightening as she clamps down around me, but before I spill inside her, I pull out of her and shudder at the loss.

But I needed to taste her. Needed to taste all the honey that was dripping all over the bed.

Before she can protest the loss, I settle myself in between her thick thighs and draw my tongue up her soaked slit and suck her clit between my lips, swirling my tongue lightly as I teased her. Her hips buck, and I reach to wrap my hand around her tight waist, holding her in place while I eat my fill.

"Yes, oh fuck yes. Shit," she cries, pushing her hands into my hair as she tugs me closer. I chuckle into the apex of her things, the vibration making her body arch as she gushes with her orgasm.

I dip my tongue into her channel and groan at the taste, needing more.

Her moves become almost desperate as she tries to push me away from her sensitive pussy. But I am nowhere near done yet. Not in the least. I am starving, and she is the perfect meal.

Aneira

I ALMOST SOB and lose all ability to think as Casimir takes my clit into his mouth, skillfully rolling my swollen nub around his mouth. Everything part of me is sensitive, and my entire world is on fire. How I survived with just sex toys, I will never understand. Because nothing, and I mean absolutely nothing, is better than the sheer amount of pleasure Casimir is able to draw out of my body.

He pins me down with a deep growl, and I reach my hands to grab his head closer...or push it away, I'm not sure which— my eyes now have a permanent place at the back of my head and are probably wreaking havoc on whatever lobes are back there. I couldn't science or biology when I had the god of pussy-licking currently working between my legs.

"Oh fuck, Alpha. This is just... too... damn good," I groan and whisper as he licks from my dripping pussy back up to wrap his lips around my clit gently, sucking my nub into his mouth while licking it gently.

I close my thighs around his head, loving the sensation of his tongue needing to work just a little harder to reach my swollen clit. He doesn't disappoint, and I hiss as he takes his time, dipping his impossibly soft tongue between my plump lips to lightly tease my clit. Back and forth, side to side, dipping his tongue lightly into my channel before coming right back.

My legs start to shake, and I almost sob as he manages to suck my clit into his mouth, sucking gently while licking me ever so sweetly, savoring me like I was his favorite meal. I feel my body shudder as he takes me higher and higher. I feel like I'm floating, and I feel his eyes watching me, and while I want to avoid meeting his gaze, needing to break this connection between us, I find myself looking into his eyes as he starts to lick just a little bit faster. I shudder at the intensity of his gaze, and as he bites down gently on my clit I find myself screaming my release, my back arching as my body shakes.

And yet, he doesn't stop. Instead, he pulls my thighs apart and descends on me like a man starved until I'm screaming out another orgasm.

"Fucking beautiful," he says as he crawls up my body and takes advantage of my parted lips to tangle his tongue with mine, and I moan at the taste of myself on his tongue.

Pulling back, he draws his hands down my body, caressing me from my rips cage to my thighs and back.

"When I'm between your thighs, I expect to taste no less than three orgasms, Aneira," he growls out, drawing his lips over my breasts, leaving marks on my body, claiming me.

I breathe out, my heat still riding me hard, and I can't say anything other than 'Yes, Alpha' as he places kisses all over my sensitive body.

"Good girl, now get on your knees," he commands, flipping me over before I have a chance to do as he asks, and wrapping his hand into my hair, he pushes inside me in one thrust, and I scream. He is impossibly large, yet my pussy sucks him right in as his knot pushes against me. I feel crazed and out of control as he lets go of my hair to bring his hands down on my ass with a heavy smack.

He growls, "This ass is fucking mine. fucking perfect," he smacks it over and over again, my pussy clenching each time until I clamp down around him with a hoarse yell.

"Fuck yes, Aneria. You're almost ready for me," he strains out. In my daze, I feel him reaching to the side as he continues to fuck me. I hear the familiar sound of my vibrator as he runs it against my clit, making me pant as our bodies slam together.

As he wrings another orgasm out of me, I suddenly feel the pressure of the vibrator against my tight hole and groan as he switches it to the highest setting, pushing inside of me. I feel impossibly full, and he groans as I go back against the onslaught, delirious with pleasure.

"You were made for me. I can't wait to use this body in any way I see fit," he grunts out fucking me harder while still fucking my ass with the vibrator, with calm, sure strokes. He plays my body like a fine-tuned instrument, and I have to wonder how he knew that I sometimes fucked myself with two toys at once. Just like this, and fuck if it isn't perfect.

"So damn good, " he shudders before he pulls out of me, leaving the vibrator inside of me.

"Turn around, Little Wolf," he says gruffly. I find myself face-to-face with his huge dick, and my eyes widen. Fuck.

My mouth salivates as he rubs the head of his dick against my lips. I dart my tongue out to run it up the slit and groan at the taste.

He hisses, grabbing my face gently as he pushes past my lips.

I open my mouth as wide as I can, barely able to get around the girth, saliva dripping down my chin as he works his hips gently with a deep moan that I echo at the feel and taste of him and at the sensations of the vibrator inside of me.

His movements become almost desperate, and even knowing there is no way I can fit him all inside of my mouth, I push him further down as much as I can, almost gagging, tears streaming down my face.

His hips buck as he looks down at me, wiping my face, "So fucking beautiful choking on your Alpha. I can't wait to make you kneel for me whenever I want, to fill your throat with every drop of my cum."

I groan as his words and gruff commands drive me into a frenzy. My wolf is mindlessly whining as she relinquishes all control to Casimir. And as much as I hate to admit it, I loved it. He knew exactly what I wanted and had no problem ensuring I knew it.

He grabs my hair, pushing himself further as his head falls back, his abs flexing as he thrusts.

"You see, Little Wolf, the first time I come will be down your throat. I want you to taste me; remember the feel of my dick in your throat as cum. Remember how you worked me over, and while you thought you had the power, it was your Alpha you were drinking down. So every time you think about running, you're going to remember that and come running to swallow me down instead," he says darkly, and I scream as he reaches over to fuck me with the vibrator while my tongue swirled around his thick cock the best that it could. He groans, closing his eyes briefly on the edge. I take the chance to dip my finger into my sopping pussy, then press them against his ass, pushing in and rubbing against that sweet spot. His eyes shoot open as he lets out a hoarse groan, grabbing my head firmly as he spills down my throat, and I swallow down as much as I can.

"Fuck yes, drink me down, Little Wolf," he grunts, and at his words, my body spasms out of control, and I scream around his dick, cum dribbling out of my mouth as I reach my release.

Casimir

I PULL my still-hard dick out of her mouth, knowing that until we knotted, I wasn't going to get the true release I needed, and she won't get through her first wave. Leaving the vibrator inside of her, I waste no time as I turn her almost limp body around, and still on her knees, I shove myself back inside her tight pussy. Only this time, I let my knot tease her each time, almost slipping in. My head spins at the sensation, and I grab her breasts, rolling her nipples as I anchor myself. Fucking her deeply, savagely.

Unintelligible moans fall from her mouth, and sweat coats our bodies as I lean back and flick the vibrator on the highest setting, panting at the sensation between the thin walls.

I groan as I grab her waist, driving myself inside her, her pussy sucking me down greedily and her screams echoing off the wall.

"Who do you belong to, Little Wolf?"

I ask, and without hesitation, she responds.

"You, Alpha!"

I smile savagely, "Yes, to me."

Grabbing her waist, my wolf takes control, and we fuck her ruthlessly. I feel my orgasm build as I lose myself in her sweet pussy, her juices and our sweat making us slick as our bodies rode out the pleasure of her heat. I lose count of her orgasms as her pussy convulses over and over on my dick. I slam into her, reaching to roll her clit as I feel my balls tightening for the second time, only this time, my eyes almost roll back as my knot finally slips in, and her walls convulse as she screams.

I don't hold back my shout of pleasure as my knot slams home, and I cum harder than I ever have in my life, her body squeezing and caressing my knot in the sweetest, most torturous of ways.

"Oh fuck, so fucking good."

Unable to move, I empty myself deep inside her with a yell, continuing to rub her sweet spot as she milks me dry.

"Yes, Little Wolf. Cum around this dick like the good girl you are. SO fucking tight and sweet."

Her body shudders over and over with pleasure, and my wolf preens as we fill her perfect pussy up with my cum. Needing this sweet torture, I reach down to pinch and roll her clit while I continue to grind myself inside of her, knowing my knot wasn't going to abate anytime soon. She whimpers in pleasure and pain, moaning nonsense words into the pillow as I keep her body on edge. Soon, her deep breathing fills the room, and I carefully rearrange us to our sides, my knot still firmly inside her. Looking at her like this, body spent, I want more of her. I needed more time to learn everything that brought her pleasure, and I don't think I would ever have enough time.

CHAPTER II
ANEIRA

I'm lost in the sensation of Casimir. Time no longer holds any meaning to me, and we fuck like it's the last day of our lives. He fills me in the best way possible, and my greedy pussy milks him for everything it's worth. Our wolves take over while we lose ourselves to our baser instincts, no longer talking, but the pounding and slapping of our flesh are enough.

This heat has been the best and the worst ever. The best because he's making me feel—fuck— I can't even describe how much he stretches me, and the knot is so much better in person than even the most realistic dildo I could find. But it's also the worst because even though my wolf keens in my chest at this bonding, and I've screamed 'Alpha' more times than I can count, there is still that niggling worry in the back of my mind that it would all implode on me, and I need to get myself out of this situation and clear my head once the bond haze wears off.

Which it finally does after eight long days of this fuck fest. I know my heat is wearing off when I suddenly need to leave the room to check on my shop. That slight worry about something other than my orgasm makes me slightly relieved that I won't be so reliant on Casimir anymore, even if he is the sexiest distraction ever.

He's asleep when I finally extract myself from his legs, which are tangled between mine, and his face is buried into my shoulder. I ignore the pang in my chest as I look down at his face as I pull out of his hold, but I need to firmly reassure myself that I'm an independent as fuck single woman that will stay that way for now, no matter how good his dick is. I will not be held accountable for what was screamed under the influence of cock. Nope. I'm going to have a shower and get back to work.

I'm sure Storm has done a fantastic job holding down the shop and the shifter wars while I've been otherwise entertained, but I need to be there myself. I've created a slice of heaven in this community. I need that small portion of control in my life, and after this week, I desperately need control. Although, admittedly, if there is one takeaway from this week, it's that relinquishing control to the right person makes all the difference. Not once did I mind letting Casimir take the reins when all he cared about was my pleasure and happiness. But now? I felt an odd pang in my chest at the thought; I didn't want to become dependent on someone else. I wanted to remain the independent omega that I was eight days ago, the one who wasn't afraid of being alone, of facing the world and whatever it could throw at me.

You are still who you are; it is your mate's job to provide for you in every way. Your job is to do the same. Stop making things difficult. I feel my wolf stretch and stir before she settles back down, completely tuckered out. I don't bother responding, choosing to step into my shower instead.

I crank the shower up to Satan's Soup level and step into the infernal elixir, which does wonders to unwind my muscles which are deliciously tense from all the crazy sex positions I've been in. The urge to go back into my nest and fall into his arms is overwhelming, but with a mental yell of 'this is Sparta' I drop kick that sensation right into a deep hole of 'fuck you.'

Ignoring the fading marks on my body, I wash myself methodically and then step out onto the cool tiles and wrap a towel around myself. My reflection is still the same as ever when I stare at myself, but there is a certain glow, a healthiness to my skin that I've never had after a heat. Obviously, this is some magical mojo from Casimir. After my DIY heat phases, my skin always seemed a bit sallow. I scowl at my reflection, cursing myself for looking so fabulous after a sex-athon. This is also not a reason to fall into the 'mate' fantasy. Clearly, all I need to do is buy some better skin products.

I leave the bathroom, heading past my nest and going into my bedroom to change. Yet nothing I see is something I want to wear. Instead, I want to grab his clothes and bury myself in his scent. Fuck me. For all I know, he could be some sort of a serial killer wolf that collects the toenails of his victims. Okay, he wasn't; that sort of depravity comes with a particular scent, but still.

I shove my body into a pair of leggings and a tank top, grabbing my trainers from my closet. My heart aches as I pass the picture of my mom while making my way out of the room. She gave me everything I needed to start fresh, and the last thing I want is to leave Cabria Falls behind. But, if she taught me anything, it was that there are no such things as happy endings in my pack. She thought she had found hers, and then my grandfather dragged her back into everything she had run away from in the first place. That's all I need—giving in to my wolf and then being found and stolen away anyway.

So while I didn't want to leave, I would if I had to. Storm might not like it if I locked her in the boot of my car, but she's my BFF, and I don't think I could live without her now. Fuck, if horse boy is her mate, then he might have to come too. Maybe if I ask him really nicely, he could shift, and we ride him away somewhere.

But maybe riding off into the sunset on my best-friends mate isn't the best idea. But I can always ride Storm. It's part of the best friend code, right? Thou Shall Shift and Carry Your Broken Friend to Paradise. I would have to figure out how to ask that question without pissing off Calian. But I did have a tendency of putting my foot in my mouth.

Just like when I was at school, and this boy I liked smiled at me, and I yelled out and asked if his pubes were as red as his hair. It was so fucking quiet in the room that everyone heard, and I didn't hear the end of it for fucking weeks.

Thankfully, he saw the funny side, but I never got a date. He ended up with Susie Jeffers after that, which made me die a little inside every time we locked eyes. Last I heard, they were mated, living together.

Blech, married bliss.

Casimir is still out for the count when I sneak into the nest to snag his shirt before leaving. I would never admit it. Not even to myself. Nope, I didn't do it.

My phone is on the stand next to the front door, and I swipe it on my way down to the shop. Fuck, it doesn't have any battery. Thankfully I have a spare charger downstairs, so there's no risk of having to go back and risk waking up the sex on legs, I was lucky he was still sleeping, but heats are hard on your partner; moon knows how many vibrators I've had to replace. Rest In Peace.

My fucking wolf whines, and I have to mentally tap her sharply on the nose to get her to heel so she doesn't fight with me and try returning to bed. Calm down, you Feverish Furball, I chastise her, when she makes a little yip in my head. I get the image of her baring her teeth at me, using that name for her, making my lips quirk into a grin.

The shop is quiet and has a little bit of a musty tang to the air, which surprises me as I thought Storm was holding down the fort. Worry courses through me as I hunt for the charger and wait impatiently while it decides to turn on.

"Come on, stupid piece of shit," I growl, tapping my foot until finally, I can call my best friend. It rings out, and then I get through to her chirpy voicemail.

Images of her lying battered and broken in a ditch somewhere, or worse, working at the Kentucky Derby, makes my adrenaline spike, and I need to find her ass. Why the fuck isn't she answering her phone? She's always answering it.

The air is cold this morning, but I'm too worried to turn back and grab a coat. Plus, I'll warm up if I jog to hers, which isn't far. My stomach rumbles as I make my way through town, but I don't stop at the delicious cafes with the enticing smells wafting out, even though my wolf nips at my heels to grab something to eat.

"Storm first, then food," I snap at her and ignore her as she huffs and curls into a ball right at the back of my mind.

Temperamental bitch.

I'm only slightly out of breath when I find myself outside her house. It's cute as shit with the ivy growing up the front of it, trailing over the rough stone. It was in her family for years, and she always said it reminds her of a mini princess castle which I always agree with. She stays humble by working at the b&b where we met, but in reality, she's rolling in old money.

My sharp knock goes unanswered, and I'm two seconds away from bashing the door in when it suddenly swings open, and I come face to chest with a— well, a muscular, tanned specimen.

Once my mouth is scraped off the floor, my eyes meet one very satisfied-looking Calian. His grin is amused as he stands there with his arm braced on the door in nothing but a towel.

Shit, what have I missed in these eight days of cum soaked sheets?

I brush past him to go inside, "Calian, we really have to stop meeting like this. I come to see someone, and there you are, like a creepy horse-shaped jack in the box."

He rolls his eyes and closes the door behind me.

I flop into the chair in her foyer, and air wooshes out my lungs. Okay, not dead. Just a whore. Although, I don't have a paw to stand on, considering my own week.

Calian stands in front of me; eyebrow raised as if waiting for an explanation of why I was in *my* Storm's house. The nerve. She is mine, my best friend.

Eyes narrowed, I take a deep breath and smell, yup, sex and horse-shifter. Suddenly Cardi B's lyrics play through my head, and I giggle despite my growing irritation.

"So... Storm decided to give you a chance then?" I ask him, looking up at him. Jesus, just how tall was he? I'm over all these tall hot men coming in and laying claim to our lives. Just clouding our judgment with their peens and taking over our lives with their 'me, mate...you, mine' bullshit. I feel my eye twitch as my emotions whirl out of control. Want, hate, sadness, helplessness. Too much is changing at once, and I don't like it. I don't care if it seemed dramatic, fuck that.

His lips quirk slightly, "So. Smells like you gave the Alpha a chance, then." His eyes twinkle.

"I have showered, you know," I grumble.

He chuckles, "You can shower all you want; the scent of a freshly mated female doesn't fade."

His smile fades and is replaced with a dark look that sends a trickle of ice down my spine. I'm suddenly looking at Councilman Swiftwater instead of Calian, and I now understand why he has the reputation he did. If this were the last look I had to see before I was sentenced to death, I would repent immediately. There should be posters of this look in all schools; kids would never misbehave. I tuck that genius idea in my back pocket.

"What's concerning is that you don't seem particularly happy. Did something happen? Will I have to work harder this week to cover up a murder? I don't relish the idea of Storm committing murder, but I would be hard-pressed to stop her."

My lips quirk even as Agatha growls at the idea of her mate being harmed.

"No murder. He's...great..." I admit bitterly, struggling to swallow past the ache in my throat. My head starts to ache at all the ups and downs, and I drop my head into my hands.

"I just don't like change, and this is all too much at once," I sigh.

He hums, his face sympathetic, "There are some things in this world worth fighting against and some worth fighting for. Being a shifter, we understand, more than most, that often it's the same battle—fighting against our natures for the sake of ourselves. It would be much simpler if, like our animal counterparts, we saw things as black or white instead of seeing the shades of grey. But fate, in this regard, is not a battle you need to fight. A destined mate is a gift, Aneira. This battle you wish to wage will only serve to cloud your senses and bring you misery."

I look up at him, the toweled equine philosopher of the new age.

"I don't want sense or facts. I want to kidnap my best friend, ride off into the sunset, and live happily ever after as old ladies who hit on younger men and make them supremely uncomfortable as we shine our dentures," I groan.

Calian's eyes narrow, "As darling, as that image is, wolf If you attempt to take my mate from me, I will hunt you to the ends of the earth and ensure you regret ever crossing my path."

I growl as I leap to my feet, relishing the anger instead of the emotional cocktail, "Storm was mine before she was yours. She is my pack, wolf or not. I call bestfriend dibs. Plotting before trotting, lupine before equine. That's how this will work here, you unbridled brute." I step into his space, and I poke his rock-hard abs to emphasize my point.

"Now fuck off; you had your time with Storm. She is mine now."

His gaze hardens as I speak, and our bonding moment is effectively over.

"I'm going to let this slide for now, Aneira because you've just found your mate and been introduced to the mating lust haze. But for the future record?" His voice deepens. "Don't put Storm in a position to choose because if she does choose you, you'll either become my new pet wolf or a new rug in my bedroom."

My wolf rolls her eyes internally. *Children, both of you.*

Traitor, I reply.

"Was that the Uber delivery—" Storm takes that moment to appear around the corner, also in a towel, looking wholly unconcerned and freshly fucked. She finally takes notice of my stance, and her mouth pops into an 'O'.

"What in the ultimate-beastmaster-hulk-out shit is going on here?" Even though she asks a question, I get the feeling she's hoping it's rhetorical as her gaze ping-pongs between us.

"Annie, how are you? How was your heat? Was he good in the sack? Sorry, I haven't been to the shop. Things have been crazy." She breaks off with a nervous giggle and plays with her hair.

My focus lands on her, and I'm shocked out of my anger. Storm never giggles nervously, ever. Her giggles are confident chuckles of destruction. What type cock-tail is Calian serving in that bedroom?

"No, the Uber delivery hasn't arrived, but now that you have company, I probably should show my face at Swiftwater, so they don't forget what their Alpha looks like." He smiles sweetly at Storm and kisses her on the temple. She leans into his touch, and a dopey grin flits across her face, making her look so much younger and vulnerable.

He pins me with a look and then gives me a broad smile as if he hasn't threatened to domesticate me, the fucker, before leaving us alone.

"Are you going to tell me about all the sex you've been having this week?" Storm gushes as she drags me into the kitchen.

"Er, bitch," I snark as I open the cupboards and grab two mugs to make us a coffee. "Think you wanna tell me about where the fuck you've been and who you've been swinging off? Last we spoke, you were a human and didn't want to be tied down. Now here you and Calian are playing my little -fucking-pony." I can't help the snap that rings in my voice.

It's not her I'm mad at. Fuck, I'm scared if I really want to put an emotion on it.

Scared that Storm will leave me now that she's found some-thing with Calian worth pursuing—straight out of a romance novel. And what's worse is that she looks completely okay with it all. Her life was rocked, from human to horse, from single to mated, from flipping pages to being flipped like a pancake in the bedroom.

Scared of my life changing, now I've met Casimir. He's not going to let me go easily; I know it. And fuck, if I didn't love that, he would fight for me in all the ways that count. Which was a mindfuck of its own.

And I'm terrified this fragile life I've created, which gives me comfort, will get shattered into a thousand tiny pieces.

#

"So you're telling me that you left him in your room, in a post-heat coma, to come and find me?" Storm hoots through the mouthful of popcorn as we lay back on her comfortable sofas with a chick flick on in the background.

"Yeah. I just..." I shrug, not knowing how to vocalize my insecurities without sounding like a whiny asshole. "It's too much." I finish lamely.

"Oh, honey." She pats my leg and leans her head on my shoulder to give me that fortification. She doesn't need to say anything, knowing my fucking awful backstory, and can see the reason for my mini freak out. "What do you need?"

Well, if that isn't a loaded question. What I need is for this all to go away and for everything to get back to normal. Maybe another Aneira in another life would be happier with having a mate—especially one as attentive as Casimir. But no matter how hard I try, the past rushes up to haunt me. I thought I was over it and beginning to heal, but the feelings building inside me make me realize that I'm just putting a bandaid over the wound.

"I think...I think I may need to get out of Cabria Falls," I say, tasting the feel of those words on my lips. They tasted like fear, and I hated it. What does fear taste like? Like unseasoned, tangy brussel sprouts.

Storm reels back as if I've slapped her and scowls, "Oh, so you've become a runner? You're going to run away from me, and the best thing that has ever happened to you because your old pack is a scourge on this earth? And don't get me started on hunting that grandfather of yours down and bitch slapping him with my hooves the moment I can shift and be mare-nificent."

I wince at the anger in her tone and the guilt that comes with it.

Her features soften, "You know it's true, Aneira. If you need to get away for a bit to help sort yourself out and come back from your confusion, I got your back. But I won't let you run from happiness."

I sigh and let my head fall back on the couch, "I'm not running from you. I'm not even sure if I'm running from Casimir, exactly. I just don't know," I jump onto my feet with a growl and throw my hands in the air.

"It's what he represents. Pack life. Wolf politics. Being a mate to an Alpha and now having to help run a pack. I'm happy running the bookshop and shifter wars. It's..."

"That is bullshit, and you fucking know it," she scowls, jumping to her feet and knocking the popcorn everywhere. Damn, that's a waste of good fucking popcorn.

"You've been content, comfortable even. But now that you found your mate, you have that final piece. So what if he is an Alpha? You wanted to find him the moment you realized he even existed. Why do you think I didn't bother trying to avoid Calian, other than that he's a romance book in the making? Because I can clearly see that a shifter can't avoid their fated mate. Why fight the chance at true love and happiness?"

"Because you're a horny bitch?" I offer lamely.

She laughs," Please, I can go without dick longer than a freshly blessed Nun, and you know it. I'm not going to cut off my hooves to spite my gallop or whatever the saying is. It's a waste of energy when I could be getting fucked senseless."

I shake my head with a mirthless laugh, "fair point. But I still need to get away for a while. Figure out how to get past this fear. Otherwise, I'll be a shitty mate anyway. He doesn't deserve that," I admit.

She purses her lips and strides to the kitchen, picking up the popcorn bowl on the way.

"Fine, but correct me if I'm wrong," she tosses over her shoulder as I follow behind her. "You mated during your heat. What does that mean for your bond? He could find you no matter where you go, right?"

I curse, forgetting that gem. I feel Agatha's smugness reverberate through my head. Storm, is right on both counts, we mated during my heat, and I claimed him even if it was during the sex-filled haze. There is no distance I can go where Casimir wouldn't be able to use the bond to find us. Motherfuck.

"Unless..." she stands in front of the microwave, salivating at the popcorn popping. "is there a way to block the bond temporarily until you can take the time you need to figure shit out?"

I feel Agatha rear back at the suggestion. I consider her words. It would take a powerful magical charm, but what was the benefit of having witches as part of your tribe if you couldn't get a magic charm to block a bond from your fated mate so you could run away and cry like a little bitch?

"The witches. We can ask Lynsday for help. Hopefully, before Casimir wakes up from the heat coma. It should keep him knocked out for a couple more hours," I look down at the time and shoot Lyndsay a quick 911 message.

"Hmm, that would work. I can't imagine Agatha will like that much; even my mare is cursing me out for even suggesting it. Apparently, it will cause you quite a bit of discomfort being cut off from your bond," her face scrunches as she listens to her mare, "and it's also unnatural. She thinks I'm encouraging you when I should...beat some sense into you and then just rally the shifters and...wow, that was very creative...well, let's just say she wants us to go kill your grandfather, get revenge, so then you can stop worrying."

I blink. Well, safe to say that Storm and her mare are one and the same.

"Can't say she's too off base. I'm totally down to plan a murder and pack takeover instead of sending you off with your bushy tail tucked between your legs," Storm grabs the popcorn and starts shoving it into her mouth.

I ignore her sage advice as my phone beeps.

Lynsday- On it, see you in twenty.

"Lyndsay will be here in twenty. I understand everything you are saying, but I need time to sort shit out. Mental stability before murder and all that."

She gives me the side eye but, luckily, doesn't comment on my crisis of conscience, and that's one of the reasons I love her. Yelling, advice, murder planning, and understanding. Pack.

We sit in silence for a while, stuffing all the buttery goodness into our mouths. Until I realized that in my drama, I never asked her about Calian or what the fuck I missed while I was otherwise occupied.

"I meant to ask you what happened with your fuckfest? I'm sorry, I am so wrapped up in my shit that I didn't ask you what happened with Calian."

She gives me a dirty chuckle, and I ignore the pieces of popcorn that fly out of her mouth.

"Cliff notes version until I can give the story the justice it deserves. A wild ride through a forest, a concussion, an annoying ass second-in-command that will probably be our new bestie, mind-blowing sex, and a mare who wants me as relaxed as possible before, apparently, the most excruciating pain ever," she rolls her eyes.

"As for Calian, is he fucking dreamy? Fuck, yes. Do I picture him as a horse while I'm riding on his back through a prairie full of flowers and majestic dragons? Also yes. But don't tell him that." She leans in and punches my shoulder, "But I'm not the one going through all the emotions. So, we're going to handle your shit so we can have a proper girls' day with diagrams and shit."

I laugh, my heart feeling full. Storm is sugar, extra spice, sinister plans, and porn diagrams. Everything a best friend should be. Every day I'm glad I met her.

I breathe a sigh of relief, "I just need a vacation, completely off-grid, then I can come back and figure shit out."

Storm leans against the counter for a beat, and then a devilish smirk takes over her face. "I think you need to have somewhere with cocktails, unlimited food, and time to be yourself."

"Go on; I'm listening."

"How about," she pauses for dramatic effect and gives me jazz hands. "You need to go on a cruise. Sun sea, sand, and lack of sexy alphas." She tips me a wink, and I let the idea claw its way into my brain.

I've got sudden images of laying on a lounger for days, only getting up for food and having drinks handed to me whenever I wanted. Then it's replaced by soft fluffy sand with aquamarine water softly lapping against it, only broken by the soft tropical music.

"Sounds fucking perfect," I smile, resisting the urge to rub a palm over the ache in my heart because, in all those images, Casimir is right alongside me.

CHAPTER 12
CASIMIR

Casimir

"Where the fuck is she?" I growl at the useless waste of space in front of me. "It has been two fucking weeks, and I've not heard a single thing about where she could be. If I don't get an answer soon, your head will be on a platter."

I slam my fist down on my desk, snapping it in half. I can barely breathe through the rage coursing through my body and fight the urge to gasp for breath. Instead, I let my claws slide out and squeeze my hand, the bite of pain making it easier for me to gulp down air like a man starved for oxygen.

But that is precisely what I was. A wolf deprived of its mate, freshly bonded or not, suddenly and without reason was like pouring acid on an open wound. I feel my heart breaking within my chest, a piece of it chipping away every second I don't feel our bond. It is a dull echo in my chest, and no amount of rubbing can ease the pain I'm feeling.

Tristan whistles, "That's the fourth desk this week, Cas. At this point, just stop replacing it."

I turn away from our tracker, Jensen, and hear his sigh of relief as I fix my attention on Tristan. My fangs lengthen, and my muscles contract as I meet Tristan's disapproving gaze.

Fuck his look. My wolf doesn't care that it's unfair to take my rage and frustration out on Jensen, and a small part of me feels so much better when a drop of sweat runs down his face and into his mouth. The rest of me knows it's wrong, but the rest of me can fuck right off. I want my mate.

"Jensen, thank you. You may go," Tristan says, eyes on me the entire time, arms crossed over his thick chest, his wolf close to the surface. As it had been since the moment, I returned to the pack losing my damn mind. He's been the voice of reason, and that should have been enough to jolt me out of whatever I was going through, but it wasn't then, and it isn't now.

I see Jensen nod from the corner of my wolfed-out eyes, and I give a growl that has him bustling out of the room faster. He and other trackers have been around the clock to find Aneira once I realized I couldn't track her with our bond. But I didn't give a flying fuck if they had to scour every inch of this universe and the next; she could not have just disappeared. I want her found.

"I know it is easier said than done, but you need to rein it the fuck in. You have a pack to run, not a pack you need to make run away. Are you ready to turn into your father? If so, I will challenge your ass for Alpha right the fuck now."

I let out a feral roar of pure rage, but he doesn't so much as flinch. Usually, I would admire that. Right now? I want to rip out his heart so that he can feel a sliver of the pain I am feeling right now. But his words have the desired effect as I take a deep breath to clear my mind. I would never become my father; my rage comes from a place of love, not one of malice. While I know that, it was one thing to understand it and another to show it.

I give a slight now of understanding. There's a beat of silence before Tristan nods and sits in the only chair I haven't destroyed.

"I still say we question the best friend. I'm not bothered; she's fucking hot."

I scoff," She's also mated to the Swiftwater Alpha. He will run a hoof up your insolent ass. Besides, I already text her every day for updates. Incessantly."

Dropping my head into my hands, I rub my temples, trying to ease the ache that was almost permanent at this point. I haven't been able to sleep well, if at all. I am exhausted, angry, and overwhelmingly depressed. I may not have expected to meet Aneira, but being without her was downright painful.

I've dragged myself from a cesspool of shitty wolves, built a strong pack, and gained the respect of all those under my charge. So how the fuck can I lose my mate after meeting her?

As for Storm, I'd love nothing more than to question her friend in the only way I know how— violently, but I respect my mate too much than to hurt her by going for her best friend. Not to mention, I don't fancy having a herd of horses trying to kill me.

When I can sleep, I'm instantly transported to the moment I woke up only to meet the cold side of the bed instead of my mate. At first, I wasn't too worried. Her insistence on wanting to be independent and her overall fear of being mated were enough for me to have a clear head. But my stomach sank when night fell, and she still didn't appear, and I couldn't feel our bond. I became frantic.

After digging around her apartment, I was able to find her best friend's information. Then I called Pierce, who was able to give me her number and where to find her. That leopard has his hands in everything, just like a cat, ever curious by nature. He even offered to come to talk to her with me since he knew her better. I tucked that in my back pocket as an option, but I opted for sending her a quick text that evening, to which she responded with;

> Storm- I would ask how you got my number, but you shifters are obviously under the impression that you can do whatever you want, when you want, and fuck the consequences. I'll have you know that mate bond or no, Aneira is MINE first. If she were missing for more than five fucking minutes, I'd be so far up the Fates' ass they would make me the fourth sister out of sheer fear alone. But not all gross and shit like the ones from Hercules. Because seriously. What the fuck was up with that shit? And no, I'm not going to rub up on a milky-ass eye, drizzling eye jizz. I mean, really, Walt? Really?! Anyways, Aneira. She needs time to get her mind right. Believe me, I tried to talk her out of it, but she does need time to sort out her shitty past; then maybe she won't fight your ass. She is under strict instructions to call me every day, or I will call Edward Cullen to rain some the sparkles of fury on that furry ass.

I chose to ignore the ranting and focused on the part about Aneria. She needed time. Time I could give her, but I couldn't *feel* our bond, which was more problematic.

> Casimir- Duly noted. Any idea why I cannot at least feel our bond? How do you know if is truly okay? This isnt natural.

> Storm- Reception is breaking up.
> Cant...Tex...Bye...

I narrow my eyes at the phone in my hand. Oh yeah, she knows exactly why.

> Casimir- Nice try. I'll be checking in with you every day. And soon, I'll be making a visit.

> Storm- As if I could ever be scared of Lassie. Go fall down a well werefucker.

> Storm- Also, I'll drop a gem on your were-ass. Being an Alpha-male doesn't mean you chase until they are too tired to run anymore. That's terrifying, not romantic. It's recognizing that sometimes chasing is a long game. Give her a chance to recognize the difference between exhaustion and love. Otherwise, you'll be chasing forever.

After a week, desperation started to leak into the very fiber of my being, and at that point the daily, 'she's okay.' Messages weren't cutting it anymore. So instead, I did something I didn't picture myself doing...ever...I found her mate's information and asked him for help. I figured if anyone could appeal to Storm would be her mate. Only to find out he is Calian Swiftwater and the area's Councilman. Whether I just made things harder for my pack or more difficult has yet to be seen, but all he did was to assure me Aneira is safe, and I should trust his word.

It was a nice sentiment. However, it didn't have the desired effect.

> Casimir- Tell me, Calian, if Storm is suddenly missing and you can't feel your bond, and you are told to sit and wait, how would you feel?"

He didn't respond. *Point proven.*

In a short time, my circle went from only Tristan and my pack to add Pierce, Ramiro, and Imelda, who kept checking in on me, bringing food, and offering a listening ear.

Yesterday, Calian dropped by to check in on me, only to say that he could not interfere but that she was fine. It didn't help. I need to know for myself that she's okay. However, he was very interested in the pack lands, even though he didn't mention legalities, thank the moon. I was not in the mindset to broach that topic at all. What I know for a certainty is that my ass isn't going anywhere, pack or otherwise, until my mate came home or I could find her.

She didn't make any promises to me. Not really. What was screamed under the influence of many, many orgasms wasn't something I could bank on, but the threats I made were absolutely worth their weight in gold. When I got my hands on her, after I inspected every inch of her to ensure there wasn't one scratch on her perfect body, I would turn her over my knee.

Her being off-grid was one of the most concerning things for me. I had called the witches in my pack to my office once I realized the bond was gone. Maddison, an empathy witch that can manipulate emotions, among other things; Asia a time witch who can manipulate time; Adaline, a dream witch who can manipulate dreams and uncover all your fears and desires and finally, Letty, an elemental witch who can manipulate all the elements. All unique, rare, strong, and amazing women.

While meeting all of them may have been serendipity, I

thanked all the stars and the moon that we ended up with the witch versions of our Omega's castaways. Yet, in their case, it was because their covens either coveted their power for nefarious reasons or were terrified of them. None of those covens saw what I saw—strong, resilient women who wanted love, acceptance, and a place where they could explore their powers without fear of judgment. They are pack, just as much as my wolves are.

They deduced that the only way to block the bond was by creating a moon-block charm. For the spell to have been used, whichever witch created it would have needed an article of my clothing, which makes sense since my shirt was missing when I went to get dressed that afternoon. I figured she wanted my scent, but she was apparently off galloping with Hermione. Harry Potter and the Hidden Moon Bond. Absolutely insanity. My life was a movie at this point.

The problem with the charm was that, depending on how it was created, it could harm her and her wolf if used long-term. Distrust in her and her wolf's bond was the least of her worries because the longer Aneira wore the charm, the higher the chance of her likely becoming feral. For however long, her wolf decided she needed to run. The bright side was that her wolf would likely return to me but would be a possible danger to the pack. This was a cluster-fuck of epic proportions. And all because she was afraid to be mated.

The witches had a few options for me to consider. If you could ever consider them as such. The first was to use an elemental spell that would undo the charm, but this could be dangerous as it could cause a backlash, resulting in Aneira's body struggling to handle the sudden release of the blocked bond, leading to extreme physical and emotional exhaustion. It could also temporarily impair her senses and abilities as a wolf shifter, leaving her vulnerable to external threats. In the worst-case scenario, the backlash could cause irreparable damage to

Aneira's wolf side, weakening her connection to her inner wolf and potentially affecting her ability to shift.

The reasonable option was to find the witch who created the charm and have them undo it. Except Storm was still as tight-lipped as ever. At least she answered my daily text to tell me that Aneira was okay. Although, I kept hoping that my side texts to Calian would eventually weaken her stance. Although, apparently, not too likely. It seems we both ended up with stubborn as fuck mates.

I can only hope that she would take it off soon, if even for a few seconds, so that I can get a read on her. I wanted her with me. Now.

My skin feels like fire as I clench my fists and let out a guttural roar of frustration. My wolf inside me begs to be released so that he can spread his fury with reckless abandon. My thoughts are chaotic, and my heart is heavy. I crave my mate. Our bond is unbreakable; I am hers, and she is mine. An unseen force chokes my breath until it comes in short gasps. Only one thing can quell this deep-seated agony - I need to run.

Before I finish the thought, I surge out of my chair and race into the forest behind the cabin, seamlessly transitioning mid-jump to land on four paws, my now shredded suit fluttering around me like confetti, as if in celebration of my broken heart.

I let out an ear-splitting howl as I leap over the chopped lumber lying by the forest's edge, eager to feel the leaves and mud under my paws as I weave through the trees. Eager to race away from the fragmented pieces of my soul, from the hole in my spirit pouring out the tears that my eyes can't let flow.

Instead, within my wolf, I relish the power flowing through my large body, my black fur moving with the wind as I breathe in the forest. The scents of pine, oak, and maple trees fill my nostrils, calming my warring emotions as my body blurs through the forest. I faintly register the sounds of Tristan keeping pace behind me, our mental links blissfully silent as he lets me wage war against my internal battle.

The questions are always the same, and I never have the answers.

Am I not enough to satisfy her? Physically, that just wasn't possible. She craved me just as much as I craved her. Emotionally, she never gave me a chance to help her heal from what was causing the shadows of fear in her eyes when discussing the mating bond. So what the fuck do I do to prove to her that whatever the fuck happened in her past had nothing to do with our bond?

I let out a low whine as my old insecurities rear up, the ones from when I was a pup, and told nothing would come of me. My father was a cruel Alpha, although he hid it well whenever the head of the Wolf Council would make their random rounds or when all Alphas had to report to their yearly summit to discuss pack matters. But he is as toxic as a wolf can be— forcing arranged marriages based on his favorites within his advising council. Fated mates didn't matter to him. Only control did, and he was loathed to relinquish it. When I was born, the idea of having a son appealed to him until I got older, and he realized that I was nowhere near as depraved as he was. I didn't tolerate the abuse of our pack members; it went against every fiber of my being. Naturally, my wolf wouldn't take part. I emerged as an Alpha a lot sooner than expected, Montgomery balking at the abuse at the hands of my father, not only to me but to my mother and sister as well. Unfortunately, my mother passed when my sister was born, but at least she was free. But my sister, Aoife, is everything light and pure in the world, and one day I will get her back.

I was thirteen, but from that day, my father never laid another hand on me. He could deny it, but he feared me. I relished that fear and basked in it. It goes to show you that 'weakness,' perceived or otherwise, doesn't determine the power of your spirit. It merely serves as a label others use to boost their own sense of control. Your true strength lies within your soul, woven into the very fibers of your essence— unable to be bound by any chains or shackled by any bonds. You will always hold the key inside you, and when you finally unleash it, its power will be unparalleled.

I should have taken advantage of that fear instead of leaving to create my own path. I would, eventually, when I was in a position to do so. It was another reason that despite the majority of the pack not wanting to be involved in shifter politics as a formal pack, it is imperative to our future. To eradicate the rot from our old pack and to save the ones that chose to stay behind out of fear of being considered 'rogue.'

I'm not sure yet, what caused Aneira to leave her old pack, but I will prove to her that my pack is different. That I am different. I just have to find her first.

Ridding myself of my thoughts, I let the forest embrace me. One paw in front of the other, I run, letting my body fall into that familiar rhythm that would push me to exhaustion if only to push myself to the brink of exhaustion. If only to fall asleep and have a few moments with Aneria, knowing she still wouldn't be there when I woke up. But for those few precious seconds...she would be.

CHAPTER 13
ANEIRA

I look at the necklace dangling from Lynsday's hands with a
dubious expression," that's going to block our bond?"

She rubbed it all over Casimir's shirt before offering it
to me.

She rolls her eyes, huffing, "Are you doubting my genius? Of
course, it will work. But, I want to say, for the record, I do not
approve of this choice. It is absolutely insane to me that you finally
have what other people literally kill and stalk to have, and you're
running away."

Hanging from a thin gold chain is a small iridescent jewel. If it weren't for the fact that I am putting my faith in your wolf to talk sense into your ass, I wouldn't even bother."

This time I roll my eyes, "Aren't you all about women's empowerment and freedom of choice?"

She narrows her eyes, "Yes, and I'm empowering you to make the right choice. This isn't about systematic oppression from centuries of gender misconceptions; this is about you finding the person that is literally made for you. The moon has given you a gift, and you are fighting against it out of fear of your shitty past. However, I will support your choice to take time out for yourself and reset because you will be back. Or, so help me, I will help Storm throw you into a kennel and bring you back howling and growling."

Storm sighs happily, "That's real friendship right there. Now, are there any side effects to the charm? She's not going to all Sirius Black and drag some sweet old man named Harry into the whomping willow, right?"

Lynsday cackles, "Man, Harry looked scared as fuck in that scene. Priceless. Anyway, a moon-block charm would normally make your wolf go feral when removed from your person, yes. IF a lesser witch had made it, it would block your wolf completely, and Agatha would lose her shit and eat a few people when you did decide to come to your damn senses. But in this case, the I only blocked the bond, you will still be able to communicate with Agatha, and your bond to Casimir will be the only thing affected. You're welcome. But keep in mind, if you take it off for even a second and he is conscious, he will pinpoint your location no matter where you are."

I stared at the charm, eyes wide, " do I even want to know how you came up with something so perfect?"

Her eyes darken, "let's just say, before I left, these types of charms were made to be almost more nefarious and leave it at that. You and your wolf will be safe. I promise you that. Now, I have to get the bar ready; since you and Storm here have been off getting fucked, I've been manning down the fort. Keep Storm updated so we know you're *safe. And come back soon, I'm working too damn hard, and I can't even drink during my shift like normal. Responsibilities suck."*

I laugh as she puts the necklace around my neck and walks out after a quick hug.

I fix a smile on my face, but the air around me freezes, solidifying my lungs until I can't breathe, leaving an icy void of emptiness that expands in my chest. I try to convince myself that this is for the best, yet my heart refuses to accept it, slowly shattering into a million cold shards that fall slowly down my body. I immediately feel...empty.

I play with the necklace hanging from my neck as a familiar flash of intense desolation punches my chest-- an unwelcome intrusion to my otherwise relaxed day. It's been two weeks since I left, and the pressure in my chest grew every day. While my bond was blocked, there are still times when I can feel Casimir's pain from my absence. It was either that or acute heart failure. I'm pretty sure Lynsday did that on purpose. During the most intense moments, it was as if my heart was being wrenched from my chest. To say it was unpleasant wouldn't do it justice. My only consolation was that I missed him too, but none of that, including Agatha's incessant badgering, was enough to make me take the necklace off. Instead, I took that time to journal and purge my thoughts and fears and look at it all objectively. But all that I could come up with was that I made a choice without knowing who Casimir truly was, and I was wracked with guilt.

After Lynsday left, Storm opened up her laptop and booked me a fourteen-day Caribbean cruise that I was currently waiting to board and a couple of weeks' stay beforehand in Barbados. When I tried to pay for it, she shoved me off and said it was her treat, promising to look after my bookshop and Shifter Wars.

My passport was already in her house as I had her look after it years ago, in case my place was raided. I gathered some of the clothes that I had in her house, including Casimir's shirt. Within the next couple of hours, I was being driven to the airport for an overnight flight that miraculously had a seat. However, I'm pretty sure Storm had canceled someone's flight and put me in instead—diabolical little woman. Just before I said goodbye, she handed me another passport, this time with my third alias, 'just in case,' and I was off.

Anything else I needed I bought once I arrived on the island and my escape...er...vacation began. To say those first two weeks were difficult was putting it mildly. While Agatha yelled and howled, I did my best to block it out.

As of this morning, she was finally talking to me again, begrudgingly. If only to remind me to get some extra food. Our appetite has been downright ravenous. So after I board the ship to make my way to my suite and change into a bathing suit, I head to the dining area to fill up a tray of food before heading back to the lounging deck area to stuff my face.

Already having done all the safety checks, the ship starts to pull away from the dock, and I give a half-hearted sigh of relief as I lay on the recliner, rubbing the ache in my chest. The two weeks at the resort were incredible, but staying stationary was grating on my nerves. Despite my alias being used, Agatha Gertrude Fitzgibbons, I felt like I was on borrowed time until Casimir finally made an appearance. While Storm is a genius, anything can be hacked, and I am sure he would be able to connect all dots if he hacked Storm's email and found a ticket matching the day I disappeared. Luckily this cruise ship is only traveling to private islands, and no other ships would be docking while we are there. Honestly, it was genius planning in such a short period of time too. It makes me wonder if Storm was some sort of secret agent.

I frown as my sun is blocked suddenly, and a shadow falls over me. "Can I sit here?"

I look up to meet the eyes of a tall blonde adonis. Before

answering, I look him up and down, and from here, the view is damn good. Tall, muscular, and despite the sheen of sweat on his body, presumably from the gym as he was dressed in workout gear, he smelled sexy and delicious. Yet...he wasn't my Casimir. So, eh.

I look at the seat beside me and shrug, "Sure, the seat is open."

"Thank you," he sits and leans back with a groan, muscles flexing. I feel my wolf get annoyed at the intrusion, and I discreetly whiff the air. Human. My wolf settles back down, not seeing him as a threat to her mate bond or she-wolf. I sigh internally, moody as ever. If it wasn't for this charm, I had a feeling we would have shifted and swam our way to land.

He takes a long swallow from a drink in his hand, "I was hoping you'd say yes. You're the only woman I've seen not leaking pheromones or shining their dentures. So I figured you were relatively safe. I'm Wilder, by the way." His voice is deep and pleasant, and if Casimir hadn't taken over my thoughts and body, he would have been just my type for a quick romp, but I had no interest in him. Or any of the other men who hit on me during this getaway. They didn't do it for me. I internally cursed this bond. I couldn't escape it, even in a damn ocean in the middle of nowhere.

My face splits into a grin. Despite the gym rat look, I don't think that was his first drink, "Gertrude, and no leaky pheromones here. Just struggling with my heart and its blatant disregard for what my brain wants. Which is for it to return to being cold and dead." I frown, and he laughs softly.

"I know what you mean. I didn't know I had a heart beyond loving my work. I would cuddle with my client list at night," he shakes his head, running his hand through his hair. "Hearts are treacherous little bitches. You think you're safe. Have everything set up. Have a plan. And in walks a vixen that knocks you off your feet. " He leans back with an angry sigh, rubbing his temples.

I laugh, "You're not wrong. It looks like we are in good company. Do I have that 'confused about love' look on my face? If so, I need to work on my poker face."

He shrugs, "Kindred spirit? Either we will drink away our woes or talk some sense into each other. The only other alternative would be to call my brothers and have them say to me 'I told you so.'"

"Hmm, I have one of those. A few, actually. They can be real witches, a tempest of meddling," I chuckle at my inside joke. I check in with Storm daily, only for her to tell me that she will let Casimir know that I am safe and that he wouldn't stop trying to convince Calian to give her up my location. Despite my feelings toward the entire bonding bullshit, this trip has served two purposes—forced relaxation and the realization that Casimir wasn't going anywhere. Not from my life nor my soul. The Fates have 'mate' their decision, and now I have to live with it. Those bitches. The entire mate rejection idea crossed my mind for all of .02 seconds before my wolf made it clear she would take over and shift until I changed my mind. Living in the woods for the foreseeable future is not in my plans.

I sit up, adjust my lounger and turn to face him completely. "So, did you realize what I've realized?" I ask, curious.

"That Hercules was probably accurate with the depiction of the Fates, and the only way to win is to seduce them?" He finishes off his drink and frowns at the empty cup.

I laugh, "I refuse to seduce those hades-loving hussies."

"That's fair," he says, leaning back with a dreamy, drunken sigh."No, I've realized it's stupid to fight something good just because I don't like change."

I nod, "it gives a whole new meaning to 'you can run, but you can't hide.'"

He laughs heartily and stops a server. He grabs two drinks from a tray, passing me one. All-Inclusive was a nice touch to this trip. "A toast to realizing that the heart is a traitorous bitch and accepting our destinies."

I reach for the offered drink with a smile and bring it to my lips. But as soon as I catch a whiff, I recoil and pull it away as I gag.

Wilder reaches for the cup in my hand with a frown, his eyebrows pinching with concern, "are you okay?"

I give a puzzled shake of my head, "Hmm, I don't know. I never met a drink I couldn't toss back like a champ," I sigh. "If it's not my heart, it's my stomach. It seems like my body's on a mission to rebel." I frown. Alcohol doesn't affect me, but it would have been a nice half-second relief.

He nods, throwing his head back to toss my drink down his throat."Can't let good alcohol go to waste," he jokes and stands up. "Thank you, Gertrude, for your help. Let's meet up for dinner. I feel we must hide from the single people on the prowl." He walks away with a laugh, and I wave.

I stand up to head back to my room, no longer in a lounging mood. Looking back on the past two weeks, I don't think I touched any alcohol. I just haven't felt the need to attempt to drown out my emotions, not with a drink. I was doing a pretty good damn job with the power of my denial. Subconsciously, Agatha may have been influencing that decision even though it took a lot to get me remotely tipsy--a trip paired with questionable actions while trying to be off the radar from my old pack and Casimir would not be the greatest decision. I open the door to my suite, strip quickly, and jump into the shower. After a thorough rinse, I dry off and open my suitcase to grab an outfit. A pack of tampons falls from the side pocket, and I freeze.

Son of a fucking bitch whore.

CHAPTER 14
CASIMIR

I stride into Aneira's bookshop and look around, Tristan sharp on my heels. Storm hovers behind the counter with wide eyes. I wasn't deterred by her fake innocent look or the fucking horse shifters helping her in the shop. I couldn't care less if they all reported to Calian that a crazed Alpha wolf with an unshaven face and red eyes was terrorizing the town. I am losing my shit.

My wolf will rake his way out of my chest and take over if I didn't get to my mate soon. It's officially been three weeks, and my patience was now gone. In all truth, I am impressed I held back this long. However, I was going to resort to bypassing any semblance of privacy and get my wolves to hack everything tech-related that Aneira and Storm owned.

I slam the door behind me and lock it. I nod to Tristan, and he moves to guard it, crossing his arms and staring down the shifters who are not so discreetly texting on their phones in haste. I stomp over to the counter, my eyes glowing.

Leaning over it, I get in Storm's face and deepen my tone. "Tell me where my mate is, Storm. Before I have to do something, I won't be proud of," My lips curl in an ugly sneer as my teeth grind together.

She looks into my eyes and laughs. *Fucking Laughs.* Waving the horse shifters away from the counter, she giggles, "Well damn, Casimir. It took you long enough to go all Alpha. It is about time." She chuckles and pulls out a laptop from under the counter before opening it to start typing.

I blink at her and lean back from the counter. My anger bleeds into irritation and I scowl at her, "You're telling me, if I would have come in here and lost my mind sooner, you would have helped me?"

She blinked, "Well, after adequate time for her to get shit sorted in her head, yeah. Which, admittedly, should have only taken her about a week. But if you weren't going to fight for her, why the hell would I help you? Texting is good and all, and it's appreciated, but when you really want something, sometimes you need to go berserk." She shrugs, "After all your mind-blowing sex and bonding, I am surprised you lasted this long. I would have burned down every house of anyone who got in my way of finding Calian," she paused and glanced over at the door.

"Uh, I suggest you ask your second to move from that door before he ends up with a hoof print on his meaty forehead," she smirks before looking down to clack on her keyboard. *Is she fucking hacking the Pentagon?*

Moments later, Tristan jumps out of the way as the door

shatters, and Calian strides in with a…cougar shifter on his heels. *Interesting.*

I watch as Tristan and the cougar size each other up, but my focus is drawn back to Storm, who looks up and scowls, "You have a fucking key, you damn horse Neanderthal. You're going to fix that fucking door."

Calian blinks in surprise at her tone and holds his hands up, "I was just coming to help you." He looks around and glowers at Tristan and me. I suppress a smile at the great Swiftwater Alpha warring between anger and looking chagrined.

Storm scoffs, "Casimir is a puppy with no fur. He wouldn't do shit to me knowing Aneira would peg his ass with no lube."

"Hey!" I say indignantly.

"Hay is for horses," she replies primly, "which is all Calian is going to be eating, instead of me, if he doesn't start fixing my damn door."

Calian sighs, rubbing his head, before going behind the counter and grabbing Storm for a kiss. After a few moments, she pulls away, her cheeks pink and her breathing shallow. "That's a better way to greet me, Stallion." Calian smiles down at Storm warmly, wrapping his arms around her, the door now forgotten. I feel a pang of jealousy in my chest. I *want my mate.*

"Now that you've come to your senses, *this* week she is on a cruise. It's supposed to dock back in Barbados in another week." She glances at the computer screen, and my chest tightens at the thought. I can't wait another week.

"Luckily, the cruise ship is docked at a small island for a couple of days starting tomorrow," she adds with glee, clapping her damn hands. "But you'll have to jump on a plane to get here," she points at a map, indicating a random island I had never heard of. "Then you'll need to charter a boat to get here," she points at another tiny island. Jesus, Aneira did all of this to get away from me? My wolf pouts before he growls, *get my mate.*

That's the plan, buddy.

"Now, you would have to leave soon. Calian can help with that," she looks back at him, and he looks down, startled, confusion marring his face.

"I can?" He asks.

"Absolutely. You are ridiculously rich and my mate. Well, I'm also loaded, but that's neither here nor there," she waves her hands in the air. "The point is that money is no object when it comes to my best friend…"

"I can afford it…" I start, and she glares at me cutting me off.

The cougar nudges my shoulder, "Don't cut her off when she is on a tangent, Bro. Trust me."

Storm gives him a bright smile, "Thank you, Ralph; you are the cat's meow."

Ralph nods sagely and gives me the side eye. Got it. Just go with it.

"Like I was saying before, I was howl-ly interrupted… my furry soul-mate sister. By the court of furry law, Aneira is your sister-in-law. Or is it sister-in-mate? Which, then, makes Casimir your brother-in-law, mate. This means he is part of your pack, and you're part of his; we are all one big shifter family. And since we will not be one of those weird families that only see each other on holidays… I mean, really, what the fuck is that about?"

We stare at her silently while she takes a deep breath. Ralph shakes his head subtly.

Right. Not done.

"Therefore, your money, my money, is their money and all that—shifter division of assets. So, we have to help. Understand?" Hands on her hips, she meets our gazes, eyes glowing brightly as her face splits into a satisfied smirk. I have this strange urge to clap that I barely hold back. Instead, I run my hands through my already mussed hair.

Calian and I glance at each other with varying shades of bemusement and awe at the force of her conviction. There was no point in telling her that shifter groups technically didn't work that way because I had a feeling it won't matter. She could probably convince a beaver it was a bear, and no one would bat an eye. She was born to be an Alpha's mate, more so a wife of a councilman. I shudder to think of the force she and Aneira would be, with Aneira's stubbornness and Storm's inner fire. Terrifying really.

Knowing that Aneria had a sister like Storm and, thereby, a family like the Swiftwaters, as she hereby dictated, made me feel a sense of intense peace. There was something to be said for a real family, even if it was one that you created yourself, despite all odds against you. I respected that, and I knew the sentiment and circumstance well. Despite the challenges of starting my own pack of misfits and the few knuckleheads we had, we made it, and we were strong as fuck. We had accumulated witch allies, almost unheard of within shifter society, and loyal wolves were saved from shitty circumstances. And due to our varying talents, we have coffers as well as accounts full of money to support our pack and our needs.

The Spiorad Pack was a force to be reckoned with, and although we were not yet formally recognized as a pack, I was working on changing the minds of the pack members. Especially if I want to keep Aneira in my life, having the Swiftwaters on our side will more than sway matters; it would solidify our place.

Calian sighs deeply, "Well, when you put it like that, mate. I suppose you are correct." The shifters in his room cough to disguise their laughter when he glares in their direction.

Looking at me, he nods, "I'll arrange transport for you. Storm is right, I have a private plane you can use, and I will call to charter a boat for your use. At island West-Bumble-Fuck," he mutters the last as he grabs his phone and starts making calls.

As Montgomery's howl of joy reverberates within my skull, a long-held dread lifts from my chest, and I can feel my muscles release as I exhale a deep sigh of relief.

Tristan slaps my shoulder, "Cas, go get your mate...distract her with your giant cock, tie her up, and bring our Luna the fuck home. I will hold down the fort here." With a nod toward Calian and Storm, Tristan strides out of the bookstore, but not before he hands over the backpack full of my clothes; we prepared, knowing that I would leave to find her today, no matter what.

I blink as his words sink in. Home, established or not, Cabria Falls is where our pack belongs. But more importantly, *our Luna*. In our old pack, our women, no matter their mate, weren't given a position that would have indicated any form of power, and while I have always, internally, thought of Aneria as more than just an Omega, to hear it fall from my second's lips, is powerful.

"Um, before you hit the airport, may I suggest you go upstairs, shower, shave, and change? You look gross. Definitely not brother-in-mate material," Storm wrinkles her nose, and I laugh, the carefree sound almost foreign coming from my lips after these past few weeks.

I jump over the counter and wrap her in a hug, much to Calians displeasure, if his low neigh-like growl is any indication.

Storm laughs and hugs me back, "I know I saved the day. I have a tendency to do that. It's a superpower. Now go bring back our girl."

As if anything could stop me.

AFTER A QUICK SHOWER AND SHAVE, I jump into a car Calian has waiting for me in the front of the shop, Ralph in the driver's seat.

"When you get to the airstrip, you'll meet my Pilot, Aurora, but call her Rory, or she gets a little peeved," Calian nods, taps the top of the car, and we pull off.

Ralph snorts as we drive away, "peeved is putting it lightly. She is a scary little thing. She hates her name because she was named after sleeping beauty— her mom has a bit of a Disney obsession—Not knowing that Rory would later be diagnosed with a neurological condition that makes her pass out when overexcited or angry. So she is a bit sensitive about her name. "

I was familiar with the condition in passing, Tristan being our medical doctor in our pack and my best friend; I was there for every study session and every flashcard drill.

I nod, "cataplexy? Wouldn't that make her being a pilot a little dangerous?"

"Nah, she has it under control for the most part. As well as a magical charm we had made for her. She is usually very easy-going. Just don't piss her off; she is more likely to stab you in the cockpit and smile the entire time without even raising her heart rate. Shifter control and all. Bird shifters tend to go with the airflow… get it?" He chortles.

I shake my head. He fills the quick drive with stories about how Calian and Storm met and how Storm was on a mission to change the shifter world, from coercing members of the shifter council to sending her own personal bodyguard, Oliver, off on secret missions.

"You haven't had the chance to really get to know Storm yet, but if Aneira is anything like her, I feel bad for whoever gets in their way of the shifter revolution she is planning," he chuckles. Before I can ask what he means, we are pulling up to the Airstrip, and I'm hoping out of the car.

"Good luck Pack-in-Mate. Bring your girl home, or Storm will make you into a wolf kebab," he laughs and pulls out of the lot with a quick wave to who I presume is Aurora, standing by a small plane with the name "Neigh-Vagator," printed on the side.

I laugh and shake my head as I walk up the tarmac to where she is waiting. If Tristan were here, he would waste no time flirting with the beautiful, tall, athletic woman with long, wavy bright-red hair and amber eyes rimmed in gold that shine the closer I get. She is wearing low-hanging jeans and a tank top that reads, 'Will Set Fire To Your Loins,' with a colorful tattoo of a Pheonix in flight that wraps around her right forearm on display. I take a deep breath, confirming my suspicions, a Pheonix shifter.

By the moon.

"I'm Rory; let's get you to island west-bumble-fuck so that I can lay in the sun while you run off to get your mate and bring her ass home," she smiles brightly, and I narrow my eyes as she almost knocks me off my feet with the strength pouring off of her.

She laughs, pulling back her power, "Sorry, I tend to leak power when I'm not paying attention. In the sky, no one cares how strong you are. There aren't any shifter powerplays; it's nice just to be free."

I nod in understanding as I follow her up the small staircase, and she waves me into the cock-pit to sit next to her instead of in the seats in the back, "you can sit up with me and give me all the juicy details. I got the low-down from Storm, but I must hear it all. We have a few hours, so sit back, relax, and give it to Dear Rory."

I laugh and sit back as she starts the plane and goes through all the checks before getting us into the air. The pressure is making me a tad uncomfortable. I preferred running through the forest, not the clouds, but whatever got me closer to my mate.

Before I decide to give a random bird shifter my entire life story, my curiosity gets the best of me, "your power...." I start and let the rest hang in the air. Who was she, and how the fuck was she so strong but working as Calian's private pilot.

She waves her hand, "Oh, my aunt is the Phoenix on the Shifter Council. I'm technically next in line because of my power, but my cousin wants the mantle. I could care less. Calian offered me a job and his guidance, and I leaped on it. No one argues with him, which works for me. I don't like the bullshit that comes with politics, you know? Playing favorites and the entire blah blah blah, you must pay for your transgressions," her voice deepens with the last, and she laughs.

I nod. I definitely understand her point. It wasn't easy running a Pack, let alone having the mantle of being responsible for multiple packs, and even then, the Council still allowed a lot of shit to fly under the radar. They needed a better system.

"Anyways, enough about me. Tell me everything, and I'll try to help you not fuck up. She ran for a reason; let's fix it."

So for the next few hours, we hash out a plan, which she names 'Operation Fiery Heart Heist,' to figure out a way to get my mate through whatever she was terrified of.

CHAPTER 15
CASIMIR

After we land on a small tarmac, Rory points to the private boat and gives me a quick wave before heading off to "recharge her flames of temptation." I shake my head with a laugh. In the short time, I've been in Cabria Falls, I've met more shifters than I ever had living within my old pack lands. It's easy to see why Calian is so well respected. He has created something quite extraordinary, not only by gaining the respect of various shifters but also providing them with a safe place to be themselves. He has created the exact world that shifters need to truly thrive instead of hiding in the shadows.

Grabbing my bag, I make my way to the waiting boat—although "boat" is putting it mildly, considering it's actually a massive luxury yacht—and give a slight nod to the man who Rory said was named Calder. Tall and powerfully built with dark hair and eyes as blue as the water, he sails, covered in tattoos ranging from tribal ink to a dragon wrapped around his massive arm. Taking a deep breath, I pick up on a scent I have yet to come into contact with myself, but Montgomery answers the question for me—*water dragon.*

I blink. Well then. Who else did Calian know? Was I going to meet a mermaid shifter next? I wouldn't put it past his connections at this point.

"You, Casimir?" He reaches out a hand as I jump onto the boat and shakes my hand.

"Yes, Calder, I presume?"

He smiles, "That would be me. You can call me Cal. Any friend of Calian is a friend of mine. His mate, Storm, sent me a text threatening to use my scales as toothpicks to take the grass out of her mare's teeth if I didn't bring you both back safely," he laughs and moves to take the rope off the pier.

I shake my head with a laugh, "Yeah, from what I know about her so far, it seems like she can wrap almost everyone around her little finger."

"Yeah, Calian needed someone like that, though; he's a tough son of a bitch. Regardless, I can stay docked at the island as long as you need, so there's no rush to get back to the boat, or if you need privacy, I can make myself scarce, and you two can take one of the three rooms downstairs. Just don't sink my boat with all the howling," he chuckles.

"I appreciate that," I say gratefully. I drop my bag and follow him to where I presume the captain's area is. "Do you have a special license where you can dock at the islands as long as you want? I thought there were certain maritime laws," I ask, curious but also trying to keep my mind occupied as much as possible to keep myself reasonably sane as the itch to see Aneira eats away at me.

I let out a low whistle as I look around the luxurious captain's bridge. The room is decorated in rich, dark woods and polished brass, giving it a regal feeling. The captain's chair is a large, plush leather seat that looks like it could swivel 360 degrees.

Calder chuckles at my reaction. "Yeah, she's a beauty, isn't she?" he says, gesturing around the room. "The boss sure knows how to live in style."

He starts flipping switches and pulling off into the open sea. "Calian?"

He chuckles, "No, me. Calian needed a favor, and here I am. As for your previous question, I can dock as long as I want because I own these islands. My pod, or a ripple as most of us prefer, lives within these seas. It's why the islands are rarely found on maps and are difficult to find."

I blink, "So why open it up to a cruise ship?"

"My cruise ship. My people run it, and it only docks here once a year. The humans don't remember the location, just that they went to an exclusive island," he smirks.

Shifters are nothing if not resourceful, I think to myself.

Suddenly, the world shifts beneath me, and Montgomery lets out a howl as I am bombarded with a surge of power that travels along my skin to every nerve ending. A low rumble escapes from my throat as I feel my hair stand on end from the pulsing energy that is now radiating through my veins. The makeshift life support system, made from sheer will alone that has kept my torn, broken heart pumping blood through my emotionally wrecked body, is now gone. Instead, there's a gentle hum that laces its way through my body as the bond between Aneira and me springs back to life. I close my eyes and take a deep breath, allowing the sensation of wholeness to envelop me like a warm embrace.

I take a deep breath, one that finally fills my lungs enough to make me wonder how the hell I've lived these weeks without our bond. I reach out and expect to feel the softness of her skin; our connection is so deep, it's almost tangible. I fight the urge to shift as a crescendo of emotions thunders through my chest until my heartbeat is pounding in time with hers, an overwhelming harmony that sends chills down my spine.

"You okay there, Casimir?" Calder's concerned voice breaks through my whirlwind of thoughts and emotions.

I exhale a deep sigh of relief and smile, "I am now. Let's go get my mate."

He laughs and smacks my shoulder, "Let's do it. The island isn't far."

I stay silent, as it no longer matters. Distance is irrelevant. Because now, I can pinpoint Aneira's exact position, like a beacon of light piercing through the darkness that had enveloped my heart. My entire being resonates with her presence, a harmonious melody echoing within my soul—a song which I will follow to the ends of the earth.

CHAPTER 16
ANEIRA

I disembark from the small shuttle boat that takes us from the ship to the island, the private island not having deep enough water to support such a large ship. I sigh with my bag slung over my shoulder. It's been three whole weeks and two days since I've been away from Casimir, and I've processed enough. My conclusion is: screw my stupid pack and all their nonsense. My mother fought for love, and she wanted the same for me. So I'm going to fight for love and devour everyone who gets in my way with a pickle. I am bone tired and grumpy and want to go home.

After getting over the shock of not having my period on

schedule, I quickly threw on a dress and ran down to the ship's medical bay, where I paid for several pregnancy tests. Like an idiot, because if I were pregnant, it would mean it happened during the heat haze, which was just two weeks ago, three if conception occurred on the first day of my heat. Although, now that I think about it, it was likely, considering I bonded with Casimir the first night with all the biting, scratching, humping, and howling.

Instead of peeing on a bunch of sticks, I threw the pregnancy tests on the bed and called Storm, who immediately picked up.

"There is no blood leaking from my vagina!" I say instead of a greeting.

"Well, that all sounds quite delightful, honey. I imagine it makes it easier for the sharks not to be tempted by all that sweet wolf strawberry sauce," she cackles.

"Seriously, Storm. Can you warn a man before you start talking about female strawberry juice? I was just about to have lunch!" a voice shouts from the background.

"Shut your whiskered face, Ralph. One day you'll have a mate and daughters, and you'll have to handle that stuff like the badass clawed beast you are becoming," she replies. I shake my head. Ralph was Calian's bodyguard and second in command, and Storm claimed him, so he was in for it.

"Focus here," I bite my lip. "At most, I would be three weeks along. The smell of alcohol is repulsive, and I've been hungry as hell. I never noticed any of the pregnant wolves in my old pack. I don't know who else to ask. Isn't it too early?" I sit on the edge of the bed and drop my head to one hand.

"Uh, have you tried asking Agatha? My mare says your wolf would have known shortly after conception. Also, shifters are more sensitive to pregnancy hormones, a tad more violent, and a lot more affectionate, so be careful. But she also said that she may not want to tell you anything since you pissed your wolf off with the moon charm. She says a lot of other stuff that you don't need to know, but yeah, ask her. I have to go, I have to see a man about a horse. I love you." She cackles and hangs up.

I blink at the phone; well, damn, it really could be that simple.

"Agatha, do you have something you want to tell me?"

She sniffs at me; *oh, now you want to take advantage of our bond and the magic that is being a shifter? You disappoint me.*

I roll my eyes, ignoring the guilt that her lecturing always brings me. "Agatha..."

Of course, I knew. I know everything that is going on with our body. Now bring us back to our mate, she snarls and goes back to ignoring me. I want to slap her. But you know, animal abuse and all. And technically, self-harm.

—

As I head to the beach, I take off my charm and gasp as I'm hit with a sensation of relief so profound it almost knocks me off my feet. My body feels electrified as our bond flares to life, and a sob lodges itself in my throat as Casimir's pain and longing hit me like a punch to the gut. Agatha howls with pleasure as our souls call out to our mate. Time slows, and I'm not sure how long I stand at the edge of the beach until Wilder suddenly appears and playfully bumps me. "Cheer up, I hear this island is the same as the other islands we've been on. Desolate and full of snacks and mimosas."

I give him a weak smile. He is a good guy, and I am rooting for his relationship once we get back to real civilization. As it is, he's racking up quite a bill for calls and internet minutes to video chat with his now-official girlfriend. Not that I care, but it turns out he's filthy rich—the owner of one of the biggest architecture firms back in New York City. He was even in some weird magazine that listed the most eligible rich bachelors under 30. It's a creepy magazine, like a list of people to poach. But what did I know? Shifters didn't do that shit. Can you imagine? May's Wolf Edition; Packs' Most Eligible Furry Alpha-hole. Nope.

"Ha, ha. You know I can't drink anything anyway. No, I will be right there on that lounger catching some sun as usual. But I'm not really hungry; maybe I'll nibble on something," I say, even though my stomach is rebelling, feeling the tug of the bond urging me closer to Casimir. Usually, I'm so hungry that Wilder is always randomly sending me servers with trays of food, like some kind of pregnancy food genie. A hungry pregnant wolf is a dangerous thing, so Agatha insists on consuming as much meat as possible to keep up our strength. Rare steak, chocolate, grapes, and cheese have been my major food groups for the past few days, and Wilder's mission is to ensure I don't need anything. I think it's his way of staying busy when he isn't on the phone with his girlfriend.

He looks down at me, concern and surprise, etching his face. "Have you been feeling nauseous at all? I hear that's a thing."

"No, I think it's too early for morning sickness. If I think back to when I would have conceived, I'm only about five weeks along," I grumble, not looking forward to any nausea, which will undoubtedly come my way soon.

"Man, I'm surprised those tests picked up your pregnancy so quickly," He shakes his head, grabbing my bag and leading us to a couple of loungers facing the ocean.

I laugh nervously. It wasn't like I could tell him that my wolf had confirmed my pregnancy. "I know, super strange. But I'm definitely feeling all the side effects minus nausea. I'm tired, grumpy, and hungry."

He laughs. "Oh, I know. I'm going to go explore the reef, but I'll send the server over with your usual order of steak and cheese cubes, just in case you do want to eat before I head off."

He waves after grabbing his snorkeling gear and heading off. Such a nice guy, I think to myself. He would have been

someone I gravitated toward had it not been for the entire
fated mate thing.

Trying to ignore the feeling of my skin on fire and the urge
to shift and swim to civilization, I strip out of my cover-up and
pour tanning lotion on my skin, my tiny bikini showing the
maximum amount of skin to tan. Everyone on this cruise was
either a geriatric couple or coupled up. Wilder and I were the
only solos here, and he was utterly fixated on his new girlfriend. Granted, this ship could have been filled with single
men and women, and I would still wear whatever the fuck I
wanted. Still, it was nice not to be leered at. However, a little
objectification would give me a fresh lunch—for the baby to
grow strong, of course. Maybe. Sigh, decisions, decisions.

As promised, Wilder sends a tray of food to where I'm
sitting. I push back the swirling in my stomach as I feel my
bond tug harder as if Casimir were close by, but he couldn't be.
I frown as I pick at the steak on the tray until I give up.

Lying back, I close my eyes, feeling restless and exhausted at
the same time. I sigh, trying to stay still, at least, until it starts
raining. My eyebrows scrunch together. Wait, there's no rain in
the forecast. I groan and open my eyes, meeting the gaze of a
very wet and very hostile wolf.

"Hello, Little Wolf, enjoying the sun?"

CHAPTER 17
CASIMIR

Calder pulls up to the other side of the island, avoiding the cruise ship docked and the swimmers. Basking in the warmth of the bond that flared to life, I focus on the tug as we get closer and closer.

"Like I said, I can stay here as long as we need, so don't worry about rushing back," he stretches. "Okay, so you have two options here. You can jump in and swim there. Or you can jump in and swim there. Personally, I like the jumping in and swimming there option," he chuckles, and I roll my eyes. Having already changed into a pair of swimming trunks, I give him a wave before throwing myself over the side of the ship.

The island is tiny and surrounded by beautiful coral reefs, but I can't admire it because I'm too busy propelling myself through the clear water, my arms cutting a path through the water as I swim to the other side of the shore. My body vibrates with tension, and I know that if I hit land, I may shift, frighten the cruisers, and probably piss off a few water dragons. Following the pull in my chest, I start to make my way out of the water, and my eyes are immediately drawn to the most gorgeous woman in the world, in a tiny bikini, looking very restless, and I know she has to feel my proximity even if she's trying to suppress it. My heart howls with joy. Fuck, I missed her terribly, and for weeks I wanted nothing more than to have her back in my arms again. But as much as I am relieved to see her, a wave of anger floods through me that I try to push down. Three weeks had passed since she left, an unnecessary trip that she took alone. She hadn't been by my side or safe in our bed; instead, I had barely slept, worrying about her, wondering if she was ever going to come back to me. So seeing her laying there, nowhere near as torn-up as I have been, a part of me can't help but feel resentful.

Still, even as pissed as I am, my heart starts beating almost too rapidly with longing. I walk closer, treading water, and take a deep breath, desperate to breathe her scent into my lungs. But when I catch her scent in the very light breeze, my brain almost short-circuits for an entirely different reason.

Biting back a growl, I stomp over to where she's lying down, with a barely touched tray of food, discomfort etched on her face, and stand over her. I take a deep breath, confirming my suspicions, and I drip water all over her.

She groans, opening her eyes. If it was another circumstance, the adorable shock on her face would have made me laugh. As it was, I wasn't sure if I wanted to choke her or kiss her.

"Hello, mate, enjoying the sun?" I ask, my jaw clenched.

"Casimir! How..." Aneira sits up, her eyes blazing with her wolf as she stares at me, the joy and surprise at seeing me again unmistakable. Before I can open my mouth to answer, she dives into my arms and smashes her body against me, eagerly pressing her lips onto mine, tasting the sweetness of her kiss. My hands wander over her curves, exploring every inch that I've dreamed of for weeks. A hot shiver runs through me as our tongues tangle together, and I wrap my arms around her tightly, pulling her in close. Her hands tug at my hair, and I deepen the kiss, groaning against her lips. The desperation of our need for each other is almost palpable in the air, and I fight the primate urge to take her right here and now.

Reluctantly, I pull away from her agonized whimper, unfortunately, aware of our very public reunion. Our wolves howl in tandem, both missing their mate. Wolves rarely had to be apart from their counterparts, but when it was a forced separation, it can pose a real danger to their mental well-being—for a pregnant she-wolf like Aneira even more so.

Pregnant.

Placing my hands on her waist, I put a little space between us. "Anything to say for yourself?" I ask my voice hard. But truthfully, I lost my steam at the look on her face, the almost desperate kisses, and her condition. I was just relieved to know she was safe and with me now. It could have been worse. Although Storm and Calian said she was safe, and I checked in with Storm every day, I still dreamed up several scenarios and none of them were remotely pleasant.

Her cheeks burn with shame, but her eyes blaze with defiance, well, attempting to, as she can't stop drinking me in as if I am not real and she can't quite believe her eyes. "Well, what do you expect? I ran away from my pack to avoid all the toxic wolf hierarchy bullshit. Living in fear for several years that those assholes would find me and they'd drag me back and force me into an unwanted marriage." I frown at that, a growl rumbling in my throat but she continues, "Then! Just when I found some normalcy, a little peace, and a sense of safety all wrapped up with a great, violent, best friend, a great book store filled with smutty amazingness, a shifter club, you come waltzing in, my hot mate," she pokes me in the chest. "During a heat frenzy, none-the-less and we mate like…like… like wolves in heat," she waves her hand. She looks around and brings her voice down to a whispered shout, realizing we aren't technically alone, "we bond and quite-frankly, I wasn't exactly willing to follow the mating path. What if you were some type of crazy serial killer, fated mated who collects toenails? But nope, the Fates decided to meddle in my life instead of minding their own business! But then it was already too late - I could see how amazing you are and I needed space to breathe and work through my fear of ending up like my mother, mateless and dragged back to live with a shitty pack. Then imagine me, trying to take time to process, and BAM, I miss my period and my wolf tells me I'm pregnant. Do you see how my life went from zero to like, fifty-thousand?"

My eyebrows shoot up at her word vomit, and there is so much to dissect there but what I did know is that she clearly wants me, she is just scared. Fear, I can eradicate. She is my mate, and I would always be her safe place.

She pauses her rant, breathing heavily and despite the warring emotions coming off of her I start to laugh. I tug her close and sit down on the soft sand, pulling her onto my lap.

"It isn't funny Casimir," she pouts with a sigh, laying her head on my shoulder, fitting perfectly.

Turning my head I kiss her frown away, "It is pretty funny. Here I am going batshit crazy and none of my wolves could track you down. Turns out you had a sort of cock-knot-blocking charm while traveling around random little islands with a completely different name and going just as crazy as I was. Although you'll try to deny it. Then Storm finally gives in after I lose my shit and I have to hop on a plane with a phoenix and get on a boat with a water dragon, to find out you're having our baby." I chuckle, shaking my head. The insanity of it all, the sleepless nights and the stress of the past few weeks finally catch up to me as I continue to chuckle.

Eventually, I calm down enough to look at my beautiful mate, her body glowing in the sun-kissed light that radiates from her skin, looking absolutely ravishing. I press my forehead against hers, "We will get back to your past, because I would like to actually know, in extreme detail, what the fuck happened in your old pack that has you fearful that you had to hide for so many years and even more so that you were willing to run from your mate. With a firm understanding that heads will roll."

I turn her body so that her legs straddle my waist and with both hands, I caress her cheeks gently, my thumbs tracing the outline of her delicate face as I tilt her head to gaze into my eyes.

"Aneira, I know there will be days that you will want to run, fear can do that to you but I will always follow you," I place kisses along her jaw. "There will also be moments that you believe there are monsters in your closet. But, Little Wolf, I will go through every closet, every night if I have to until you understand that I am the biggest and scariest monster to anyone who poses a threat to you. The only time you will have to run is when we chase our son or daughter, under the moonlight and then bring them back home safely - with us, together. Always together. Your heart belongs with me, always with me."

Her bottom lip quivers and her eyes fill with unshed tears, "but what happens now? I've fought so hard to make a life for myself and now things will change." A tone of despair laces her words as she looks at me as if I have all the answers. And maybe I do, murder being one of them, especially as my wolf snaps at the chance to destroy whoever hurt her.

Gently I brush away her tears with my fingertips "Now," I reply softly, "we make a new life together. We are mates, you will be bringing the most beautiful baby into our lives, but nothing else has to change. At least not in the way you fear. You will still have your bookstore and Storm, you'll just have a few more things on your plate." I pause to look at her, making sure she understood my next point clearly, "however, we will be talking about who I have to kill."

She gives me a watery smile and laughs, "Baby steps."

I lightly place my hand on her stomach, and for a split second a thrill of excitement races through me, and I'm overwhelmed as the reality that we created a life together, sets in. "Literally," I tease. Montgomery howls with pride, *strong wolf, strong swimmers*. I roll my eyes internally, choosing to ignore him.

She groans with a smile, putting her hand over mine. "Now I'm hungry. Once I even think 'baby' my wolf wants steak."

"So let's feed our baby," I lean over to quickly capture her lips, slowly and thoroughly before I pick her up, place her back on the lounger, and stand up. I frown at the forgotten cold steak on the platter next to her chair and I look around in search of a server.

"I'm going to get you something to eat and then we'll go home," I say with a reassuring smile. Aneira's eyes almost narrow at the suggestion, but she slowly nods her head in agreement. I can see her urge to fight simply for the sake of her independent streak but I can see her wolf riding her hard. When pregnant, wolves can get overwhelmed by unfamiliar scents, sights, and sounds. The charm may have helped her cope, but she needed to be home, craved the familiarity of her surroundings and the ability to protect her territory. Aneira couldn't fight her instincts. No matter how much she rebelled in the human state, deep down inside, she was still very much a wolf.

As I turn to try to find her food, I hear someone shouting her alias, a tray full of steak, grapes, and cheese in his hands.

He approached us and sets it on the lounger next to Aneira, and looks at me curiously. "Gertrude, I finished exploring the reef. Same as the last place, reefy." He chuckles and passes her the tray. "Hello, I'm Wilder," he reaches out to shake my hand. I grab his in mine firmly, and my wolf breathes in his scent and, sensing nothing but sincerity, gives me a slight internal nod and backs down slightly despite being annoyed that someone was around his pregnant mate, taking care of her the way we should have been.

"I'm Casimir." Even though my wolf is happy, my voice still rumbles out with a growl.

He doesn't even flinch. Instead a smile almost splits his face in two, "The Casimir? Well, it is certainly a pleasure to meet you. Gertrude and I bonded over pining for our significant others. But how in the world did you get here?" He looks around with a furrowed brow. A hot zing of pride settles in my chest, knowing that Aneira had been talking about me and pining, as Wilder said.

Aneira scowls, her mouth full of steak. Swallowing, she looks up briefly from her plate, "plane, chartered boat, swimming." We both look at her as she goes back to eating. I admit, she is quite terrifying when hungry. Reminder to self, have steaks in the freezer.

"You chartered a plane and boat?" He groans, "I have no idea why I didn't think of that." He slumps down on the lounger next to Aneira, angling his body away from her while she eats. Humans may not always know about us, but they still sense something is different. In this case, his instincts are telling him to back away from the hungry pregnant she-wolf.

I look at him curiously, but before I can ask, he explains, "I left behind someone too. I even left my business to my brothers to handle, which I never do, to try to clear my head on this cruise. I know everything about corporate stocks and architecture but love? No idea. But after just one talk with Gertrude, I called Kalissa and caved in. I am tired of living the same day over and over again, you know?" he sighs, his face fixed on the horizon and arms now crossed. I can tell from his steely expression that he wasn't used to talking about himself, yet something about Aneira's presence seemed to help him relax enough to open up. It was almost as if this trip had cast a spell on both of them, allowing Wilder to finally let his guard down and share his thoughts and Aneira to process whatever burdened her. Sometimes you just needed an almost deserted island and a listening ear or two, I suppose. Whatever it is, I am grateful.

"Well, we are going to head back when Ane...Gertrude finishes up her meal. You can come with us if you want to grab your stuff from the ship. We don't mind."

Aneira grunts in agreement, reaching for the water on her tray and washing down her finished meal.

"That is a great idea, Cas." Her face lights up, and I grin in response to her joy, lightening every bit of darkness I felt these past few weeks.

Wilder nods, a determined look on his face, and stands up from the lounger, "absolutely. If you give me your suite key, I will square things away from the reception desk and grab your bags for you too."

"The boat is on the other side of the island. You can't miss it. If you tell the front desk that you're with Calder and Calian's group, you should have no problem, and they should give you a lift, too." I say. I wasn't sure, but it seemed like a safe bet. I also wanted some time with Aneira before we set sail.

We had some...remembering...to do.

WHEN YOU RUN...
YOU RUN TO ME

You're Due For
A Punishment

CHAPTER 18
ANEIRA/CASIMIR

Aneira

Casimir tugs me into his arms, my legs wrapped firmly around his waist, and, nuzzles my neck while he strides at an unnatural speed toward the other side of the island.

"Remember when I said that if you ever wanted to run, there was only one place you should be running to?"

I moan softly as he licks his way up my neck to tug at my earlobe, "yes."

He hums, "That means, Little Wolf, that you're due for a punishment."

One hand falls hard to my ass, and I let out a gasp as heat floods my core.

He growls as his lips capture mine. I lose sense of time as I'm lost in the sensation of his lips as they move over mine, and his tongue teases mine. Suddenly I'm being laid down on a bed as Casimir undoes the ties of my suit, his hands roaming all over my body as his lips stay on mine, capturing my moans.

The heel of his hand presses against my core briefly, and the heat that builds is almost overwhelming. He pulls away with a dark chuckle, "Oh no, this is for me. I'm going to use your body, as I see fit, as my personal pleasure toy. You'll get release when I am good and ready to give it to you and not a moment before," He bites down on my bottom lip and kisses me savagely while his heavy hands cup my breasts, teasing my nipples roughly until they are hard and sensitive. I break the kiss, gasping for air, as my back arches. He takes the opportunity to trail hot kisses down my neck, his hands still exploring hungrily but avoiding my aching center.

Unable to stop myself, I reach down and stroke his hard cock through his swim trunks, feeling it twitch under my touch. He groans, the sound sending shivers down my spine. I want him, need him inside me.

He pulls my hand away, "On your knees, Aneira. You want my cock; it's going to go into your mouth like I promised it would be."

He turns me onto my knees, and my mouth salivates as he drops his trunks, and I waste no time running my tongue from the underside of his cock to the swollen head, stretching my mouth as much as I can to take him into my mouth. He wraps his hand into my hair and lets out a hiss as I suck.

"Fuck yes," he grunts. His familiar scent envelops me, and I can feel myself getting wetter as I bob my head as much as I can. He grinds his hips, making my mouth water as I gag on his length, and my eyes roll back in pleasure as I savor the taste of the salty pre-cum that drips into my mouth.

I swallow as best as I can as he tosses his head back, the cords of his neck showing the strain as his hips move restlessly.

I whimper as he reaches down and pinches my nipples.

"You left me, Aneira. That won't happen again, do you understand me? Now shut the fuck up and choke on this dick like a good girl." He thrusts harder, voice rough, and my wolf howls in pleasure as he takes complete control, his eyes flashing.

"That's it, your throat, your pussy, your ass, your body belongs to your Alpha," he grunts.

Without warning, He pulls his cock out of my mouth with a pop and grabs my hips, positioning himself behind me. His rough hands glide over my ass and squeeze coarsely, fingers digging in and making me gasp.

He runs his tongue down my slit and thrusts it into my core, "Fuck, you taste so good," he moans.

My body trembles, and I feel my wetness coat his fingers as he sucks on my clit lightly, swirling his tongue around and around until he releases it and sucks on my lips. He spends time teasing my entrance, thrusting his fingers deep inside of me, curling and rubbing against the spot he became well acquainted with a few weeks ago.

I feel the pressure building, but he pulls back, and I almost cry but. I bite my lip as he presses himself at my entrance, and he slowly slides inside me, filling me up completely until I cry out in pleasure.

"Fuck I missed you, never again," he murmurs as he starts to move faster, my pussy clenching as my head thrashes wildly.

He pinches my clit, and I'm thrown off the ledge as I find my release. "Fuck yes, Alpha," I scream as he thrusts savagely, my body made for his, taking him completely. I feel his knot at my entrance, and I'm panting for it.

Except he pulls out and turns me onto my back before settling between my thighs, his eyes dark with desire as he looks down at my core and kisses it as if he will never get enough.

He's hungry.

I can feel it.

I know it.

Heat builds within me, threatening to consume what's left of my sanity. I let the feeling consume me, let it carry me away.

I cry out his name like a prayer to the moon.

Don't ever let this stop.

Casimir

As HER HONEY coats my tongue, I crawl my way up her body, placing teasing kissing on her feverish body, pausing to pull her nipples into my mouth, biting as she wraps her hands into my hair.

No more words are needed as I push myself inside and keep my eyes on hers, a silent command to keep eye contact. I wanted to watch her eyes glaze over with pleasure as I fill her with my cum, as her body greedily milks me dry.

I let out bodies guide us as she wraps her legs around my waist, making her sweet cunt impossibly tighter as electricity sparks between us, pushing us higher until she is finding her release and my knot finds itself fully inside of her, locking us together as our bodies milk one another.

I know that no matter what happens, I'll always want her.

Aneira

SOMETHING SETTLES in my chest the longer that I'm with Cas. He soothes the wolf within me, and although I know, I needed the time to process, part of me feels guilty for going to such lengths to run away. I couldn't call it anything else at this point. I ran. Made our wolves suffer. But the other part is relieved that he not only gave me the chance to figure things out, but that he was also checking in on me every day via Storm and came to find me and bring me home. Home.

I am grateful that I also had the opportunity to meet Wilder. After my cheeks stopped flaming when Casimir and I finally came out of the cabin to Wilder and Calder, who struggled to keep the smirk off his face as he introduced himself, we set off to where the plane was waiting.

#

As we disembark the boat, Calder stops Casimir and me, "I will be seeing you both soon. If Calian's mate has anything to do with it, she will single-handedly unite all the shifters." He laughs and rolls his eyes, and I turn my head in confusion.

"You'll see what I mean. In the meantime, it was a pleasure to meet you both. A little less running next time, okay?" He directs the last at me, and my cheeks heat.

With a wave, he heads back to his boat, and we make our way to the plane.

"So my plan worked?" A gorgeous woman pops her head out of the plane, and her hair catches the setting sun. For a second, I think her hair is on fire.

Casimir chuckles, tugging me closer to place a kiss on my head, " I actually didn't need to kidnap her and set fire to the evidence."

She pouts, "Well, that's lame. Fire is always fun. I'm Rory, by the way. It's a pleasure to meet you."

I laugh softly, " You sound like Storm. It is a pleasure to meet you too, I'm Aneira, and this is my friend, Wilder," I point to Wilder, who looks up from his phone with a dopey grin on his face and waves.

"Ah, another person in love. I recognize that look anywhere," Rory jokes.

"Alright, let's get this show on the road. I gotta see a lady about a bird," she cackles and jumps into the plane.

"You have some interesting friends," Wilder murmurs.

I laugh, "Oh, you have no idea."

After we get off the plane, Wilder and I exchange numbers and promise to keep in contact before he jumps into a private car. I can't lie; I want to meet the woman who has him all in knots. No pun intended seeing that he's a human. But still, she sounds like she would fit right in with Storm and me.

Casimir grabs our bags, and we walk to a private car that Storm must have arranged if the sign on the back reading, 'Tail-Waggin- Taxi' is any indication. I roll my eyes, "Oh, I'm going to have the best fucking time coming up with shit to call her when we get home."

Casimir lets out a low chuckle, deep and sensual, as we get into the car and pulls me onto his lap. His strong arms envelop me in a warm embrace, and I can feel him smiling against my cheek.

"I like the way that sounds," he muses. "We. Home."

I grin, allowing my body to melt into his. I curl up against him and sigh contentedly as I let my mind wander. Home. Together. Whether that time would be spent on his land or at the bookstore was yet to be seen, but I have a feeling he will make it work no matter what. It's strange putting so much trust in Casimir, but as I let myself relax into his body, I realize it doesn't matter. It feels right.

The car comes to a stop outside of Storm's house, and I glance up at Casimir in confusion. He shrugs with a warm smile that sends electricity through my veins, "I figured you'd want to see Storm."

My lips spread into a wide grin, and without warning, I lean forward to crash my lips onto his. Our mouths move together hungrily, and he deepens the kiss until we are both breathless —wolf trap.

Where was I again? Oh, Right. Storm. I shake my head to clear the lust.

I jump out of the car before we give the private driver a live porno and stomp to the door, Casimir's laughter following me like a mocking caress.

I push open the door, " Honey, I'm home! The store was out

of milk. It took me a few weeks to get back!" I yell loudly with a cackle.

I walk through the house with a huff. She should have been at the front door to greet me and worship my furry paws.

I take a deep breath and follow my nose until it takes me to the backyard.

"Oh where, oh where, is my little pony? Oh, where, oh where can she be?" I sing softly to myself as I follow the sounds of soft neighs coming from the backyard.

"God, I hope they aren't humping in horse. I am not prepared to be traumatized," I whisper to Casimir, who is hot on my paws.

A deep, hearty laugh radiates from his lips, sending shivers of warmth through me. I pause and turn to drink in the way his handsome face lights up, his grey eyes crinkling with amusement. His neatly trimmed beard catches the sunlight streaming through the window, and I can't help but feel a surge of regret that I missed out on three weeks of his smile.

Feeling my guilt, his laughter fades away, and he pulls me into his arms, "Little Wolf, you're here with me now. We may not be able to get those days back, but that just means we have to stay up later to make it up," he kisses me lightly, and I laugh.

"That works for me; just extra steak, please. I'll need it for all the cardio." I tease.

He growls lightly, and I pull out of his arms, trying to resist the urge to jump into bed and lose myself in him.

Focus, I think to myself as I turn on my heel, and I make my way through to the kitchen, to the large French doors that lead outside.

My mouth gapes open and I let out a peel of laughter. Gasping, I manage to get out, "What in the My Little Pony is going on here?"

There is a huge chestnut shire prancing around with a smaller chestnut that has a star on its forehead. Although huge was putting it lightly, I have to wonder if they were injecting this horse with some type of pony steroid. I laugh as they take turns lunging towards each other, the smaller chestnut squealing while it strikes its front hooves out.

"Looks like we've found Storm," Cas chuckles, pulling my back against his firm chest and wrapping his arms around my middle. "And she's managed to shift too. A chestnut mare, why doesn't that surprise me?"

His comment is rhetorical, but I'm still mesmerized by this display before me, so I shuffle a little in his hold. "Why doesn't it surprise you then?"

That infernal chuckle rumbled around me like a washing machine set on high...one that I'm sitting on and taking for a wild ride that General Motors did not intend it for. But I digress.

"Chestnut horses are damn crazy. Ask anyone, and they will tell you one with that coloring are wild and unpredictable, needing a bit more patience...or maybe an extra feeding of hay laced with mare-ijuana," he laughs.

A smirk tugs at my lips. Ahh, redhead syndrome. It didn't surprise me; Storm is one of the spiciest women I have ever met. Although, seeing as how best friends naturally saw each other naked, I can attest that the carpet did not match the drapes. Or, in this case, is it 'the pelt did not match the felt'? I shrugged internally; either way, she was naturally a brunette.

Suddenly their ears prick up as they realize they aren't alone. I mean, besides the fact that we've been standing and staring for the better part of five minutes. I watch in fascination as the Hagrid of horses stuffs all that stallion back into a human body and turns into a very naked Calian.

A very hung and aroused, naked Calian. My jaw drops. How the hell did he fit that Galloping Girth inside my tiny best friend? Okay, logically, shifter bodies are made for their mate, but Luna guide the chariot or something like that.

I nudge Casimir and whisper, "Are you seeing what I'm seeing?"

"You mean the Wild Pegasus Power-Piston?" He whispers back.

"Yeah, the fucking Trotting Treasure Torpedo. Do you think Storm sings a variation of Horseplay Hallelujah when it hits her cervix?"

Calian scowls, although the effect is completely lost as he reaches for a pair of pants and shifts the earth's axis.

"I can hear you, you know," he says wryly, now clothed from the bottom down.

"Well, we can *see* you," I chortle. Then gasp as Storm barrels into me, wrapping her legs around my middle, butt ass naked.

I laugh as I easily hold her weight and spin us around. Casimir diverts his gaze with a chuckle as Calian tries and fails to wrap us in a blanket.

Storm nuzzles my neck, "Annie! My moonbeam. Yum, you smell so yummy. Like warm cinnamon buns dipped in warm milk chocolate, is it because of the baby? Pregnancy smells good on you!"

I laugh and set her down, and Calian immediately covers her with a frown.

"Pregnant?"

"You knew?"

Casimir and Calian have matching angry expressions as they speak over each other. Storm shrugs sheepishly. Well, she tries, but she doesn't look the least bit chagrined.

"If I had known she was pregnant, I would have gotten her location from you sooner and sent Casimir to get his mate," Calian growls.

"Well, my loyalty is to Aneira," she sniffs, chin high. " Besides, she was perfectly safe. She was on a cruise ship owned by a damn water dragon and on an island in Barbados full of Osprey shifters. Do you think I would send her off without hacking your council computer systems, which are super weak, by the way, and threatening their lives if she were hurt in any way? I mean, I am no amateur. Even if I weren't a shifter, I would have hacked every damn system to keep an eye on her. It's part of the best-friend stalker code."

I blink, "you did what?"

She smiles maniacally," The charm was also a tracking charm. I texted Lyndsay right after you did. You're my emotional-support lycan. This was the closest I could get to getting you micro-chipped."

I'm mildly impressed, yet not the least bit surprised.

"Who are you?" Casimir questions, an adorable glazed look of shock on his face.

"That's what I'd like to know," Calian murmurs, a hint of pride and wonder in his voice.

Storm waves them off, "Never mind that. I'm just an evil genius in the making. Call me the Alpha Night-Mare," she laughs and grabs my arm to steer me inside.

"Let's get my niece or nephew some tea. Then you can go take a nap."

"I think, maybe just nap. I'm exhausted," I yawn into my mouth, suddenly overwhelmed with the need to fall into my bed. Casimir sweeps me up into his arms before I can take another step.

I smile gratefully as my eyes droop. Cas tucks me firmly into his chest, and it becomes an enormous effort to keep my eyes open before darkness edges into my vision and sleep starts claiming its hold on me.

His chest rumbles as he says his goodbyes to both of us and let the soft motion of his walking lull me into a deep sleep.

Content and happy for my mate to take me home.

CHAPTER 19

CASIMIR/ANEIRA

Casimir

I strip Aneira and play a game of "juggle the mate" while I get us both into a warm bath. I pour some oils into the water and settle us into the large tub. The entire time, she stays asleep, and I take that time to drink in her perfection, hungrily. Unable to resist, I place soft kisses on each eyelid, admiring how her long eyelashes rest on her cheeks, highlighting her delicate features, while her lips take my breath away every time I look at them. By the moon, she is gorgeous, I think to myself as I trail my hands down her arms and back lightly, tracing her sensual curves, that scream of sin, and golden skin.

I lie there for what feels like hours, lost in the blissful silence just barely punctuated by her deep breathing; the steam from the hot bath wrapped around us like a cocoon. As much as I want to close my eyes, I resist for fear of missing another moment. We stay in the warm water until Aneira starts lightly stirring from her sleep. I softly stroke my fingertips over her face, tracing a few of its contours before lightly kissing her forehead as she blinks open beautiful gray eyes.

"Hey you," I whisper as she looks up at me from beneath heavy eyelids and smiles sleepily in response.

"Mmm, what time is it?" she murmurs back, stretching against me as if trying to burrow deeper into the safety of my arms.

"Time for us to get out," I chuckle lightly. "But it's okay," I whisper in her ear, wrapping my arms around her and drawing her closer, "you can sleep a little longer."

She snuggles into me with a content sigh, before drifting off to sleep again. I wait a few moments, before standing and shifting her just enough to drape her in a fluffy towel. I don't care if I'm wet, as long as she doesn't catch a chill.

The fact that she sleeps so deeply while being maneuvered around like a, loved, sack of flour is a testament to how safe her wolf feels with her mate; otherwise, she would be ripping out my throat. Pregnant wolves can be very volatile.

I dry her off and tuck her into the bed, and my heart swells at the sight of my pregnant mate in bed, the moonlight streaming through the window caressing the skin covered in my scent. I lay my hand on her tummy and feel my eyes flash golden as a wild fervor courses through me; a wave of pride, possessiveness, protectiveness, and the urge to keep her and my child safe.

She doesn't know, yet, the hold she has on me, the firm hold she has over my once-dark heart. The power she wields that with one gentle, sassy look from her would bring me to my knees in the sweetest of ways.

I quickly dry off and get into the bed, pull her into my arms, and watch as the waves of her hair fan over the pillow.

Sleep, I will stay alert. You cannot protect if you are dead on your feet, Monti's gruff voice echoes in my head, and I heave a sigh of relief as I let my body drag me into sleep. But instead of sweet dreams, my sleep is filled with darkness, claws, teeth, and a broken Aneira lying in my arms; her dead eyes looking up at me as life slips away from her body.

🦟

I AWAKE with a growl in my throat, to a loud pounding at the door and the sun streaming through the window, chasing away the darkness from my nightmares. The pain in my chest threatens to consume me, and in a panic, I reach for Aneira and breathe a sigh of relief when I see her sleeping peacefully beside me.

"Wake up, sleepyheads! The sunshine shines down on another day of shifter depravity and howling good times. So let's greet the day with a growl," Storm taps a beat on the door before laughing and walking away.

Aneira groans, "Ugh, it is way too morning to morning. Wake me up in a few years." She grabs a pillow and covers her head.

I laugh half-heartedly, the nightmares still tugging at my consciousness, trying to drag me back.

Aneira pulls her head out and looks at me with a frown. "I happen to know that I am hilarious, and your laugh did not reflect that. Also, I feel your heartbeat racing through the bond of fanged destiny. Are you okay?"

I sigh, pull her into my arms, and breathe in her scent. "I am now. Just a bad dream."

"Okay then. Just a word of warn—"

Her words trail off as another bang sounds on the door. "I said wake up. I will not tolerate this disregard for my morning demands!" Storm yells.

"ing... she won't stop," she finishes with a growl.

"I'm going to claw out your fucking heart and eat that shit with a fucking pickle dipped in vanilla ice cream and your liver enzymes!" Aneira yells back, pulling herself out of my arms.

I rub my head; it's way too early for sun salutations and murder threats.

"Rude. I have steak!" Storm replies.

Aneira shoots out of bed and starts tugging on clothes while racing to the bathroom. I hear the tap start and the sounds of her brushing her teeth.

In less than two minutes, she's rushing out of the door and barrels into Storm's smiling face; Calian hovering behind her, rubbing his temples. I give him a sympathetic look.

"Food." Aneira commands before shifting her head slightly and sniffing. "Never mind..." She rushes off, and Storm cackles, following behind.

"Please tell me there is coffee?" I ask Calian, who is still hovering by the door.

He nods, a frown affixed on his face. "Copious amounts," he sighs and turns to follow the girls.

I have to agree with Aneira... It's way too morning to morning.

✦

Aneira

I FOLLOW the scent of steak downstairs to the bookstore instead of the kitchen, where I would have expected the food to be. Instead, I walk towards the back of the shop to the plush couches and coffee table piled high with steaks, orange juice, and fruits. The effect is lovely, bloody steaks and a floor-to-ceiling view of the forest, lit up with the morning sunlight.

I hum in appreciation as I sit on the plush couch and reach for the food. But before I can grab the steak, I catch a whiff of two unfamiliar scents that set my wolf on edge. My hackles rise, and I feel my eyes flash golden, and I can't help the first words that fly out of my mouth, "Whoever the fuck is here, better stay the fuck away from my steak." My voice is gruff as my wolf pushes her way to the forefront.

I watch two unknown men shuffle forward, their hands held up in supplication, and I scowl as my senses pick up everything at hyper speed, and I process several things at once. Number one, the scents are all so deeply tangled up with Casimir's and Calian's that I know these shifters, a wolf and a cougar, must be connected to them somehow. Number two, they pose no danger, but I pose one to them if their stomachs grumble even slightly.

Big men mean bigger appetites, and they are not eating my fucking food.

Storm walks into the room, holding tea, and I say nothing as I reach for my food and glare at the two shifters as my claws come out, sinking into my meat. I ignore the juices dripping down my chin as I chew ferally, a threat or a promise; I have no idea at this point.

"Should I get you a bib, or are you going for the full wild wolf look?" Storm says wryly. I say nothing as I continue to stare.

"Oh, I forget you haven't actually met yet. This is Ralph, the cougar I told you about before. He's Calian's bodyguard and technically second in command too. Also, he is going to totally be the new bestie," she points at the brown-haired shifter with amber eyes and arms that look like they eat the bench press. Like usual, cougar shifters were just massive fuckers.

"That is Tristan, Casimir's second. I haven't had a chance to vet him too much, but oh, I will dissect his very essence," her eyes narrow, and Tristan's green eyes widen. He should be scared. No matter how muscled and intimidating he looks, Storm is a tiny tornado of terror.

Calian strides into the room with Casimir on his heels. They both pause to stare at me, then at Tristan and Ralph.

Casimir raises an eyebrow, "The way you're eating your steak, I'm not sure if I should be turned on, jealous, or terrified."

A growl erupts from my throat. Usually, I wouldn't mind their presence, but apparently, pregnant Aneira means my hormones are all over the place, and I'm violent as fuck. I pull the table closer and shift my body to hover protectively while reaching for more. My belly felt like an empty pit, but I savor each swallow.

Tristan moves to do that weird man hug with Casimir and whispers, "Terrified. Fucking terrified. This is like watching a bloody massacre."

"I think it's hot. So I vote for turned on," Ralph adds, and Storm cackles into her cup.

I scowl, "I'm not sure why there are two more shifters In the bookstore at the ass crack of 'fuck-off,' I comment, reaching for some juice and leaving a bloody print on the glass.

The two men exchange glances and shrug and move to lean on the wall before Tristan finally speaks up, "Well it was either this or watch the pack build more houses. Over it." He says with a smirk.

Ralph huffs before adding, "I'm here for one reason only. To make sure that Storm doesn't hack into anything else. Since our Alpha is completely whipped," he points at Calian, who has moved to put Storm in his lap. I eye his proximity warily. But as the tray is now empty, I'm happier.

I sigh, and Casimir appears with a wet towel in hand and sits beside me. I smile gratefully, and it must be a terrifying sight, but his eyes still do that gorgeous melting thing that makes my stomach do backflips.

"Okay, so now that the feral pregnant wolf has been fed," Storm starts as she waves Tristan and Ralph closer to the empty chairs.

Calian clears his throat, and Storm smiles sheepishly, well, attempts to.

Calian sighs heavily, "You're going to be the death of me, woman." I smirk. Accurate.

"Casimir, I'm sure you are aware of the rules when it comes to settling within any territory. I can ignore the fact that you moved into the territory without a formal request, seeing as, from what I was able to deduce, you are essentially a pack filled with wolves that were in precarious situations--I'll be asking for more details on that so I can get the bigger picture. However, you are not an 'official pack which means you are technically classified as rogues, which is an automatic death sentence," I feel Casimir tense.

"In this case," Calian continues, "I give a formal exemption for settlement since you are all technically escaping a precarious situation and have become a sanctuary of sorts for wolves and witches. As long as you guys are here to heal and rebuild, I won't raise any issues. I also have to note that there is a reason why I have no wolf packs within my territory. Cumbria Falls is a high attraction for human tourists and wolves aren't seen in this area, let alone large shifters that are twice the size of normal wolves, if not bigger. Detection is the least of our worries. But unwanted attention and questions from the Shifter Council are the worst. Luckily, they hold me in high regard..."

Ralph scoffs, "More like they are terrified of your violent unpredictability."

Calian glares at him, "Semantics. I've chosen to get in front of rumors and reached out to the Shifter Council for a formal meeting, and while you were away, we got word that they will be honored to meet you and discuss making your pack official."

A shiver of trepidation and excitement flows through our bond. What Calian was offering is a big deal..for anyone else. But the truth is, I didn't want to rejoin shifter politics. The system is flawed—too many Alpha's flying under the radar.

My eyes fly to Storm's, and although she gives me a reassuring smile, an entire conversation flows between us. Fear bolts through me like lightning, and I struggle to swallow. As Casimir's bonded mate, becoming formally recognized requires me to give my real name - the same name linked to a past I have desperately been trying to escape for eight long years. One that officially marks me as becoming the next 'mate' for the next Alpha of our pack. It didn't matter that I was already mated. To my grandfather, I am property, just like my mother before me, and while I know I have the protection of those in this room, all I can imagine is being dragged back.

And I will die before I ever go back.

Casimir

TERROR RIPS through the mate bond, and my eyebrows furrow as I turn my head to look at Aneira, whose face is ashen. I squeeze her hand. We still haven't discussed, in detail, her past, but she has to know that I will protect her and keep her safe. Hell, between all of us, she will never come to harm.

I send reassurance through our bond as I look at Calian, processing the bomb he just dropped on me. There is a level of safety and relief as an official pack. Overall, being formally recognized would mean that we would be required to submit quarterly financials and be called when needed to aid other shifters and packs. It also meant that we would be subject to more rigid shifter laws. We have been living beyond council rules because I had a feeling my father was too prideful to admit that he had several defected wolves. In fact, I'm sure that was the case for a lot of the other wolves in my pack that stayed behind. In the end, wolves were prideful, and multiple defections would be them admitting that they were failing as a pack. I could imagine the reaction of the Council if they found out not one but about six wolf packs had members that left, and one of them that had multiple Omegas defecting at once as well. There would be complete chaos.

Calian is correct, though. Defected wolves were often considered 'rogue,' meant to be crazed, attacking humans and other shifters. Depending on the case, those wolves were considered beyond saving and were hunted and put down before they could cause harm or more harm. However, my pack proved that that wasn't always the case. It made me think about all the other wolves who were hunted down. Were they really 'rogue', or were they quiet dissenters that were put down before they could bring about positive change? Every wolf in my pack is strong, loyal, and we don't harm shifters or humans, not intentionally anyway, or without cause. However, if we were to be attacked by another pack, shifter law would be on the side of the pack that is within the Council's rule. Not to mention if we had been reported formally to the Council, we would have hunted down like...no pun intended...dogs. With Calian's declaration, we were officially safe, for now. But what if it were not a factor? We were fortunate during this time, and while I understood my packs position, if we want to bring about change, we can't do that from the sidelines, especially not as an unofficial pack.

Of course, I'm not a tyrant. If they feel uncomfortable about setting roots down, they will be free to come and go as they wish, and I will always have a spot for them at the pack home, unofficial or not.

But I cannot put into words how much I need the council to approve the pack. This is life-changing news for my pack, and my future family. No more running. Just setting up roots and being a part of the shifter community. Something that I never wanted until meeting Aneira.

Still, it is complicated. I have to acknowledge that the rest of my pack may not be on board, and that's putting it lightly. Their opinions matter greatly to me, as they should. The council was neglectful at best and not held in the highest regard. Now, after being 'free' from shifter politics, I will have to convince the rest of the pack that this is our best choice.

I look at Tristan, who looks hopeful. And something in me settles.

My play of emotions must show plainly on my face because Calian nods, "I understand your apprehension, Casimir. But you'll convince your pack. By becoming officially recognized, you'd have access to resources and protection you wouldn't otherwise have. Also, from what I see, your ideals, the ideals that have brought your pack together, align with my own. We can work together to change outdated shifter laws and traditions that don't align with those beliefs."

"Besides," Storm jumps in. "The first steps are already done. The pack is official in terms of a refugee pack. Now we just need to sit, look pretty and try not to stab the useless motherfucker in charge of the wolf shifters when we see them tomorrow. Aneira's home is with me. I am here. So you can't go even if you tried to. I'll change my name to Canta-ruella Hoof-ville and then 101 Dalmation the fuck outta of all of you. Chase you all down and…."

Calian scrubs a hand over his face and rubs his temples. Ralph and Tristan chuckle. Even without Storm's threat, I wouldn't, in good conscience, remove Aneira from her life, bookstore, and home.

I look at Aneira, who hasn't moved an inch, a faraway, haunted, look on her face. An expression that I will do everything in my power to erase. Because formal recognition also means my child and mate would be protected if they did come into danger. Something in Storm's rant registers. "Did you say tomorrow?"

Calian clears his throat, eyes shifting to mine, "They would like to see where you are going to set up the pack and see what you have established so far as soon as possible."

Ralph scoffs again, "What he means is that those nosey

fucks jumped at the chance to come to Cabria Falls, seeing as how Calian has declared this a Council Free Zone. Choosing to handle most of his shit in-house."

"Thank you, Ralph." Calian growls. His diplomatic response ruined. My lips twitch with a smile.

"It goes without saying, but if it wasn't clear, I will, of course, vouch for you," Calian adds casually, as if like it isn't a massive deal for a shifter of his standing to come to the aid of a new pack that hasn't been formally established yet. "After all, that's what brother mate-in-laws do for each other," he adds wryly, looking at Storm, who preens.

Storm beams with joy beside Calian. Whether luck or destiny brought us to Cabria Falls without a definite plan, it didn't matter—everything was coming together. The Spiroid Pack now has a member of the shifter council on our side, and I have found my destined mate. I was damn lucky.

"Part one complete," Storm claps, her eyes taking on a manic gleam, her voice taking on a feral tone. With a watchful eye on Aneira, she adds, "Part two, plan a murder. Part three, name this family unit."

We exchange confused glances at her words.

All except Aneira, who finally stirs beside me, her body shuddering as her claws shoot out and her eyes blaze with savage fury, "Let's fucking plan a murder," she growls through gritted teeth, a fire raging in her voice makes the hairs on the back of my neck stand up and my dick hard as fuck.

CHAPTER 20
ANEIRA/CASIMIR

Aneira

I'm not sure why I received a summons to come into the Alpha's office. It was rare for him to even acknowledge me, let alone see me. But despite wanting to avoid him completely, it was better to pick and choose my battles. As I walk into the office, I can feel his eyes on me, cold, cruel, and calculating. I stay standing, choosing to ignore the chairs in front of me. I resist the urge to shudder and fidget, as he observes me silently.

He leans back in his chair, his grey marks that look exactly like mine hardening at the lack of reaction from me. Yeah, fuck you asshole, I think to myself.

"I am sure you're wondering why I called you in here today. So let's cut to the chase. As the heir to this pack, you have a duty to this pack. Your mother didn't recognize that. I blame myself, I should have beaten her more often. Still, you now have the opportunity to make up for it."

I feel my eyebrows fly up, but I don't respond. Because my mother warned me that every word ever uttered from his mouth is a weapon. So I let him lay his proverbial arsenal on the table in front of me, knowing I would sooner pick one up to stab his ass than do whatever it was that he wanted me to do.

"I have received word that the alpha from the Redwood pack will be arriving tomorrow to discuss the marriage arrangements," my grandfather continues, his voice clipped.

I stiffen at the news, feeling a surge of rage that has me speaking before I can hold it back, "The fuck you did. "I won't marry some alpha you've picked out for me," I say with a snarl.

His expression darkens and he chuckles darkly. Somehow that puts me more on edge than if we would have leaped over the table and punished me. I let my limbs loosen because if he changes his mind, I'm going to make sure I bring this motherfucker down with me. Little did he know, the communes were a little more than training grounds for those of us who were tired of the treatment of Omegas. When we would use our skills, I have no idea. But the fact that we could, make us all feel a little bit more secure.

"You will do as I say. You are little more than a chess piece, but still, you will be of use to me. That is...unless you would like to see your mother beaten every day until you obey? I can make that happen."

I feel my wolf churning inside me and my body shudders as she fights to break free and rip out his throat. I force myself to nod, hearing my mother's voice in my head. Pick and choose and when you *choose prepare for the consequences and the blood bath that will come with it.*

"You may go," he waves me off. As I turn on my heel he adds, "Oh and Aneira? You'll be guarded, in case you decide to run away like your useless mother. Except this time, when we bring you back, you won't live to tell the tale."

That night, my mother and I killed six guards and she sent me off with an account number and a safety deposit box key. She stayed back to cover my trail and I'm not sure if she was still alive, but what I do know is that I wouldn't let her sacrifice whether it had been with her life or blood, be in vain.

Casimir
Next Day

"STOP FIDGETING; EVERYTHING WILL BE FINE." I clasp Aneira's hand with my own to hold it down by my side. She looks stunning this morning in a soft navy blue dress that clings to her curves in all the right ways, distracting me to no end. "This is just a formality. Calian will ensure that your name isn't exposed."

I hear the words flowing from my lips, but after Storm and Aneira made their declaration, Calian asked for a better expla-

nation as to why we were planning a mass murder. Under-
standably so, seeing as how we would be needing a ton of
shovels or a big fire. Safe to say, we were all on the same page.
But even more so, the need to make sure we became officially
recognized is even more important, if only to start clearing the
corruption that was so clearly present.

I have to admit, I'm also nervous. We may have Calian on
our side, but the truth is, I'll be exposing my pack and making
them vulnerable, bringing down our shields to bring several
shifters and their guards into our safe space.

Aneira sighs, "Easy for you to say. You don't get all 'I'm
going to rip out your throat' if someone looks at your dinner.
Everyone is in danger if they look at my baked potato," she
pouts. I burst out laughing, and my tension eases.

She smiles cheekily. Aneira, 1. Me, 0.

"Okay," she continues. "Run me through the day again, so I
know what to expect." We stand outside our home, which is
still being constructed, in the soft morning light. We both
needed the fresh air and also needed to get out of the way of
the wolves building.

But my nerves aren't just because of the meeting. Last night,
the dreams took hold again, only this time, I held our newborn
daughter as I watched helplessly while Aneira fought against
six wolves before she was slaughtered. I woke up in a cold
sweat and gathered her into my arms. I can't shake the sense of
foreboding in the air. A dark stain threatens the peace of my
territory.

Last night, I gathered the pack and explained my decision,
and asked for their input. The majority of them were happy to
stay, wanting permanent roots somewhere, being sick of
constantly running to a new place and uprooting the children
several times over.

A handful decided to leave before the council arrived,
holding a personal grudge against the lack of care the council

has shown in the past. I wished them well and told them we always have an open door here. I think they will be back; it was a safer bet in the long term.

"So, I will receive the members along with Calian, as the member vouching for me. You and Storm will be by our side. Storm hasn't been formally recognized as the Swiftwater Pack Alpha Mare, but that won't mean much to her or Calian. We will do a walk around the pack lands area, where we will explain our plans. Then there is dinner and a formal meeting straight after, where the pack will become official, and then you'll be recognized as both my mate and Luna of our pack."

She exhales and nods, and I pull her into my arms. "As for your old pack, if your name is brought up, which is doubtful considering how I doubt your grandfather has declared you rogue, just like my father hasn't, Calian will smooth it over. Anything else that comes from it, we will handle it together. One dead wolf at a time."

She chuckles.

"Guys. Can you just tone down all the love?" Storm sidles over with Calian in tow. "We all know what happens when mates hug, and I don't think the council wants to meet you with your bare asses in the air." She pauses briefly and waggles her eyebrows, "Bare. Bear. Get it?" She cackles, and we roll our eyes. But hers light up.

"Fuck I recognize that look, everyone sit down and prepare," Ralph walks up, Tristan at his side, with his hands in his trousers, and sighs.

"Okay, rude." She glares at Ralph but then smiles. "But also accurate. I've met the bear shifters at shifter wars. And of course, the pack that runs the wilderness shop, 'Bear-ly Surviving,' for the tourists. Clever name, by the way. So I did some digging in the Council Archives…"

Calian scowls, and she waves him off, "Consider it free labor. I find the holes and patch them up. The point is that the bear pack in Cabria is super unique, the only pack apparently with green eyes. So naturally, I got curious about all the Council members in case I needed to dig up dirt and blackmail them at any point in time," her eyes shifted to Calian whose face darkened by the second.

"Fucking genius," Tristan murmurs.

Aneira nods in agreement. As Alpha, bad Storm. As Casimir, fuck yes.

"A lot of these fuckers are getting up there in years, and, while shifters live a fuck ton more than humans, we can start our revolution to Phil Collins the shit out of the shifter world. Harmony, peace, and all of that. We need to schmooze, get into their heads and find out if they are assholes or good shifters. So tonight, operation Phil Collins commences. Okay?"

Aneira bursts out laughing and high-fives her, her nerves forgotten. "Genius. Once we compare notes, we can figure out whose life we are upending. Then, we can talk to the witches and bring all the good shifters to Cabria Falls; it will be a mating revolution."

Storm holds her hands in the air, mimicking fireworks, "Sex, sex everywhere. Mate bonds, more sex. Revolutions. More sex."

At the mention of sex, Aneria looks at me with heat in her gaze. "Works for me. More time to be with my Fido."

"I know what you mean," Storm nods sagely, "there is something about that Kentucky Derby dick, for me too. I mean," she pauses to fan herself dramatically while she slaps hands with Aniera, ignoring while Calian scowls, his face matching mine. She called me fucking Fido.

While the girls laugh, I bump Calian's shoulder and murmur, "Have you ever had to tolerate this much disrespect before?"

He crosses his arms and sighs, a dark look on his face belying the slight smirk gracing his lips as he stares at Storm,

"Seeing as how I never tolerate a hint of disrespect, ever -I would have shifted and crushed the skull of anyone who thought it- At this point, the clan is so in love with her fierceness and quirkiness that the word vomit tendencies don't bother them. Even my grandmother is absolutely taken with her. Although, between you and me, I think they are just secretly laughing behind my back, thoroughly enjoying seeing me whipped. You should have been there when I introduced myself to her. If I hadn't mentioned Aneira giving her blessing, I would have been horse meat," he shakes his head with a laugh.

"I'm going to need that story," I laugh and clap his shoulder.

"You'll need a long night and toilet paper for that shit show. Just wait till you meet her serial killer guard dog...." Ralph starts, and Calian glares at him.

I look at them with my eyebrows raised. *Serial killer?*

Calian sighs, "Suffice to say, it's a damn good story. Let's get over this hurdle first," he replies with an eye roll.

I nod with a chuckle and tune back into the girls.

"I have to introduce myself more to the pack and get to know them all. Want to come with?" Aneira asks.

Storm smiles, "We are a big furry family now. Horse and Wolves, Wolves and Horses. Horves! Wolses! If you need me there, I'll be there."

Calian's face tightens, but he doesn't say anything. Storm, ideally, should stay near him while the council was here as a formality to his position within the Council. Storm isn't just the Swiftwater Alpha-mare; she is the mate of a Councilman. It is pretty significant. But even more so, he would want Storm right by his side to show her as his equal. Little power plays go a long way, and it would show the start of his plan to initiate change.

"First, let's meet this fucking council of fuck wits, and then we can escape," she adds, reaching to hold Calian's hand, whose face splits into a grin.

"What? Do you think I would leave you unprotected? I wore a dress with a split on the thigh. This is prime, ass-kicking gear," she teases.

I look at my watch and expel a deep breath; the council is due at the property line in a few minutes.

"Ready?" I look at Aneira and hold out my hand.

She smiles brightly, all trace of nerves gone, "Let's change the fucking world, Mate."

"One purple nurple at a time," Storm adds as she strides forward purposefully.

We hasten behind her, and all I can think is, *fuck, please don't twist the Council's nipples.*

Oh, how my life has changed.

CHAPTER 21
CASIMIR/ANEIRA

Casimir

Aneira moves closer, tightening her hold on my hand as a faint blue glow in the trees appears and gets painfully bright until suddenly, there are several men and women standing before us. The witches had brought down the shield beforehand, and they will set up another perimeter after the council steps over the boundary line. Although, it won't be as strong since the Council is a protective force of its own. Or at least they like to think so. I prefer extra precautions.

I fight the urge to widen my eyes as they stand in a loose semi-circle around us, wearing robes that look like they came straight from the movies: they are made of a deep navy blue velvet, with intricate silver embroidery forming runes on their chest and back. The cuffs are lined with white fur, and golden rings hang from the waistbands. The robes have a slight luminescence to them and billow slightly in the breeze. A bit overkill.

Despite having been a part of a formal pack, I've never formally met the Shifter Council. Meetings were reserved for actual Alphas or major events, neither of which I was allowed to attend.

Calian bows his head, and we follow his lead.

"Well met; may blessings be bountiful," Calian murmurs, his fist to his chest. They all incline their heads in greeting, raising their fists to their chests as well before pulling down their hoods.

I recognize Pierce, Calder, and Rory immediately. Except while Calder has the council robes, Rory is standing in a pair of torn jeans with a t-shirt that says, 'Phoenixes Do It With Fire' next to a woman who looks strikingly like her, who, judging by the disapproving look on her face, must be her aunt she had mentioned. She sticks out her tongue, and her aunt's disapproving look deepens. Not that Rory cares. Pierce is standing next to what, in several years, would be his carbon copy, and I deduce that it's probably his father. I admit, it feels good to see familiar faces.

"Calian. So good to see you again. How's the herd?" A woman purrs at him from one side of the circle. Her dark hair flows down to her waist, and even from here, the purple of her eyes is electrifying. But something about her is...off. Her smile doesn't quite reach her eyes, her posture is too stiff as if she's constantly on guard, and the way her eyes roam... It's as if she's searching for something or someone to sink her nails into.

"Kathleen. Great to see you," Calian grits his teeth, his tone completely at odds with his pleasant words. "The herd is great. May I introduce you all to my Fated Mate, Storm?" His tone softens, and a smile lights his face as he pulls Storm closer, placing a kiss on her head.

Kathleen's face contorts with a feral smile as she looks at Storm up and down. Storm narrows her eyes at her briefly before turning to everyone else, "Well met."

"We've spoken," Calder responds with a chuckle. "It's nice to meet you in person. I admit I expected you to be slightly taller. Tell me, Storm, do you still think you can use my scales as toothpicks?"

Storm laughs. "Miniature exterior, ferocious interior, or in my case, miniature mare, force to beware. Besides, Calder, you should know more than anyone here. It's not the size of the boat but the motion of the blood-red ocean."

Calder gives a booming laugh while several of the members and their entourage snicker. Calian smiles softly with a shake of his head.

A large, imposing wolf-shifter moves closer, his robe billowing in the breeze, his Scottish accent thick with an air of authority. "Having dispensed with all the threats," he begins, a small smile on his face, "Safe to say that you are Casimir?" He directs the question at me. There is something vaguely familiar about him; in fact, he reminds me a bit of Aneira.

I step forward and extend my hand, which he shakes firmly. "Yes, I am Casimir, Alpha to the Spiorad pack."

He grins widely, creases forming at the edges of his eyes and gray irises sparkling. The expression is at odds with his rough exterior: he must be over six and a half feet tall, with long, black hair tied back, and a deep, jagged scar that runs from the top of his forehead all the way across his left eye, which is still intact, down to his bottom lip. The smile is one I've seen before, and I resist the urge to look toward Aneira.

"Pleasure to meet you. My name is Harailt of the Hellraizer Pack. I know this may all seem sudden and unexpected, as it's not often that the famous," he says sarcastically, "and esteemed Calian asks for our presence in any sort of capacity. It's even rarer for him to recommend a pack to be set up in his jurisdiction. In fact," he glances around at the other members of the council, "I think this may be the first time he has ever asked our help with his beloved Cabria Shifter Falls."

I keep my face carefully blank, but his comment grates on me, and if Aneira's suddenly tense body is anything to go by, it pisses her off too. *They rush to meet a pack for the sake of gossip, but when it came to protecting shifters, they moved at a glacial pace?*

Another man chuckles throatily, stepping closer to us. "That's a nice way of saying we are a bloody nosy lot, and we scrambled here faster than eggs in a pan! This is the first time Calian has invited us anywhere near this shifter oasis."

"You know damn well why, Kenai," Calian says, a frown on his face.

"Yes, yes. You're a private man. We get it." He clears his throat and looks toward me, "Apologies. My name is Kenai of the Collins Grizzly pack," he nods his head with a fatherly smile.

I raise my voice to drown out Storm's small squeal and subsequent humming of the Brother Bear songs, ironic, really. Kenai's eyes flick her way, and he stifles a laugh before waving a hand to the rest of the members, prompting them to introduce themselves. Rory's aunt, Mila Daria of the Feralis Pack, who is head of the bird shifters, and Pierce's father, Jonas of Leopardo Pack, head of all feline shifters. Kathleen is their mage liaison who is paid to protect the council and assist them with instant travel. Everyone else in their party, other than Pierce and Rory, were either guards like Ralph or Seconds like Tristan.

"It is a pleasure to meet you all. My pack and I are grateful for your quick visit. I hope to prove to all of you how our pack will be an integral addition to the shifter community as a formally established pack. Before I take you around, may I formally introduce you to my second in command, Tristan, as well as my mate, Aneira?" Tristan nods respectfully as I turn to grab Aneira's hand and bring her closer, tucking her into my side, if only to keep her from losing it as rage and annoyance reverberate through our bond.

"It is an absolute pleasure to meet all of you," she smiles brightly, her voice slightly strained.

Harailt makes a soft noise in the back of his throat as he looks at Aneira, as if in a dream, before shaking his head.

Kenai clears his throat as he looks at Harailt curiously. "Well then, let's not waste any time, shall we? Casimir, lead the way please. I am sure Calian went over a few basic things, but we will walk around your pack land twice, once with you as our guide and then again without your guidance so we can ask your packmates a few questions. We will then have a formal sit-down with your pack, followed by a quick deliberation, and our decision will be after dinner. In this case, Calian has also requested that, if everything goes favorably for your pack, for us to formally acknowledge your mate bond and accept Aneira as your chosen. While this is usually done at the yearly Alpha-shifter meetings, in your case, Harailt has already had his yearly meeting. No sense in having you wait when we are all here."

I don't respond. Instead, I briefly lock gazes with Aneira.

Her eyes flood with understanding, and I feel a surge of confidence flood our bond as she presses herself against me---my arms instinctively wrapping around her.

"Show them your heart, Casimir. When they see what I did from the moment I met you..."

"They'll run?" I tease.

Her warm laugh envelopes me, and she reaches on her toes to press a kiss on my lips," "They will fall in love so hard, they will have no choice but to accept your greatness and your vision."

My pulse quickens as I fall into her eyes. Calian clears his throat, breaking the spell. I take a deep breath and gratefully squeeze Aneira's hand, feeling the tension in my chest dissipate.

Steeling myself, I move forward, wondering how I can show them my heart when I was just looking into it's eyes?

Aneira

I HANG BACK with Storm as Casimir leads the council on a tour of the pack lands. Although I had been formally introduced to the pack myself after a quick walk-through the afternoon before, I'm still interested in learning a bit more about the pack and what was in the works for them as a whole. Part of me feels like a tourist to my own pack lands, and that's a mind-fuck itself—the fact that these lands are technically mine now too. "Sure, just give me a moment to channel my inner quest-giver and transform into a wise old sage," Storm deepens her voice to mimic Casimir as she keeps pace by my side.

I laugh softly, "part of me wanted to pretend they were talking to me so I could say, 'Right, then. First years this way, please! Come on, now, don't be shy! Follow me!'"

"Fuck, Hagrid. That was way better than mine," she says softly as Calian shoots her a look. She sticks out her tongue.

"I admit, in a short time, he has pulled a fucking HGTV miracle," Storm marvels a few minutes later, and I smile with pride as Casimir showcases the new buildings and their features, starting with a state-of-the-art library—swoon—that he says is soon to be filled with books donated by various charities he has ties with. I have to agree with Storm. When Tristan mentioned being tired of seeing the wolves build homes, I was picturing a quaint rustic town, but the architecture here would make Wilder faint.

Casimir moves from the public meeting hall to an area that has been transformed into a lush garden with winding paths, dotted with fruit trees, and is attacked by a group of pups.

"Tristan, call the Council! We are under attack!" Casimir shouts, jokingly.

"I'm running for my life; these little ones look feral!" Tristan replies as one child pretends to gnaw off his neck.

"Alpha Casi, are you almost done?! You promised we would play Wolves and Robbers!" A little girl, who can't be over five, whines, her bright green eyes so striking that it takes my breath away.

Casimir chuckles, "Break!" he calls out, and they all stop immediately.

"Hot and commanding. I like it. You can keep him," Storm whispers, and I laugh.

He looks my way and winks. "We will be finished by lunchtime, Lacey, and then I promise I will come and play. But first, you have your morning lessons at the schoolhouse, and if you miss those…"

"You'll be the wolf, and we'll be the robbers," Lacey pouts.

I burst out laughing along with several of the council members as the kids run off at top speed, apparently afraid of the big bad wolf, Alpha Casi.

"Calian mentioned refugees, but there are certainly quite a bit of children here," Harailt says.

Casimir nods, "Unfortunately, we have quite a few Omegas here that came from precarious situations. Lacey, for example, came with her aunt—her sister having been injured and unable to escape their old pack. Still, the children are adjusting well, despite the moving around. Let's continue. I have a game of wolves and robbers to win at high noon."

He chuckles but turns, effectively cutting off any further questions. Questions that are burning in Harailt's eyes. Everything else can be addressed later, but right now, he has to show them, beyond words, why the pack is worthy of being formally recognized.

I'm not sure how long we walk, but every minute is filled with new surprises, from medical offices and homes built specifically for single moms and elderly wolves to the communal kitchens, where everyone within the pack is encouraged to take part in meal preparation together. And with every minute that passes, I know without a doubt that Casimir is every bit the mate that I never let myself dream of, and I'm glad because I don't think the dream would have come close to reality.

🐾

AS CAS FINISHED THE TOUR, Storm and I broke away. The Council moved along to do their own walk around and get to know the pack while Casimir disappeared to handle pack matters and a certain game of robbers. I took the opportunity to eat, shower, and change into another dress for dinner.

Still, as Storm and I head for dinner, my stomach gives a rumble of anger, and I'm seconds away from eating the next person with the council entourage, that looks at me curiously as they mill around. I'm not sure when it started happening, but every few moments during the morning tour, Harailt would look back and stare, eyes filled with wonder as if I was a fucking painting in a museum. Then a few members of the guard started doing it too.

Storm nods her head, indicating the council group directly ahead of us. "Hot Grandpa wolf keeps looking back at you again," Storm murmurs softly in my ear as we follow the path to the dining hall.

Despite my sensitive hearing, my ears strain to catch her words over my grumbling stomach. I appreciate the discretion, as I was just going to bring up the same thing, albeit much louder. My patience is warring with my hunger.

For the most part, we stayed silent during the tour as Casimir confidently moved, answering questions and introducing members of the pack. What he has accomplished is nothing short of incredible, and it was clear, by the nods and smiles, that the council felt the same way.

I would have basked in finally having a pack to be proud of if it wasn't for the stares from Harailt—his very familiar stare. Part of me felt like I knew him, and with how he kept looking at me, I wondered if I did. Even if his face wasn't memorable, and it certainly was, I know I would remember meeting a shifter that exuded so much power. His demeanor screamed, 'I'll fuck you up and laugh while I eat your heart.'

"I know. It's grating on my fucking nerves, but I swear, Agatha recognizes him to some degree but doesn't know how." I shake my head.

"Don't want to point out the obvious here, but he looks a lot like you, sweets. I mean…if you were the male byproduct of The Rock, Vin Diesel, The Terminator, and Jacob Black, in a hot dress. Which in his case," Storm looks at Harailt up and down "may very well be exactly how he came to be. We should look into labs that are splicing genes or something," she adds, her head turned as if she is really considering it. Although, in her case, she probably is.

I laugh softly, "Please don't hack into top-secret databases to test your theory."

She gives a dramatic sigh, "Fine. Party pooper… Still, the idea has merit."

I shove her lightly, and she laughs. I look over at the wolf councilman, and my heart thumps wildly as he looks away when our gazes meet. I never met my father, but my mother was sure he was dead. The safety deposit box had a hastily penned letter with the same account number on the slip of paper she had given me, with instructions on how to access the account. The pack was relatively wealthy but not wealthy enough for my mom to abscond with several million. I figured in those fifteen years, she had set up lucrative investments, and the rest was a life insurance policy that paid out when my father was pronounced dead. I now wish I had the courage to ask her more questions. I catch myself as I stare mindlessly while I muse and shake my head to rid my thoughts. No. She was sure they had killed him when they found her and dragged her back. Said her mate bond was destroyed, and if it weren't for me, she would have given in to the pain and let the moon take her to the next life. You couldn't fake something like a bond break. Maybe Harailt is related to my father?

I push all thoughts to the back of my mind as Casimir calls my name when we enter the dining hall. Although 'dining hall' is putting it mildly. The hall boasts multiple levels—one for children during school hours, one for dining parties, and then the main floor. The entire hall was constructed with more than just the pack's comfort in mind. The ambiance feels like an extension of a home, a place to belong. The high ceilings and large windows let in plenty of natural light, while crystal chandeliers hang low from the dark oak beams. Tables of cherry wood of various sizes are strategically placed throughout the room to accommodate families of any size, with chairs that match the polished dark wood flooring. Then to top it all off, there is an open-style kitchen that bustled with wolves, allowing them to feel as if they were dining with the pack instead of hidden away. It is perfect.

With a slight smile, I tug Storm with me, following Casimir's beaming smile like a beacon. I settle at the table in the front of the dining hall, seated next to Casimir, with Tristan on his opposite side. Storm makes her way to sit next to Calian, who is waiting for her, at the council table. While we set the seating up to promote integration, out of a show of respect, the council has its table on a slightly raised dais. Otherwise, they looked like they were part of the pack.

My eyes search for steak and grapes when Harailt clears his throat, drawing our attention.

Agatha grumbles in my head. *So the speech can't wait until I feed the child? Rude. Advise that wolf that I will soon rip out his heart if I do not get my meat.*

I hold back a laugh but nudge Casimir and point to my stomach discretely. He nods and moves his hand behind us with a signal I assume means, 'get my mate some food before she kills us all and eats our souls for dessert.' Roughly.

Harailt stands, nodding respectfully at the pack. "I must confess when Calian invited us to visit a newly settled refugee pack, we felt a bit apprehensive."However, The Shifter Council commends the progress you've made in a short period and while we acknowledge your pack's accomplishments, we require additional information before making a formal decision. Therefore, we invite the chosen pack Alpha, Casimir, to lead us in the more formal proceedings of this meeting."He sits down, and I feel Casimir take a deep breath beside me, and I squeeze his hand as he stands up from his chair. I nod in encouragement, and he briefly bends down to kiss my lips, "Here's to our future, my love."

As his words wash over me like a warm wave, my heart skips a beat. He flashes me a playful wink, and I can feel my cheeks flush. *Fair is fair, I suppose*, I think to myself, remembering my earlier declaration. But, fuck, I *do* love him. Fate has spoken, and I am finally listening.

"Thank you, Councilman Harailt. I agree. Our pack *has* made incredible progress, and seeing as I understand the importance of transparency, I'll be completely open with you. I was born an Alpha, not just in terms of inheritance but also in the sense that I recognized being an Alpha is more than just a title; it's a responsibility that should never be taken lightly. But those two ideals clashed, leading to the formation of the Spiroid pack two years ago when a few loyal wolves and I chose to leave our old pack behind." Casimir pauses as Kathleen scoffs. *Just who is this bitch?* A hired mage sitting with the council didn't make any sense. So what made her valuable?

I stew on that while a sharp look from Harailt shuts her up, and he nods at Casimir to continue. The air is heavy with Casimir's declaration. Defecting from a pack without reaching out to the council for alternative placement was tantamount to a death sentence.

"The truth is never pleasant," Casimir says with a humorless chuckle. "But it's necessary. Our old pack, Pack Peilt, abused their power, and this abuse was cleverly concealed by my father. Our Omegas were treated as political bargaining chips and suffered both physically and mentally. I understand that each pack has its own leadership style, but allowing our wolves to be abused when they should feel safe within our packs didn't sit right with me. When I brought up my concerns to the

Alpha, my father, he dismissed them. I realized that for the safety of those who trusted me, it was best for us to leave and try to start our own pack."

"Why didn't you contact the council in order to be placed in another pack? Surely you realize that was an option and the correct thing to do?" Jonas, the head of the cat shifters, inquires. No judgment in his tone, just curiosity.

Casimir shakes his head sadly. "With all due respect, the council might have taken too long to re-home several dozen wolves or simply ignored our pleas." Casimir raises his hand as some council members murmur in response. "No, this is just the truth. If you check your backlog of requests, you'll find several from Casimir of the Peilt Pack. Despite the rules, I assume the council doesn't favor allowing wolf abuse to continue when it can be prevented?"As Casimir finishes his last statement, I watch Hairalt's face twist with outrage while the others gape. I lock eyes with Storm, and I can tell we're both thinking the same thing—what the fuck were these Alphas discussing, or in this case, not-discussing during their meetings that allowed so much to be under the rug? Not every Alpha can be an evil mastermind, so what is it?

"I thought so," Casimir nods. "Despite the laws, we struck out on our own. Over several months, while we searched for a place to settle, what had started as a small group of wolves grew larger as we encountered other outcasts or abused wolves with backgrounds similar to ours." He pauses briefly as he looks around the room.

"However, our journey didn't lead us to just wolves. We were lucky enough to cross paths with several witches seeking their own way too. As a whole, our pack has moved beyond the basic transactional relationship with witches that used to be the norm, embracing a more symbiotic one instead. Our pack lands remain impenetrable, and our movements, considering how we have grown, were concealed. The witches protected.

These witches now live within our pack lands and have become an integral part of our community. They *are* pack. More importantly, we are a family. While we aren't conventional, we all agree that we want peace. A pack where wolves no longer have to worry about not finding their true mate through a forced political alliance or be constricted by archaic rules that seem to vary from pack to pack to suit their ideals. We were fortunate to feel a call to Cabria Falls, although I like to think that particular call was fate rather than luck," he jokes lightly.

"I know our choices are tantamount to a death sentence, but why? For wanting and needing change? For wanting a better future? I ask that you look at what Alpha Calian has created here in Cabria Shifter Falls. This town is a community of shifters who work, live, and grow together despite being from a different genetic makeup. Witches pepper this town, as well as several hundred humans. It is time that we look beyond trying to maintain a firm foothold in traditions and look into integrating in order to build a safer community and world for us all. Furthermore," he takes a deep breath, steeling his spine, and takes a moment to look at every councilman in the eye before looking directly at Harailt.

"I can see that the news of abused wolves and the misuse of power has caught you off guard, Councilman Harailt. I wish I could say I sympathize. However, if the shifter council were more than just a figurehead and dispenser of judgments, our packs would be held to higher standards, and such abuse would cease to exist. I understand why we are here today, and while it's important to my pack and my growing family," Casimir glances at me before continuing.

"To become formally recognized, it must be done with the understanding that we share a collective responsibility to cleanse the wolf packs, or any other shifter packs, of the corruption that has taken root. Our pack plans to lead the charge against this corruption because shifters aren't just being threatened by external forces. We're under attack from within by our own kind — Our packs are being torn asunder by pride, greed, and the darkness festering within the hearts of those who are supposed to lead and protect us. It is our duty to create a better future for all shifters, where we can not only survive but truly thrive.

As we have grown, I have continued to ensure a safe place for my pack, witches, *and* wolves. I hope my pack has proven to you all today that respect, power, and progression can all go hand in hand."

He bows respectfully before retaking his seat. Grabbing his hand, I give him a gentle squeeze before leaning over to place a kiss on his cheek.

Storms stands up and starts clapping, "Well, shit. Casimir for president." Calian pulls her down, and I hear her whisper, "What? Dude, that speech made my mare-bits tingle with the flame of vengeance."

I laugh through the ache in my chest, my throat burning with tears as I grab Casimir's face to bring his eyes to my level. "I am so proud to call you my mate." There is nothing else I can be. Casimir's vision for progression, not only within the wolf packs but for all shifters and beings, is exactly what we need and deserve.

Before he can respond, a slow clap echoes around the room, this time not from Storm but from somewhere near the entrance to the dining room. Confused, we turn, and our eyes clash with Casimir's stunt double, if Casimir was 40 years older, flanked by several wolves I don't recognize. Agatha's hackles rise.

Casimir's body goes taunt, and a low growl escapes his lips.

"As stirring as that speech was, I have come to exercise my right as the Alpha of the Pielt Pack, reclaim the wolves that belong to me, and end the treasonous wolf who dared to lead my pack members away - my son." The room goes deathly still, silent.

Fuck.

Storm exhales a deep breath, "Oh shit, this just got *good*."

Double fuck.

CHAPTER 22
CASIMIR

Casimir

My blood boils as I stare at the pitiful alpha who was once my father. He may cut an imposing figure, an older reflection of me, in fact, but if you peeled back his skin and muscles, and plucked out his bones, you'll find a soul as black as his heart.

Keeping myself in control, I force my face to remain blank while I casually lean back in my chair. My father's eyes flash with irritation, and I mentally mark a win. After all that my pack has endured, if this piece of shit thought he was going to take it away, I'm prepared and more than willing to rip his bones out of his chest and eat his heart for dinner.

"Considering you are interrupting a formal Shifter Council meeting with a potential new pack and have come inside protected pack lands, uninvited, I suggest you tread lightly, Alpha," Harailt's growl pierces the silence.

"Apologies, Master Alpha Harailt, for the intrusion," he says coolly, eyes blazing with fury, not a single hint of regret in his tone.

"If you allow," he grits out, "Once I heard that my estranged, son, was petitioning to become Alpha and start his own pack, I made my way here immediately. I have not formally denounced him as my heir, and therefore, as written in our bylaws, he cannot form his own pack," he smiles, mostly teeth.

I roll my eyes, ignoring the bullshit spewing from his mouth. Something is nagging me, several things actually, like how the fuck he knew our location or got here so quickly. But right now, I'm choosing to focus on how the fuck he crossed into our lands. The witches were careful to set up a light perimeter because of the Council's presence — a decision which will piss me off for a long time—so how did he cross the borders of our lands without setting off the alarms? And why didn't he just turn back when he sensed the Council? He was always a cocky son-of-a-bitch, but reckless? Not usually.

"I also think our bylaws are firm against the abuse of power," Tristan leans forward, his canines extending as he fights for control of his wolf. His quarrel with my father is a bit more complex than most but that is his story to tell.

My father laughs a deep sinister rumble. "Tristan, how is your dear mother? Spoken to her recently?" he says with a smirk, venom seeping from his words. On the surface, it seems like a simple question - but I know better.

Tristan roars and I pull him back as his wolf tries to take

control. My eyes flash and my voice deepens with command, "Stand down, Tristan."

Tristan struggles, I lean forward with a, barely there, whisper, "Don't let this piece of shit win. Reign it in."

I glance at the council, who is looking at the events unfolding with interest, and I almost feel their minds whirling. In reality, my father's presence may be more helpful than detrimental. I'm going to let him talk himself into an early grave, assuming Tristan doesn't put him there first.

My father seems unfazed, a smug look on his face as he folds his arms across his chest, "Clearly, there is a lack of control here. Regardless, our bylaws protect an Alpha's choice, how I choose to run my pack is none of your business, you *chose* to leave."

Aneira stands and looks at the Council table with a serene smile on her face that belies the rage I feel vibrating through our bond, "Alpha Harailt, if I may?"

Harailt nods, rigid in his seat.

"Our bylaws are in place to protect our people first. The fact that an Alpha can lead their pack, as they choose is second to that. Alphas who choose to ignore the basic rights of their people, who believe in ruling with an iron fist with no justice, are the reason so many wolves are broken and defecting from their packs. They are also the reason you and the rest of the council are here today. These wolves have been through enough, *my* pack, has been through enough and yet they still have enough fortitude to rebuild, time and time again. That is a testament to Casimir's strength, not a by-product of their pack of origin…" She pauses and looks at my father up and down with disdain.

Her rage spikes, and I touch her side briefly. My father's eyes sharpen as he takes in the small touch, and Montgomery snarls in my head at the interest that flares in his eyes.

"Omega's do not have a voice. Therefore, your opinion

means less than nothing to me. Especially since you are the whore of a defected wolf, nothing more," my father's lip curls as he spits his vitriol.

All hell breaks loose as growls fill the room, making the hair on my body stand on edge as I shove my chair back, ready to tear my father's limb from limb, Council presence be damned.

Tristan rises to his feet angrily, teeth bared and claws out as he partially shifts, "You will treat my Luna with respect, you worthless murdering son of a maggot."

Storm hisses and pulls off her earrings. "Oh, hell no. This Snout-Sniveling, Moonlight Malcontent, got my family all the way fucked up. Stand the fuck back. I'm going to shove my hoof up his dickhole and then tie a unicorn horn on my head before I shift and plunge my glitter-covered razor-sharp horn right into his worthless, shriveled asshole." For a split second, all eyes flick in her direction, and I swear I see fear flash in my father's eyes before they go blank. I mean, a sharp horn up the ass will make most people run.

"That is enough," Calian's voice boomed throughout the room. "Mate, sit your gorgeous violent ass back down in that seat before I take you over my knee," his voice dark with promise.

Sensing the seriousness in his tone, Storm sits down but not before grumbling, "he acts like that's not something I want anyway."

A fleeting smirk graces Calian's face before he directs his blazing gaze around the room, unleashing tendrils of his power. The air becomes so thick that it feels as if you're swimming in pure molasses. It's a testament to Calian's power that Harailt isn't the one to rise and confront the blatant disrespect shown not only to wolves as a whole but also to an Omega wolf. Despite the rot that has seemed to take root in several packs across the country, Omega's are precious and are to be protected. *Agreed-to* political alliances notwithstanding, forcing

Omegas to marry or to abuse one physically or verbally takes a wolf of pure evil. It goes against every natural instinct we possess.

Another surge of power fills the room, and my gaze quickly shifts to Harailt. His eyes are wide, fur bristling, and fangs lengthening as his wolf struggles for dominance. It suddenly dawns on me why Calian is the one stepping up in his place - to give Harailt a chance to regain control before he unintentionally scares the very wolves he's meant to lead, particularly now that he knows about the abused Omegas within our pack.

Aneira stands up straighter and laughs, *laughs*. Calian looks at her curiously, and she smiles at him gently. "Forgive me, but this," she waves her hand at my father before she turns her body away, effectively dismissing him as a threat, "sorry excuse of a wolf, just proved our point that some packs are rotten from the very core. His overall existence may be a complete waste of space but at least now the council sees, first hand, why despite the laws about defection, wolves still choose to leave their packs. I don't think anything further needs to be said." She nods at Calian before taking her seat.

"Thank you, Aneira," Calian says before turning his gaze to my father, who is poorly controlling his anger. The wolves with him, very obviously, take a step back as the full gaze of the Shifter Council falls on him.

"I think we can all agree that this meeting has been most enlightening." Calian's voice grows deadly quiet, and he leans, palms down on the table in front of him, staring directly at my father, "Alpha Casemiro of the Pielt Pack, you have been abusing your power. Bringing physical and emotional harm to your pack Omegas and the other wolves under your charge. In fact, your sheer ineptitude as Alpha, has resulted in multiple wolves defecting. All of whom you never reported. If these wolves did pose a danger to society, the result of that poor choice would have been detrimental to all shifters. And yet, despite knowing the Shifter Council would be present– which we'll discuss shortly – you show up to do what, exactly? Threaten your son? An Alpha worth more than a hundred of your pathetic hides?"

My father sputters, "You are not a wolf; you do not understand the way we do things in order to stay on top of the food chain."

At that, Harailt leaps over the table and, in a blink of an eye, strikes my father, his claws leaving bloody marks across his face.

"Silence!"

Calian continues as if he wasn't interrupted, "You insult the sanctity of a Shifter Council meeting, breaking all of the usual protocols, including, but not limited to, speaking out of turn, disrespecting a Council member, and insulting a female, the mate of another Alpha. Then let's add to your long list of egregious offenses, not calling a formal meeting to discuss your grievances, instead choosing to hide the rot within your pack. Instead, you choose to bring members of your pack with you, now making them equally as responsible. Tell us, how many wolves will you have left if I kill everyone present tonight?"

My father's face pales, and I smirk and sit back, grateful I don't have to address the cluster fuck that was my father. There are some serious perks to this brother-in-mate business.

"Let's add that he is also a slobbering, fang-fumbling douche," Storm pipes up, and Calian lets a laugh escape. "Although my mate speaks out of turn," he looks at her with a mock glare, "We can add that to the list as well." He nods at Harailt, who looks to have himself under control, finally.

Pinning my father with a glare, he turns to the members of my pack, "It looks like I have failed all wolf shifters. I put too much faith in our Alpha meetings, trusting that the Alpha's under my command would be truthful. For that, I am truly sorry," he bows to them.

"From this point forward, we will be investigating all packs with in-person reviews, and I think I speak for the entire council when I say we plan to ensure that all complaints are pulled, heard, and rectified immediately."

I feel elation pour through Aneira, and a rush of warmth fills my chest. This is what we needed, both as a people and as a society of shifters. Who would have guessed that my father would be the catalyst to uncover the rot?

"Alpha Casemiro, although that title is heavily under question, you are to leave these lands immediately and await your punishment at your pack house, where you will be held accountable for your crimes. Although at this point, you may as well use that time to make peace with the Moon Goddess. Guards?" Harailt nods, and their guards, seemingly float out of thin air and escort the intruders out of the hall.

"Now that that unpleasantness is done, I move that we enjoy a meal together before the council announces our decision. We have been given a lot to consider, and we will discuss it amongst ourselves during our meal," Harailt nods as he strides over to reclaim his seat. Calian smiles encouragingly at us, and I close my eyes briefly before I match his smile, nodding gratefully.

I turn to grab Aneiras's hand and place our joined hands on her belly.

"Time for steak?" She asks, hopefully, and I laugh.

Feed the pregnant mate, then celebrate. I can do that.

CHAPTER 23
ANEIRA

I descend on my food like a vegan osprey let loose in a meat factory- Scarily rabid. The Council's eyes flick towards me in alarm as I growl at anyone who comes too close, except for the servers, they can keep coming. Storm sits down next to me with a sigh, " How long are you going to be the Buffy to your steak?"

I don't spare her a glance as I respond through bites, "As long as it takes you to swallow your Jockey's Joy Javelin that you have the nerve to call a penis. We all know you require a wheelchair now and are using hay magic to walk upright.

Calian should be brought up on charges. There is being dick whipped, and then there is being whipped by a dick."

Calian's eyes fly up, and he glares. Storm cackles.

"Stop talking about another man's penis," Casimir leans over with a scowl.

"She talked about my meat first!" I growl, "now back the fuck up or this will be the only meat near my mouth for the next few months."

He rolls his eyes with a laugh, kissing my cheek before he turns back to Tristan, who is doing a poor job hiding his laughter.

"Thank god the worst is over, shit was stressful as fuck," I shovel a piece of steak into my mouth and moan in appreciation.

"Jesus, if this is how you eat as a pregnant wolf, how much do you think ill eat when I eventually get pregnant?" Storm stares at me in awe.

I grab a cup of water to wash down the food in my mouth before I respond, "No idea but don't worry, I'll make sure we have plenty of grass for you to graze on."

"Bitch, it better be quality grass," she laughs, turning to her own food.

"I wonder why the other council members didn't talk more during that cluster fuck. Although their faces said enough, they have shitty resting bitch faces," she says around a mouthful of food. I laugh.

"Well, since Calian brought our formal introduction to the Council, and he is the head of this area, it falls to him to control the floor. Harailt, being that he is the wolf representative, would also share the responsibility, although I got the feeling that he was trying to control himself more than anything. He is having trouble with his self-control." I frown as I looked over to their table, and the closer I look, the more I can pick up the signs of strain on Harailt's face, the slight sag to his shoulders.

"I wonder why?" Storm asks.

Casimir leans closer to us, clearly listening in on our conversation, nosey ass. "About 25 or so years ago, Harailt lost his true mate. The fact that he didn't succumb to depression and be put down is a fucking miracle. The stronger the shifter, the harder the fall, and that's saying something. Even after all this time, the loss of a true mate will still affect a shifter. I think that finding out that so much has been happening under his nose, even more, so the abuse of Omega's, doesn't help his self-control. Then Casemiro insults a pregnant Luna, right in his face? Overall, tonight could have ended with a lot more bloodshed."

"In all honesty, he was within his right to punish Casemiro publically, but the fact that he didn't kill him despite his obvious blood lust was ridiculously impressive," Tristan's fixed gaze fell on Harialt, who was in deep discussion with the other council members. He forgets to blink for a few moments before he snaps out of it.

"You seem half in love there, Tristan," I tease.

He rolls his eyes, "Bah...he wishes I liked men. No, I simply admire restraint in the face of adversity. It's why I will always follow Casimir, despite his shitty father. One needs more than good fighting skills and pretty words in order to lead," he shrugs.

Casimir smiles, "Stop flirting with me. I don't like men either."

"You wish I would warm your bed. I'll have you know, my knot will change the world," he snarks back.

Storm rolls her eyes, "Boys, boys. We all know my Alpha brings all the Mares to the yard, okay? So let's not do this— It's embarrassing. Back to the formalities," she directs back at me, "if you call the meeting, the ball is in your pack. The shifter representative also has a say, then the council comes together, and they all make the final ruling. Genius, really, voices get heard instead of being drowned out, and shit gets accomplished."

"Yeah, it was a method put in place by the Swiftwaters decades ago. Apparently, Calian's great-grandfather lost his shit when everyone kept talking over each other and had a full-on trot attack. Since the Swiftwaters are the only original family on the council, what they say holds a lot of weight. You felt Calian's power. Shit is unreal," I shove Storm playfully, wiggling my eyebrows, and take another bite of my food. Okay, I shovel half a steak in my mouth and swallow with minimal chewing. Semantics.

"What the fuck ever. It just means more work for me to bring him down a peg. I admit, though, it is fucking hot," she sighs wistfully, staring at Calian, who looks up briefly and winks at her.

She smiles saucily before grabbing her fork to stab at her food, "although he is turning me into a saddle straddling, hoof hussy."

I laugh, "I would say it gets easier, but with mates, it just gets...harder."

"Gee, thanks," she says drolly, and I laugh harder.

"Oh, by the way," she smiles brightly, reaching to pull a small box out of moon knows where, and passes me a small box. "I wanted to wait until the Council made their formal announcement, but I think it safe to say that if any other decision is made, they are aware that I will hide under all of their beds and pull out pubic hair while they sleep until they change their minds. So I can totally give you this now."

Calian sighs, rubbing his temples as the rest of the Council stares at Storm in varying degrees of confusion and a hint of fear. So basically, the way most people react to her. Calder laughs with a shake of his head before calling everyone's attention back.

"What I say?" Storm asks as I roll my eyes and open the box to find a stunning gold bracelet with a horse and wolf charm.

She waves her wrist in my face to show her identical bracelet, "It's our official, 'book-whores to mates, soul-sister bracelet! And when your litter is born, we will add more wolf charms, and when I have tiny vaginal trotters, we will add little horses!" She claps with glee, snatching the bracelet out of the box to put it on my wrist herself.

My eyes fill with tears as I look down at my wrist. Years ago, I would have laughed in the face of anyone who told me that I would not only be happily mated but also have a human, turned horse-shifter, best friend. Now I can't picture my life any other way, and fuck; it feels good to love and be loved. Now, I just have to kill my grandfather. Baby steps.

I wrap her in a hug, " I love you, Storm."

"I love you too, Annie," she says softly.

As she squeezes, I suddenly feel the urge to pee. I pull away, and I go to push myself from the table. Casimir, Tristan, and Storm go to move with me, and I scowl, "Guys, I am pregnant, not a damn invalid, and I have to pee. Sit back down."

"Storm can go with you, or I can wait outside for you. I don't like you going alone knowing my father was anywhere near here," Casimir frowns.

"Cas, he was kicked out. Despite all the shit-talking, your father is a pussy. Agatha would rip his head off. Feel free to bring more steak to the table. I'll be right back. I am surrounded by our pack, with the Council a few feet away. I also really have to pee, so I don't wanna keep talking," I cross my legs and lean over to give him a peck on the lips before I shuffle my ass to the bathroom.

I feel eyes follow me the entire way to the bathroom, and I roll my eyes. Dramatic. I lock the bathroom door behind me and the small stall and sigh in relief as I empty my bladder. If this urgency came on at only a few weeks pregnant, I can imagine how desperate I would feel when I am several months pregnant. *Shit, I may just wear an adult diaper.*

Stepping out of the stall, I move to wash my hands, and my nose twitches as a familiar scent tickles my nose. My eyes fly up to the mirror, and a flash of recognition flits through me before I see a fist fly toward my head. The only thought going through my head is, *this is why women go to the bathroom in groups of 63* before I black out.

CHAPTER 24
ANEIRA

I bite back a groan as sounds start to filter through the darkness. But what really brings me back into the land of the living is the hot nausea that is sweeping through me. It takes all my mental fortitude not to hurl.

There's something tight around my face, but I fight to keep myself from trying to rip it off. *It's okay Aneira, just a regular run-of-the-mill kidnapping. Be cool. Don't let these fuckers know you're awake.*

With my sight taken away from me, I rely on my other

senses. I try to roll my hands, and the sharp bite of pain has me almost blowing my cover. *Silver cuffs? Motherfuckers.* Okay, can't see, can't move, and I won't be able to talk to Agatha with the fucking cuffs of doom. *Well, this is just fucking peachy.* I take a quiet breath and focus on my hearing instead. Mumbled voices carry over the loud noise of a car, and I strain to hear what is being said as the car hits a bump and a buckle stabs me on my side, and the cuffs tighten. From this position, the vibrations send another wave of sickness through me. Not fucking ideal. Neither is the fact that whoever is driving this lupine limo thinks they drive for Nascar and considering I have no idea how long I've been out for, I can't gauge my location. When I get out of these cuffs, I was eating someone.

In my effort to contain nausea and rising blood lust, I try to tune back into the murmur of voices coming from the front of the car. They're speaking in low tones, but even over the roar of the engine, one of the men sounds familiar, although I cannot for the life of me place it while my head is in a fog.

"When we get back to the pack, you need to make sure that she is separated from the rest of them. The last thing I want is to send the others into a frenzy once they get a whiff of her."

There's a scoff and then a beat of silence before the other — familiar voice speaks again. "Don't worry about that. This little omega is going to be very busy before long. She has a lot to live up to and make up for." The tone in his voice sends a chill through me, and combined with another wave of nausea, it's too much, and I can't control it before I'm choking on my vomit.

The black sack covering my head rips off, and I suck in some air. My hands are trapped underneath me, but a napkin gets wiped over my mouth with a little more force than necessary, I might add.

"Ah, you're awake little Omega. We are so close to your new pack and call it the excitement of revenge or the vindication of righting a wrong of history, but I'm looking forward to you seeing it. But I've said enough, can't ruin the surprise." I groan and lift my head as the man in the passenger seat turns around, and I can't contain my gasp.

I'm looking at a carbon copy of Casimir if he was about twenty years older. Almost instantly, the fog clears, and my memories come rushing back. The familiar scent in the bathroom, the flash of his face in the mirror before I was knocked out. Casimir's father.

Can't even pee in peace. Although, how he got back into the pack dining hall after being escorted out is beyond me right now, seeing as vomit-smeared, silver-cuffed, nauseated Aneira is not the character arc I was going for.

His face twists into a gleeful grin as he watches recognition dawn on me. I grimace as his bloodshot, half-crazed eyes flicker with his wolf's presence. "Ahh, I see you finally remember," he taunts. "Don't worry, my pretty little Omega. All will be revealed soon."

Rage burns away the rest of the nausea as I rear back and spit into his face. "I'm not *your* anything, you flea-bitten hound."

The car takes a sharp turn, tossing me around before speeding up and making another sharp turn. I can't right myself with my hands cuffed behind my back, and as I flail around like a baby giraffe, I throw up again.

"Ugh, can you do something to stop the bitch being sick all over my car?" The driver asks with derision.

Casimir's father slaps the back of his head. "Just concentrate on getting us there, and stop with the stupid comments."

"Sorry, Casemiro," the guy mumbles but doesn't say anything else. This must be his beta.

Yeah, focus on getting us there so I don't have to slide around in vomit…wait…

"Where the fuck are you taking…" I trail off as he turns

around and snarls in my face. Truly, an impressive snarl; the perfect amount of spittle with just a slight hint of 'I watch you while you pee' vibes. If I weren't his prisoner, I would ask for a tutorial—the snarl, not the urination stalking. I have to have some type of morals.

I'm losing it. It must be the lack of steak.

"Listen here, little bitch. You need to shut that mouth and keep quiet. There is so much I could do to you that by the end, you will long for death. Don't. test. me." He swivels around to the front and laughs happily. I blink. *What in the ever-loving fuck?*

If I weren't already sure that I was in a precarious position, the fact that he is quick to jump from 'my omega' to murderous fuck, to 'Chuckle The Clown' removes any doubt.

I give myself a few minutes to have a mini breakdown as I bite back a sob. Visions of my new family disintegrate before my eyes. The thoughts of big Christmases with baby horses and wolves disappear in a cloud of chloroform-scented smoke. If this motherfuckers idea of warm and cuddly is a quick kidnapping and a ride through darkness, I don't fucking want it. *Check, please.*

The rest of the journey is made in tense silence, punctuated by Casemiro's quiet, off-tune humming of 'Who Let The Dogs Out.' But it's not the song choice that worries me, although ruining the Baha Men is a sin in itself, no, it's the way his body tenses and relaxes randomly with a slight twitch in between that sets me on edge. Then I finally pick up the slight tang of addiction in the stale air, and panic unfurls in my belly. Not only is this kidnapping asshole a song-butchering psycho of epic proportions, but he's an addict as well. Drugs and shifters just don't mix. But an Alpha Wolf and drugs? Fucking disaster.

"We're here, Little Wolf, no need to panic. You're home," Casemiro sings happily when the car rolls to a stop. I try and breathe through the mounting fear when he gets out and opens the door, hauling me out like I'm a ragdoll. He takes a huge sniff of my neck, and a low chuckle rumbles through his chest. "I'm going to enjoy having you here."

I snarl at his proximity, feeling Agatha push past the silver restraints, her protective instincts rearing, "How about you let me out of these restraints, and I'll help you enjoy the afterlife." My eyes flash, and I feel my claws extend.

He frowns, and while I echo his confusion, I smirk. In all honesty, the silver should have prevented any change. My wolf should be shoved so deep inside that there would be no hope of her coming out while I was shackled.

"Interesting," his eyes flicker with something akin to desire, and I shudder in disgust as my wolf fights harder for supremacy, wanting blood and wanting to protect her baby.

He wraps his hand around my throat, squeezing painfully. "Ah, ah, ah. None of that now. You have a baby to protect, after all."

My eyes narrow at the implied threat, and I force my breathing under control before I snarl at him, "Casimir will find me, and if my best friend gets her hands on you first, you'll be fucking begging to be saved." I squirm against his hold, but it's no use as his hold on me is like fucking steel.

He moves his hand up my leg, a little too close to my apex for my liking, but it makes me go still. "That's what I'm counting on. Him finding you, and then we can settle our little family dispute once and for all." The beta sniffs, but I can't quite see his expression. "Then, once his head is mounted on a spike, I will enjoy breaking you."

Miro— I refuse to call him anything, starting with Cas because it makes my stomach rebel with disgust— keeps me held tight against him as we move past a few spaced-out houses that blend in with the forest around it. The trees are more sparse here than at Cabria, but it still seems private—no chance of being seen by anyone that can set off the Bat-Horse-Wolf signal. The very few shifters that are out and about don't spare us more than the odd curious glance, which makes me think that weird shit goes down here often. For them not to really bat an eye at a pregnant Omega in silver cuffs and a drugged-out Alpha, this must be a relaxed sort of day.

He pauses at the largest cabin/mansion at the end of the pack lands. The outside has a perfect blend of rustic and modern, and it appeals to my tastes… which really offends me. He should be living in a mud shack, not in architectural porn. Fucker.

The beta darts forward and opens the door for Miro, who strides past him without so much as a thank you.

And here is the part I hate; bad decorating. My stomach curdles, and my lip curls in disgust. The foyer is huge, like a hunting lodge, and is covered, and I mean, *covered* by animal heads. Miro lets go of my arm, and I force my legs not to give out at the sudden shift. I look around silently because, truly, there are no words that be uttered here other than several spells to summon the spirits of these animals so they can eat Miro. And seeing as how I don't know any, I stay quiet.

"You like it?" He asks proudly, misinterpreting my silence. "I like to hunt in my wolf form and keep all the kills. I feel like anyone that comes in would see my wolf's strength in the flesh and second guess about taking me on."

His words are laced with a threat, but he keeps an amiable expression. I really want to say it makes him look like a raging psycho, but I don't think it will go down well. Don't tell a murderer his body collection isn't pretty—survival 101.

When I stay silent, he continues, "When your pups are grown, they can add to the wall in the library." He guides me up the stairs, which dominate the middle of the foyer, and takes me up to the second floor. We wander down the hallway and past some doors until he stops at one near the end.

"This is going to be your room for a while. Make yourself at home." He swings open the door and reveals a huge bedroom, sparsely decorated and filled once again with an array of stuffed animals—birds in particular. Although, I don't think they would help me clean the room and do laundry if I sang to them. Cinderella-flavored necromancer, I am not.

I find my voice, "No." I hiss, placing my hands on my hips. "I am not staying here until you tell me what the fuck is going on. I've been pretty reasonable, considering I am encrusted in vomit, but now you need to tell me what is happening. I'm pregnant, and you've torn me away from my mate, and—"

I let out an annoying squeak as Miro propels me into the wall, holding my throat in his hand. Again. Oh, the joy. It doesn't hurt, but the threat is apparent that he could easily crush it without a thought.

"Since you would like answers rather than having a rest, I'm benevolent enough to give them to you."

I resist the urge to roll my eyes. Crazy? Strung-out? Tiny dick syndrome? Yes.

Benevolent? Not a chance.

"It doesn't matter what I say anyway," he mutters. "The wheels are in motion, and by the time my useless excuse for a son finds you, it will be too late." He removes his hand and guides me toward the bed. Nope, not going there.

I get a spike of adrenaline and kick him forcefully in the balls, and when he doubles over, cursing up a storm, I run away from him and down the corridor. When I try a door on this level, I can scream when I find it locked. Instead, I turn and make my way down the huge staircase and skid around the corner, only to run slap-bang into the beta from earlier.

"Going somewhere?" he asks with a bored tone. A roar from upstairs makes us both cringe and Miro vaults, fucking vaults from the top of the stairs all the way to the bottom in one jump. My anxiety ratchets up at the sheer anger coloring his face, the whites of his eyes are prominent, and I instantly regret my decision to run. *I'm so not going to get a coupon for the Kidnapper's Hotel Spa now.*

"If you want to act like that, it comes with consequences Omega," he spits, hauling me into his arms and strides down the hallway and through a door that leads down some concrete steps with a small cot bed in the corner. He pushes me to the bed, a lot gentler than I was expecting, and I bounce a couple of times. "It could have been a lot nicer for you if you cooperated with me. Such a shame that you decided to take the harder route."

He looks down at me as I try to straighten myself, his gaze blank as I struggle with still being cuffed. His head turns, and he lets out a hum, "You know Aneira, yes...I know your name, even before I was hovering outside the Council meeting," he says as my eyes must give away my surprise.

"In fact. I imagine I know more about you than you do. Anyways, despite my view on Omegas in general, you are quite tempting with your spirit. Omega's in this pack learn their place quite quickly," he chuckles darkly. "I haven't seen spunk like this in quite a long time. I admit I am intrigued, and if your little display in the car was any indication, you are quite strong as well. Hmm, half of me is quite proud that my son tried to settle for a strong mate."

My eyes narrow, "What do you mean, tried? I am his mate. There is no try about it. It's all been recognized in front of the council, and we are it, for life." Although I may not have been there for a formal announcement, I feel the truth in my words. Even without the damn announcement, we were fated, mated, and bonded. Which, I think, with savage glee, makes Miro even more fucked than he was before. Not only did Harailt pretty much effectively take away his position as Alpha of this pack, but he also kidnapped an Alpha's mate. Can he be killed twice? Well, make that three times, I want my round.

Wait, The bond!

Keeping my face blank, I reach deep within my soul and try to feel the bond between Cas and I. *Nothing.* I choke back a sob of panic as I feel my pulse thrum throughout my body, my heart squeezing painfully. Inside, Agatha is frenzied, throwing herself against the confines of my head. The need to be with my mate makes me almost delirious, but no matter how hard I try, our bond feels muted. Fuck, me. I feel almost frantic as I take in the dark void in my heart where Cas fills it so thoroughly. Logically, it has to be the cuffs. The silver is blocking the bond. Otherwise, I'm dealing with a moon block charm that was not made by one of my friends.

He smiles at my internal struggle. "Semantics. You're here now, arent you? Do you know how long it's taken for me to find you?"

"What do you mean?" My voice is thick with holding back unshed tears, anger, and annoyance. I try to clear the madness taking hold and play it as cool as possible. *Hope it's working. Otherwise, I probably look constipated.*

"I mean...I don't know how you evaded being found, but, " he shrugs, a crazed smile taking over his face, "we have been searching a little more actively for about a year. If you are still confused, your grandfather has never stopped looking for you. In fact, the bounty for your return is quite high now, obscene, really. It was a pain in the ass, but you'll be worth the stress." He turns away to leave the room but not without a few parting words, "Oh, and if you are trying to reach Casimir through your bond, you can stop, those silver cuffs are laced with a special charm. Your bond is muted. And soon, it will be severed. The perks of blood magic."

My ears ring as his words sink in. The door slams behind him, and a lock clicks into place. My grandfather? My bond is going to be severed? Blood-magic? My breathing turns shallow as my head spins, and the reality of my situation punches me in the face. Despite my very bleak predicament, or maybe because of it, I feel myself teeter on the edge of unconsciousness. I know I should fight it, try to figure out a plan to escape, but despite trying to stay conscious, I feel the blissful darkness take over. *I'll fight later, clearly, I need a panic nap.*

I GROAN as I come to a few hours later. Oh, Consciousness, we really have to stop meeting like this. In the past few hours, I've been unconscious more than at any other time in my life, and I can certainly do without it. At some point, while I was passed out, my cuffs were removed but still left to dangle from one wrist. Still blocked, but at least I can choke someone the fuck out.

I push away the fact that someone was in here while I was vulnerable, and I pull the thin sheet that covers the mattress over my body as I realize how freezing it is. Although, it does nothing to take away from the cold seeping into this room. My stomach rumbles, reminding me that I haven't eaten in a long time, but there is nothing I can do about that I focus on what I can do, which is…nothing.

Fuck, okay. Strategy.

Miro said that my grandfather has been looking for me, which I figured as much. But that effectively puts me in the path of two asshole Alphas. One who I have been planning to murder and the other who I would eat if he weren't seasoned in parsley-laced cocaine seasoning.

Then there is the whole blood magic thing which, assuming it is only used to break the bond and not turn me into a mind-less attack wolf, I can't worry about, seeing as it's nothing my fangs or claws can fight against. So what *can* I do? Right now, I have a sheet, a mattress, and vomited-covered clothes. Weapon-wise, unless Miro suddenly develops OCD, I am sorely lacking. I bite back a growl of frustration.

"Good morning, Omega, or should I say afternoon?" Miro's voice comes from the outside of the room, and a clang verberates throughout the room as the lock disengages. I was so focused on how to utilize a mattress to cut off a head that I never heard steps coming toward the door. I barely notice the door closing behind him and the lock sliding into place, locking him in the room with me as the smell of food permeating the air in his wake is enough to make me hyperaware of my gnawing hunger.

"I brought you some food," he says in a cheery tone, and he steps closer, dressed in a tux and holding a large tray with steaks. "I'm not going to have you passing out again," he adds with a sneer, as if my passing out is offensive, and places the tray in front of me.

I inhale everything on the tray in record time and wash it down with the juice. One day, I'll tell my children that I held out for 42 months and walked a thousand miles in the mud to escape, but right now, I wanted more fucking steak.

Miro's smile stays frozen in place, and he blinks."Well, that was mildly disturbing," he says, taking the tray from me and putting it on the side. "Now. We don't have much time before you're needed in your new pack, so you might want to get in the shower to get the stench of vomit and depression off."

"Sorry, my imprisonment offends you. " I'm not sorry. "How about you take the time to ease that inconvenience by expanding on your earlier bad-guy speech? You say that my grandfather has been looking for me, but you fail to mention any other details."

I'm stalling him, keeping him here as long as possible to hopefully give Cas time to figure out how to unmute our bond and find me. Or that Storm hacks the Pentagon and uses satellites, Shia Lebouff, and the Transformers to locate the allspark...aka, me, before I'm moved around again.

Hopefully, it's not painfully obvious.

"I did say that I would give you answers. And I'm aware of what you're doing. Stalling me."

Damn.

"It's actually...adorable." He says the last as if the word hurt comes out of his mouth. He stands and starts pacing the floor while I hold in a shudder. I don't want Daddio... okay, no... Miro, calling me any words of endearment. He makes me feel so... ick. He stops and whirls around to face me.

"My son does not deserve a mate as unique and beautiful as you, do you know that?" I reel back like I've been slapped.

"What?" Reduced to beauty? Instead of the dazzling ferocious lupine, I am? Rude.

"My son is a useless tool. I tried to drown him as a pup, but unfortunately, even then, he was strong. Figured it was a sign that he would be worthy of my time. Shame that he amounted to nothing. The final insult is his trying to establish a new pack. He should be here, with me, sharing the legacy. At least, with the deal I've made, Casimir's offspring will remain with me."

My blood runs cold at his words, "There is no way that I will let you have my child."

He darts forward and runs a finger down my cheek, and I fight the flinch. "Oh, my darling. You don't have a choice in the matter. You're an Omega. It's sweet you thought, even for a moment, that you have a say in things, but you really don't. As much as I admire your spirit, my patience wears thin. I will break you, and you will realize that you are nothing more than a beautiful, *silent* breeding machine. "

I shoot to my feet and ignore the head rush at getting up so suddenly. "As someone who claims to know my grandfather, you seem to have little knowledge of me at all. You won't break me. The fact that I'm an Omega or that I am pregnant doesn't factor in here. Those are titles that you use to make yourself feel a little bit more powerful. But how about you remove the bracelet and give me full access to my wolf? I will fucking show you just powerful I am," I step closer and get a thrill of satisfaction as he takes a small step back. "The only reason Cas is my mate is because *I chose him*, and he knows this. Our bond goes beyond fate, it is stronger because I made that choice without coercion. You and my grandfather still operate under the very wrong impression that removing a choice is a weapon...not realizing that whatever you weaponize can be used against you. Tell me, Miro...how is that working out for you? Got your entire pack? Your heir? Willing pack-members?" I say mockingly.

"Pity. It looks like all you have is your drug addiction and a pack full of derision. You're a self-made timebomb. Congratulations, you must be so proud of your...what was it you called it? Oh, legacy." I snort. Agatha fights a little harder to get out, and I hide the shock of her increasing presence from my face.

Despite my desire to rip his throat out, a quick flick to the door makes me remember that the door is locked from the outside, effectively stopping any plan of attack that is whirring in my head. I can't imagine anyone, despite what a shitty person Miro was, would take kindly to, 'Hey, I killed your Alpha, let me out now, please.' I step back with a growl and sink back into the gross bed, placing my head in my hands to rub away the ache that starts. *Fuck me,* I say for the thousandth time.

Kidnapping and incarceration while pregnant, 10 out 10, do NOT recommend.

Surprisingly, he drops next to me and rubs my back. "I have to admire your strength, little omega. I still stand by what I said. You are far too unique for my son." Back to snuggly Miro, then.

"That's not for you to decide." My head is still in my hands, but I can feel his hand tense on my back for a second before he pulls it away.

"You know, after a year of actually trying to search for you,

you have become quite an obsession. Your grandfather can be very persuasive, though. At first, his offer didn't appeal to me, I mean, why bother putting in effort for a *female?* But after a couple of minutes, I saw the merit of taking what was owed to me. Even if it were a generation late, I mean, wolves are long-lived, you know, our circumstance wouldn't be too odd. With that and now throwing my traitorous son into the mix, I now have, even more so, a personal investment." He stands and leans back against the wall facing me, and I grimace, finding it difficult to follow along as he quickly rambles, spittle flying out of his mouth.

I feel a flicker of apprehension as I try to piece together his seemingly nonsensical words. A generation late? My grandfather's promises? Owed to him? A sinking feeling settles in the pit of my stomach.

He takes a staggering breath, although it does nothing to dispel his heavy breathing and the veins that are beginning to throb on his neck and face. Drug haze. His eyes narrow as he meets my gaze, "If you still haven't connected all the dots, I will share." he steps off the wall and claps once in glee as he gets to his point.

"I was once promised to be your mother's mate," he scowls, "so imagine my surprise when I get to your pack lands to find out that the bitch ran away, and fifteen years later, the whore is brought back, pregnant. Spoiled goods. Useless. A shame, she was a real beauty, breaking her would have been a distinct pleasure." He mutters the last.

"But... I am pregnant," I point out.

He shrugs, "With my genes, technically. Casimir looks so much like me...it works. Besides, I think I am more than glad that it didn't work out...you're more beautiful than Esmeralda, and that is saying something." He reaches down to touch me, but I slap his hand away. His growl fills the room, "You'll get used to my touch Aneira because as I was saying, after talking to your grandfather, when your initial mating to the Redwood pack didn't work out, he kept it relatively quiet. There was a bounty, but it wasn't worth too much effort. But now? We agreed that I would find you. And when I did? As is my due, you would be my new mate...in penance for your mother's fuckup."

CHAPTER 25
ANEIRA

My mouth gapes, and I just stare at him. I was expecting some sort of fuckery, but not HBO-worthy fuckery. Moon, I hope this ends better than Game of Thrones.

"You…mom…mate?" I ask my mouth not quite catching up to my brain.

Slouching against the wall, his eyes have taken on a faraway quality. "Your grandfather and I had a longstanding agreement. Esmerelda and I were going to be mates since we were kids. My father owned this pack, and her father owned theirs. We would be mated, and together, we were going to be a super pack, a formidable presence in the UK." He rubs his chin as he rakes his gaze over me suggestively.

I want to recoil but will myself to stay quiet and not react. How the fuck could this man want to be my mate?

"How the fuck do you plan to be my mate when I already have one? It will never work." Welp, there goes my will.

He moves forward and grips me by the back of my neck, forcing me to look at him. "Did nothing I say penetrate your thick skull? Your mom fucked it all up for me, so it's only natural for me to have you. It's unfortunate that you're with my son, but I've broken a bond once. I can do it again. A little benefit of blood magic."

I stare at him, slack-jawed. *Look at that...more dragons in the air.*

His eyes soften, and he coos, "Does that shock you? Don't worry, you'll have a mate worthy of you. Your eyes will be fully opened to the true power of our world." He pulls me up against his chest.

Take that suit, day-old vomit. Small victories.

"Now, I need you to go and get dressed. There will be plenty of time for talking and more...later." Faster than I can register, he bangs on the door and the moment it's unlocked he grips my hand in his and tugs me up the small stairs, through the house until we are retracing our steps from last night.

Pulling me inside the bedroom that was supposed to be mine, he closes the door behind him, "We will get you cleaned up and put in a nicer outfit," Miro still holds my hand as he drags me through to the bathroom and then shuts the door behind him—Locking us both in here. Did he think this was a community bath?

The shock wears off, and I yank my hand out of his, "Despite the really good drugs you must be able to afford that are completely scrambling what is left of your brain, I'm not going to have a shower with you in here."

A sharp crack followed by a stinging pain draws a growl from my lips, and I bring my hand up to rub my cheek. My eyes flash, and I feel myself start to lose it. Kidnap me. Choke me. Throw me in a small room with a shitty bed, and have several long-winded soliloquies, but I'm drawing the line at being a punching bag.

"You will never disrespect me...I warned you that my patience was running low. You are mine. I am going to be your mate and alpha, so you better get used to it." He brings his face into my neck and slowly licks up the side of it. "You will love it eventually, and after all, I'm a better-looking version of Casimir, and I've heard bitches love a sugar daddy." He presses his lips to mine in a possessive kiss.

Nope. I feel my claws burst from my hand as Agatha surges forward with a howl. Using every shred of strength, I rake my hand down his face, leaving four long red lines dripping with crimson liquid. He jumps back with a strangled yelp. I look at the still dangling silver cuff and, pushing a partial shift, I slip it off. I feel a surge of power race through my body and reach for my bond. Still there.

Before Miro recovers from the shock, I move forward, and holding his gaze, I press my claws into his neck, drawing fresh blood with every word that flows from my mouth. "Let's get several things straight. I am going to fucking kill you. Then, I am going to kill my useless fucking grandfather. But first I'm going to shower and get dressed. Then, if you're a good little bitch, I'll give you a head-start before I fucking rip your head off. Or Casimir catches up to you. Either way, your lifespan just became very, very short." I rear back and slam his head into the wall behind him with every ounce of strength and watch him crumble with a satisfied sigh.

Did I say *I* would die before going back to my grandfathers? Change of plans.

KEEPING an eye on his crumpled form, I take a hot shower, scrapping the ick off of my skin. I feel my bond tug, and I send waves of reassurance. I know Casimir would be coming, preferably with an arsenal in tow, but first, I needed to get to my grandfather. There is no future with him in it. Miro was one chess piece in this long game my grandfather was apparently playing. I step out of the tub and grab a fluffy towel and hum as I dry myself off. Miro stirs behind me, and I skip forward happily and slam his head back into the ground. Insurance.

I'm not sure if I can get out of the pack lands without some form of protection. An unconscious alpha seems like a pretty good one—a dead one…not so much.

I jump slightly at the sound of a knock on the door. Taking a breath, I scent an Omega, so I open the door slightly. A girl, looking to be a little younger than me, stands just outside the door with her hands raised as if afraid that I would strike her. I shake my head sadly, "I'm not going to hurt you. I'm one of the good guys," I toss in with a smile.

Eyes cast on the floor, she murmurs, "I'm sorry to disturb you, Fa—I mean, Alpha wanted to make sure that you were dressed for the occasion, and he said for me to tell you that if you decline to wear the dress he chose, it will be not only disrespectful for him but also to the pack." Her tone wavers ever so slightly with a hint of anger.

Injured, but not broken. I can help with that.

Something she *almost* said snags at me, "Wait, is the Alpha your father?" She flinches again, and I know I'm on the money. "Holy fucking shit, he is! What's your name?"

She presses a trembling hand over my mouth. "Aoife. Please. Don't say I said anything."

I laugh and push open the door, showing her Miro's unconscious body. "Even if I did, he can't hear much right now."

Her eyes fly open, and wonder laces her tone, "How?"

I wave my hand, "Ah, you know, hell hath no fury like a pregnant she-wolf and all that jazz."

"Anyways, I have a plan. Get dressed, go to my grandfather's house. Kill him. Then I'm going back to my mate…" I pause with a turn of my head. "Wait. Your Casimir's sister? I'm his mate!"

"Change of plans then," I say as I move forward, spotting a

white gown on the bed. I whistle, Miro is fucking psycho, but he certainly had good taste in dresses. I toss the towel and start to tug on the dress as I look back over my shoulder. "You're going to come with me. We are going to blow this fucking popsicle stand. Then Storm and I are going to toughen you up and show you how to kick some ass." I pause and frown. Wait. How the fuck am I going to get out with Casimir's sister and his father? I try to channel my inner Storm. What should I do?

Well, first. You're going to wait right fucking there until we arrive. We are about ten minutes out, Council in tow. Then, we are going to fuck shit up. I have a plan. A majestic one. Don't fuck up my entrance.

I blink. That was way more than a metaphorical channeling. It was almost as if...

Yes, bitch. It is me—the bracelet. I've upped my microchipping game. Lynsday had it made for us.

Well, then... this works.

CHAPTER 26
CASIMIR

Now

Moments before we cross the boundary of my old pack lands, I feel my bond come back to life, and waves of reassurance flood through. I expel a sigh, and my eyes flick to Storm, who is dressed in all black with war pain on her face, "I feel her now."

She claps softly, "Fuck yes. I should be able to talk to her then. Great success!"

I resist the urge to bolt across the pack lands, get Aneira into my arms, and chain her to me so she never leaves my side again. The idea has promise. As it is, I'm having a hard time trying to tamp down my emotions so that I wouldn't alert anyone to our presence. It would be ineffective for the witches to shield us if I gave us all away by going on a rampage. My father was unpredictable at the best of times. But with Aneira pregnant, I need to play it safe.

Shortly after Aneira went to the bathroom, the Council stood up to congratulate us on officially becoming the Cabria Falls Wolf Shifter pack. Everyone cheered, and my head swiveled as I looked for Aneira, wondering why it was taking her so long to use the restroom. The Council went on to formally accept her as my mate, making her the first Luna of our newly established pack. They even went as far as formally accepting Storm's position as Swiftwater Alpha-Mare. Still, when she didn't show, I started to panic. When I felt our bond grow cold, I went into full-blown wolf mode and shifted. Frantic.

I ran for hours, trying to scent her. Pierce had called his leopards and his best trackers. Rory had shifted to take an aerial view. But her scent was gone. It wasn't until I was almost falling over from exhaustion and grief that Hairalt was able to force me to shift back; my wolf finally compliant enough to retreat.

Storm? Calm as fuck. A quiet fury raging through her.

🐾

6 hours missing

"YOU LOOK LIKE SHIT," Storm says as I enter the dining room. I sent the rest of the pack off to bed, but the Council and their entourage stayed behind to devise a plan of action. Having someone taken, an Alpha's mate at that, right under their noses is nothing short of a grievous insult. They insisted on staying behind to make sure justice was swift and permanent. Although now, admittedly, they all look uncomfortably out of place as Storm hovers over a map, several notes, and her open laptop.

I growl at her and tug at my hair. I probably did look like shit. It took hours for Monti to be tired enough for Harailt's alpha voice to call me back. If he wasn't so concerned, he might have been impressed. But, even after all of that, I'm still on edge.

"Well, while you were out with Harailt, playing a game of howl and go seek. I've been swimming in the black market. Aneira has always been afraid of her grandfather finding her, so I put myself in his shoes. I said, 'Storm, if I was a psychotic stalker grandfather with no boundaries or respect for women and probably a micro-penis, and my grandaughter ran away just like her mother did, what would I do?'."

Harailt's ears perked up as he walks to stand behind Storm and look over her notes. I throw myself in the seat next to her, "Okay, so what would you do?"

There is only one way to get information from Storm, play her games.

She smiles, "Well, obviously, I would set up a bounty. Then, I would increase the pot every year she wasn't found. So I cross-referenced eight years of bounty increases and the area where Aneira is from. That was the easy part. So far, the bounty is at twenty- million. That's a lot of K-9 advantage."

I nod, urging her to continue. I look over at Calian, who is standing behind Storm with a dark look on his face. Clearly, he wasn't aware of all the shit Storm is capable of. Though, to be fair, I don't think that Storm knows everything she is capable of yet.

"The hard part was tracking down everyone who put in for the bounty and then silently killing off their IPs. Those losers weren't worthy of being bounty hunters. I mean, really. Fucking useless," she sighs.

I rub my temples.

"Storm," Ralph says gently, "Focus." My eyes flick to his, and he smirks. Play the game. Got it.

"Oh, yeah. I found Aneira about ten minutes after you ran away to buy the milk—the bracelet on her wrist, tracking charm. She's been in the same location for the past two hours and arrived around midnight," she adds brightly.

I blink and shoot up from my seat, "why didn't you lead with that? Let's go!"

"Sit down. We can't do that…yet," she smiles ferally. "When I cross-referenced the Council Database, the location is your old pack lands. The bracelet should allow me to talk to her, but that is blocked by the moon-block charm that is on her person somehow. I suspect handcuffs and if she hasn't broken them off and killed everyone yet, it's probably because they are silver cuffs."

"She's pregnant, Storm. Those silver cuffs can cause more harm the longer they are on," I growl. Calian shoots me a warning glare. Fuck him. He has his super-secret ninja mate; mine was kidnapped by my psychotic father, who has a history of abusing Omegas.

"Normally. But the charm is also for protection. The silver will weaken. So while yes, we will all bust in there like the Transformers trying to get the All-Spark, we need to hang back. If we play this right, we can kill two motherfuckers by the end of tonight," she says.

I look at Calian and Ralph, who shrug.

"She was waiting for you and Harailt to come back before telling us the rest of the shit she found out," Ralph adds.

"Yes, well, now that everyone is here. I hacked Casemiro's phone records, text message history, and emails. He has been hunting Aneira for several years but ramped up the search in the past year or so. Makes sense, considering she is of breeding age…."

I can't stop the rumble in my chest, "why. Would. That. Make. Sense. Storm?"

"Aneira was promised to your father to be his mate. He let her grandfather know that he had found her, and they will be going to his house for dinner. Where apparently they will have Aneira's bond severed tonight and they will force her to mate him, instead."

I explode out of my hastily tugged-on clothes, and watch as they flutter to the ground, like morbid confetti. I start to pace, frantic. *My mate bond will not be severed. We need to leave now.* Monti growls

"Well damn, you certainly put Jacob Black to shame. You're so pretty. Oh, I can't wait for the baby. I'm going to cuddle that puppy all day long," Storm sighs wistfully.

I growl and swipe the papers from the table. Storm looks at me, unimpressed.

"Dude, Aneira may need rescuing, but she doesn't need saving," Storm rolls her eyes.

"Alpha! Control yourself," Harailt's voice bellow, and I growl at him, ready to rip his head off if he gets in my way.

"How the hell does he plan to break a fated mate bond?" Tristan asks.

"Unnatural magic," she frowns and then looks around the room. "Now let's see, what witch was once here but now isn't?" Storm asks.

Everyone looks around, confusion plain on their faces.

Kathleen is missing. Suddenly it all dawns on me, the weak-ened border, the block, the way my father could come back undetected. Unnatural magic. Blood magic. Fuck.

Aneira is in more danger than I thought. If my father is dabbling in blood magic to break a bond, there is no telling what he would do to prevent being cornered by the Council, especially since his death sentence was already handed down.

"Exactly. She has been working with the Council, she knows too much. I mean, seriously, you guys need to tighten the fuck up. I knew the moment I met her; she was shady. And not just because she is clearly trying to take a ride on my Prancing Passion Pointer," she rolls her eyes.

"Anyways, we can't rush in. This is why research is important. Even though her grandfather is the one that will break it, we need to assume your old lands are protected as well. To go in safely, we will need some form of protection. Casimir, the witches part of your pack, I will need you to call them here. Well, when you're not furry, anyway...Then, operation All-Spark is fucking on. My entrance will be fucking majestic..."

Casimir
Operation All- Spark (22 hours since taken)

DOUBLE CHECKING that the necklace weaved with protection is still around my neck. I signal Tristan forward. He had been on edge, knowing we were returning to our old pack lands, but I needed him to focus.

Tristan, at my side, I turn to face the group, "The main house is the objective. He doesn't usually have more than a couple of pack betas there. Aneira would be there, as he would want to keep her close. Calian, Ralph, Storm, and I will retrieve Aneira. The rest of us must split up and subdue the rest of the pack. If things are still the same, about 100 meters to our right is where the Omegas and children are, Harailt, you wanted to take point on retrieving them. Tristan most of them will recognize you, so you will be with them as well. Rory, if you go with them, the women will be less fearful. Beyond the women and children, anyone who doesn't submit can die."

Everyone nods, their eyes blazing.

"Uh, Cas. Quick update: Aneira bashed your dad's head against the wall a few times, cut his face up to ribbons, and is now with your sister. I told her to stay put where they were as we are a few minutes away from having a majestic entrance," Storm says proudly.

I blink, and my chest fills with pride; well, that's one part handled.

I nod, "Okay then. Is everyone else good with their directives?"

They don't respond. Instead, they fan out quietly, melting into the forest. It wasn't dark out yet, but at least in the forest, we had some form of concealment. With a nod, we move forward silently. As we get to the Alpha pack house, I frown at the lack of activity on the grounds. It was only 6 in the evening. There should be plenty of wolves about.

"Has it always been as exciting as a graveyard rave here?" Storm asks softly, voicing my concerns.

I shake my head, " there should be many more shifters present. Pielt is one of the largest packs on this side of the country."

"Maybe they are inside their houses?" Ralph suggests.

Calian surveys the area silently, taking several breaths, "Unless they are all concealed with some sort of magic, the only scents I can pick up are the women on the other side of the property and a handful of wolves in that house. Two which I recognize and two which I do not."

My response is cut off by a roar, and, fucking protocol, we all rush forward.

CHAPTER 27

ANEIRA

I give Storm a quick run down while also telling Aoife the plan. How Storm is able to carry on with six different conversations and multiple tasks at once is mindboggling. Because this is far from easy. Again, neuro-divergence is a superpower.

"Okay, your brother and my best friend are on the grounds. The Council is also here. Before we do anything, are there any other shifters in the house?" I ask.

Aoife nods, "Pack beta downstairs. That's it. It's Saturday, so everyone is on strict instructions to stay indoors."

I frown, "why is that?"

"It's when Alpha gets his weekly drug supply. Usually, he heads off the property right after. We aren't allowed to roam when he is away usually. Those who are allowed are doing whatever job was delegated to them before he left," her voice is small, and I want to go wake up Miro and knock his ass out again. I look at the bathroom. Sounds like a good plan.

"Useless sack of shit," I growl. "Okay, one beta to kill, then Miro, then my grandfather. My laundry list keeps getting longer," I sigh. "Can you zip up the dress? I want to walk out of this bitch looking majestic. "

She giggles softly, and I smile at the sound; she will be okay. Several hours of Storm and me and some self-defense classes, and she will be good as new. There is nothing like the confidence that comes with the knowledge that you can protect yourself.

While she zips up the back, I look in the full-length mirror and gag. What I thought was just a pretty white dress is actually a pristine, low-cut, white wedding gown dotted with jewels. Miro was pretty fucking confident that tonight was going to go according to plan. Gross.

I shove my feet into the slippers on the floor, "right. Well. Ignoring the fact that I look like a wolf-shifter Barbie, let's go knock out a beta. I'll let Cas throw out the trash," I point to the bathroom where Miro's slumped form was visible. He just looks so peaceful. I'll let him nap.

We move to leave and silently pad down the hallway and stairs. I pause as I pick up the scent from last night and follow it to a room that is, yup, filled with more stuffed dead animals. Seriously, did this guy attack every Disney village he ever encountered? There is a fucking bunny, for moon-sake. We stop short as we notice the pack-beta on the floor, convulsing. A heap of powder spilled across the floor.

"Fuck," I say, rushing forward. But as I reach him, his body stills, and his heart stops.

"What kind of fucking drugs is your father fucking getting? AJAX?" I ask, staring at the form on the floor.

"He must have found the fake stash," Aoife mutters. I look back at her blank face—clearly no love loss between these two.

"Just when I think this asshole can't get any worse," I shake my head and turn to leave the room.

We get as far as the staircase when we hear a voice, "Going somewhere, Mate?"

I spin around, my eyes flashing as Casemiro makes his way down the stairs, fixing the sleeves of his tuxedo. I would tell him that the effect is completely lost when paired with the powder streaking his face but with his fangs extended, as his wolf fights the effects of the drugs he must have just ingested, I don't think it would be well received.

"Ah fuck," I mutter. Okay. Nothing to worry about here, just an unpredictable, violent Alpha Wolf that is more than one hundred percent likely to be stronger.

I push Aoife behind me, "going somewhere? Me? Nope, just off to get some milk, Dear."

The lines around his eyes and mouth deepen as his brow furrow, his lips peeling back with a snarl-like chuckle, making spit drip down his face. *Fucking gross.*

I meet his gaze, watching as they flicker from human to wolf, tinged with red and completely blown out like a preter-natural optical illusion. Somehow, I don't think he wants to make amends. In fact, as he leaps the last few steps and crouches, I'm sure all thoughts of wanting me as a mate are long gone. This is a crazed wolf who wants revenge and nothing more. I could have saved him the pomp and circum-stance if he would have just skipped to the attempted murder part.

Agatha pushes forward, and I feel my own eyes flash as time slows and the room takes on a golden tinge. I force my breathing to slow as he launches himself toward me with a snarl. He barrels through the air, every muscle in his body taut, like a coiled spring. His claws extend, and I sidestep his attack, the dress tearing as he grazes it.

Super sharp claws got it.

He growls as he spins, gouging deep furrows into the floor.

"I was under the impression you wanted a mate, not an art project, Miro." I goad him. He would already be unpredictable, but any edge I can get, I'll take it.

The veins in his neck pulse as he takes in ragged breaths, "I think I will prefer you dead. You. My worthless son and your child."

I narrow my eyes at his threat, "nice talk."

Agatha howls with a feral glee as I crouch and propel myself forward, leaping over his head before I turn and kick the middle of his back, making him crash onto the floor.

He snarls as he hits the floor, and I swipe my claws across the back of his knees, cutting the tendons. He lets out an ear-splitting roar as he tries and fails to push himself up, blood pooling around his knees.

"Guess you also didn't know that I run a fight club? Probably not. The first rule about shifter fight club is don't talk about shifter fight club," I say savagely as I leap onto his back and start smashing his head into the ground. "You stupid, worthless motherfucking fuck twat. You don't get to threaten my family and fucking live to tell the tale. I'm going to kill you and bring you back and kill you again and again. You hear me?"

I punctuate each word with another smash and start to laugh uncontrollably as a red haze takes over my every thought.

"Babe, I don't think a smashed brain can hear anything," Storm's voice pierces the haze, and I look up to see Calian, Casimir, Ralph, and Storm staring at me with varying degrees of shock, pride, and glee. Guess whose face has which expression.

I blink, but the red haze doesn't abate. I frown as I look down, Miro is definitely just brain matter at this point, and the red haze is actually the blood dripping down my face. I probably look terrifying, damnit, I hope Storm has her phone.

"On it, babe. Say 'death to the patriarchy'!"

A grin splits my face as I pose on top of Casemiro.

"What the fuck," I hear Tristan mutter as the rest of the council and the guards gather at the door.

I shrug, "No one lays a finger on my Butterfinger."

CHAPTER 28
CASIMIR

The sight of Aneira on top of my father's mangled corpse finally processes and I rush forward to pull her into my arms, capturing her lips with mine.

She pulls away breathlessly with a laugh, "You're all covered in blood now."

I laugh as I look down at her. Even covered in blood, chest heaving, and dressed in a torn, bloodied wedding gown, she is absolutely breathtaking. A vision in red. Literally, as blood drips into her eyes.

"I can't miss the opportunity to kiss the bride," I tease.

She shrugs, "The artistic thing is totally Vogue now. We are ahead of the curve."

"Okay, I got all the murder pictures! Annie, let's get you changed so we can go kill your grandfather and go the fuck home, okay? I need to snuggle with my Thoroughbred Throbber. And I would like to point out, you ruined my majestic entrance. So now I need to make sure that the next venue can accommodate my requests." She cackles.

Calian sighs and leans forward to place a kiss on Storm's head, "I love you very much, Mate. Go help Aneira get cleaned up. We will handle things here."

Storm beams at him and pulls Aneira away.

"You did a beautiful job. The brain paint? Perfect touch," Storm says as they head up the stairs.

I shake my head with a laugh and look at Casimir, "Do you think we will ever have a moment of peace?"

He shakes his head with a sigh, a smile on his face as he looks at the direction that Storm went, "Not at all, but fuck if the thought doesn't make me happy as hell."

I laugh and he claps my shoulder, "I'll call a clean-up crew, and post guards so we can head out. The Council also wants to follow through with the rest of the evening, we move out in thirty."

I nod gratefully. I look down at my father's body and feel absolutely nothing but joy that he is finally gone.

I turn away as a body barrels into mine with a happy laugh that I haven't heard in a long time, "Casi!"

"Aoife?" I marvel as she wraps her arms around me and squeezes. Taking her into my arms, her 5' 2" frame dwarfed by mine as I spin her around.

"You look absolutely beautiful," I say with a laugh as she pulls out of my arms with a scowl.

"I still don't like being spun around," she frowns. The

familiar made my chest ache. Two years lost, two years with a monster where I couldn't protect her.

"Hey," she says softly, "you're back now. That's all that matters.

"Family funerals and family reunions all on the same night? This is the stuff hallmark cards are made of." Storm says as she comes down the stairs, and she wipes a fake tear from her face.

"Aoife, Aneira wants to know if there is anything here she can change into for her grandfather's funeral?"

Aoife laughs and races up the stairs, " I know just the thing!"

As I watch them run up the stairs, I sigh. Only one thought crosses my mind.

They are going to corrupt her.

CHAPTER 29
ANEIRA

A couple of hours later, I'm being driven through a town that smells like rancid memories and my stomach drops as we pull into a long, sweeping driveway I'm very familiar with. *Home Sweet Home.*

The plan we have is solid. Tristan would drive me and the Council, a few of their guards, Casimir, and Storm would all wait in the woods, undetected under a spell, while I go in alone. I will tell my grandfather that Casemiro sent me ahead while he handled pack matters and will be along momentarily. The witches cast a charm on my bracelet, and the entire 'murder' party will be able to hear the conversations held inside. Then, once they get what they need, they will move in. And, as I take in the number of wolves on guard, I am grateful they are hidden—one less thing to worry about.

I press my hand to my belly, willing the nausea to go away. Whether my pregnancy sickness is making a permanent appearance or the thought of being back here is getting to me doesn't matter. I don't have time to vomit, nor do I have another outfit. While, luckily, Miro had an entire closet full of gowns that fit me, *fucking creepy,* I didn't bring a spare, so I have to reign it in.

Okay, Aneira. It is time to Luna up and give these fuckers something to remember. I am not the child who left here so many years ago. I'm stronger, smarter, mated, and a fucking Luna. My grandfather can suck it.

"Remember. You're the fucking Luna of the Cabria Wolf Pack. So give them fucking hell and save a murder or two for me," Tristan looks back in the rearview mirror with a roguish smile.

I laugh, "You got it."

As the car rolls to a stop, a massive shifter in tactical gear opens the door, and I step out of the car, my slippered feet touching the cool marble of the driveway. I spot several wolves dressed similarly, and I pause. What in the Pedigree is going on here?

Calian says, if Kathleen is working for your grandfather, she probably tipped them off that we would be coming for you.

I resist the urge to nod. That certainly would make sense.

10-4, momma-wolf preparing to infiltrate.

His warm laugh echoes in my head, and I smile. I'm not sure if the formal recognition triggered something in our bond, but the ability to speak to Casimir mind to mind is a damn gift. Him realizing it when I was sharing our sex stories with Storm and Aoife…not so much. Storm had reluctantly given Casimir the bracelet so he could communicate with me without inter-ference.

I'm sure she will be having a shit ton of them made now for backup.

I move past the guard and my eyes take in the sprawling staircase and large oak doors that lead into the pack house all the while taking a mental tally of who is posted where and how many, and relay that information back to Casimir. Safe to say, if I tried to murder and run, I would be captured faster than a Brit drains a cup of tea.

When I reach the doors, I'm led inside until I'm facing a small group of wolves. But I ignore them as my eyes are drawn to the two people that I never thought I would see again—my mother and grandfather. Well, one that I hoped I wouldn't.

She is alive.

A soft 'Aneria' falls from my mother's mouth before she is silenced with one look from my grandfather, and I struggle to fill my lungs as I'm hit with the overwhelming urge to run into her arms.

Breathe. You will get that chance, my love.

I take a calming breath to clear my thoughts as I take in their fancy designer gowns and suits. They were dressed...for a wedding. Pushing my shoulders back I smile brightly, "Grandfa-ther. Casemiro is a bit delayed, so he sent me ahead. He said to carry on with dinner. He is waiting for a package of some sort."

My grandfather's eyes flash in irritation before they go blank. Ah, so he is aware of Miro's addiction. Not to worry, it won't be a problem anymore, I cackle to myself.

As I step closer, my mom takes a breath, and despite my grandfathers' previous look, her eyes are frozen in horror as she takes me in. She mouths the word, *pregnant,* and I nod. Her eyes steel, and I feel her mind working double time. I can't tell her that there is nothing to worry about, so instead, I bite back a smile because not only has she not changed, but my grandfather has not broken her.

My grandfather pauses as he looks at me up and down, taking in my designer gown. He looks at me expectantly, waiting for me to acknowledge him as the pack's Alpha. But I stare at him blankly. "Duncan," I say dryly, calling him by his first name.

He frowns, "Aneira. I'm so glad to see you home, back into the family fold where you belong."

"Yeah, well. Aiding and abetting a kidnapping will certainly do that," I reply.

My Grandfather looks at me disapprovingly but claps his hands together loudly. "Anyway. We must convene for dinner. There is much to discuss, and I think it's time you knew the truth about your family." He turns on his heels and strides ahead.

My mother hangs back just slightly and whispers, "I will get you out, my baby."

"I have a plan. We will both get out. ," I mutter, give her a nod and follow my grandfather and his 'party' further into the house. Which hasn't changed at all since the last time I was here. Strangely, my life has changed so drastically, yet it's as if I never left. Pictures of me as a child dotted the walls. Photos that I fucking hated. I spent most of my childhood within the commune with the other Omegas, but he would have pictures taken of me when I was playing, looking happy, and would hang them around to appear like a doting and forgiving Alpha and grandfather, despite my mother's crime of defection. Toxic.

"Whisky all around?" Duncan asks but doesn't wait for an answer before pouring a healthy amount into the glasses and handing them out to us all. I take it with a grimace as my stomach rebels at the scent of watered-down troll piss coming from the cup. Either he hasn't scented my pregnancy, Kathleen hasn't had a chance to tell him, or he doesn't care. Either way, I rather it not make it a topic of conversation. I'm sure it would just take him down a trip of memory lane, and as long as he plays nice, I can gather information *before* I kill him.

We filter through to his stuffy sitting room, which also has a few animal heads gracing the wall, but is nowhere near as morbid as Miro's place.

Duncan props himself up against the bar and raises his glass. "A toast. To family. After all, if we don't have that, what do we have?" He raises his brow and waits for us all to raise our glasses. "To family," we echo in unison, although mine falls flat.

If it isn't Vin Diesel talking about family while driving fast cars, I don't want to hear it.

Taking a seat on a small couch, I tip the glass over the edge of the armrest, letting the whiskey soak into the ugly, outdated carpet. Twenty million for a bounty but can't get a new carpet? I mean, he should thank me.

"You stupid bitch," my grandfather shouts, his voice slightly hoarse, as he strides over to me. He stands over me, and in the same tone as one would take with a petulant child, he says, "Do you know how much a single drop of that whiskey costs? There will be no more for you now."

"Gee, can I still stay up and watch cartoons?" I roll my eyes.

He shoots me a dark look before he clears his throat, "This would be a good time to adjourn to the dining hall."

"If you could all, please make your way out to the dining hall," a small voice announces as a server pops in out of nowhere.

We follow Houdini as he directs us to a ridiculously large table which I'm sure he stole from the Hogwarts Dining Room. If I had Filch's number, I would text him immediately.

As we settle into our seats, my brows furrow at the sight of an empty place at the table next to my Grandfather's seat.

"Sorry for the delay. We're just waiting for a VIP guest to

arrive. She's positively...bewitching." My grandfather grins at me.

I roll my eyes in response. Yes, yes. You have a nefarious double agent on your team, and you think you're being coy by dropping hidden hints. Too bad I already know. In the distance, a sharp staccato rhythm makes my eye twitch, and when the owner of the annoying heels round the door, I grin.

Gotcha bitch.

CHAPTER 30
ANEIRA/CASIMIR

Aneira

"So sorry I'm late. Got caught up with a certain hairy situation," Kathleen says as she enters the room.

"Not too late at all. I was merely toasting family. Now that's done, we can commence with the dinner," my grandfather smiles.

She places her manicured hand over his arm and pushes her fake tits into his face. "Oh, I love a good toast; after all, family is the most important thing, isn't it?" She kisses him on the lips and tips me a wink when she catches me staring and wipes off the crimson lip stain marking his mouth.

Gross. *Conniving, witchy little turn-coat, cougar hunting, shifter groupie.*

"While dinner is being brought out, can we please discuss why I am here? You went through all this trouble to get me here so it would be nice to have the full picture." What I really want to say is, get the fuck on with whatever bad guy speech you're going to give.

"Do we have to discuss family drama at dinners? I find it so tacky," Kathleen whines, her nose wrinkling with distaste. I'm sure she thought she looked adorable, but, in fact, it looked like she had a severe case of sinusitis.

"Not as tacky as being a shitty double agent, but alas, here we are," I reply with a song.

"Aneira. Enough." Grandfather uses his alpha bark, but I am a Luna, and he is not Harailt. So he can stuff it.

"Kathleen is a guest, and you will treat her with the respect she deserves," he adds.

My eyes narrow. I don't think he actually picked up on what I said. Either that, or he doesn't want to ruin his version of the big dramatic reveal about why she is here. Like a cheesy sitcom, I feel it percolating.

"What do you say?" he presses me, glaring at me intensely.

"Apologies, Grandfather." Those words tasted like ash but… small sacrifices.

If you're a good girl, I'll let you take my knot tonight. Casimir whispers through my head, and I suppress the pang of lust that shoots through me.

If you keep on, they will think I have a weird apologetic kink. He laughs in response.

"Right. We can get it over with. I've waited long enough for you to hear it after your little temper tantrum and waltzing off," my grandfather says as I tune back in.

I swallow my pride just to say the next words, but they are so necessary to get him to speak. "I'm ready to hear the story, Grandfather."

Yes, give me all your misgivings on a platter.

"I knew you would see sense." He leans back in his chair and drums his fingers on the table. "Right. Let's start from the beginning, shall we?" He nods to my mum, who still has her head cast down at the table. "I never wanted a daughter. In my opinion, bitches cause excessive drama, and I've yet to be proven wrong." Kathleen huffs a laugh as she picks up a bottle of wine and pours a large amount into the glass.

He takes a sip of his whisky and casts a disapproving eye over my mum. "I thought when she was older, she would prove herself a little more useful and mate to a prominent alpha of another pack. That way, we could grow our pack. Stronger, more numbers."

"We arranged the day, and the Council was due to arrive that morning. But then something happened. My little bitch of a daughter decided to run away. Then? If that's not bad enough, after fifteen years of searching, we find her mated to her fated mate and pregnant. Now, the mate bond? We had a way around it. But the pregnancy? Rendered her useless for a political alliance." He shakes his head in disgust. "My own daughter decided that love was greater than her duty to the pack. Pathetic."

"Still, I allowed her back into the pack. Let her keep her pregnancy. But we got rid of that mate bond." He chuckles the last.

I take a glance at my mother. I don't think she knew. He said mate-bond not mate. Suspicion rising, I took a second to look at Kathleen and catch a smirk flitting across her face. Yeah, my mom has no idea her mate is alive.

I had to wonder just how many wolves, or shifters as a whole, this is being done to. Removing a mate bond with blood magic is a crime against nature. I mean sure, you will always have your bad eggs in every group. But fuck, Kathleen skipped right over that and became a bad chicken.

My mum, not realizing the nuances in her father's speech, swipes at a tear from her eye which Duncan notices. "Oh, stop with the pathetic shit, Esmeralda. You gave up your life when you decided to have the child."

"Because I made a deal with you to keep her," she blurts out, and my heart jumps at her admission.

"A deal that was null and void because you were too damn depressed to marry anyone from any pack. Fucking spoiled goods! No Alpha wanted you once they saw the state you were in. A useless slab of meat. A fated bond," he scoffs. "You were absolutely useless. So now I need to take what is owed from your daughter."

My mom freezes.

"I think we might need to get back on track with this conversation," it grates on me to be civil, but I have to keep him talking.

He smiles," It might have cost a pretty penny, but once we discovered your mothers' location, we staged a coo and had the mate bond severed. We couldn't kill the wolf she was mated to for political reasons, so this was the best bet. However, the mage didn't mention that a severed bond was worse than a dead mate. So when she pleaded to keep you and said she would marry, I agreed. But she was too broken. In the end, she ended out in the commune with all the other common whores. Right place, I suppose."

Despite trying to keep myself calm, I can't let this one slide. "She was the lucky one in the end. She didn't end up with you and all this bullshit. Our 'commune' was loving. Kind. It was everything a family should be. You call those Omega's whores, knowing that you are the one that prevented them from being mated. You created the pack laws, you created the conditions we were subjected to, and then dare blame victims? It's our fault for attempting to survive the best that we can? You can live in your guided bubble of lies if it makes your nightly colon cleanse work better, but we all know it's still shit. The only whore I see in this room is the one sleeping on both sides of the bed, right next to you."

"How dare you, you little bitch?" Kathleen jumps out of her seat, ready to throw down. "You would do well to respect me. I can make your life a lot more difficult. After all, it was my magic that muted your bond. And it will be my magic that rips it apart."

She slowly sits back down and spreads her hands out on the table. "Imagine my surprise when I'm told to transport the illustrious council only to find out it was Casemiro's son. Oh, I called him immediately. My loyalty is to your grandfather and his allies, after all. But the icing on the cake was when Casemiro spotted you and told me that you were the spitting image of his intended mate. A quick call and a few dead Pielt sacrifices later, you were on your way to Casemiro's, bond muted. How poetic is that? The son and daughter of intended mates getting together. Shame it's not going to have a happy ending. For *you* anyway," she sneers the last, and cold fury sweeps through me.

This bitch was using Casimir's old pack as fodder for her blood magic? She is murdering wolves for her gain? How fucking long has this been happening?

She must see the question on my face, and she laughs. "The council leads me right into their homes. Ask yourself, how many tragic accidents happen in one year to shifters? But the truth is there was no need to raise suspicion, not when I had two packs so willing to offer their throwaways in exchange for power and drugs."

I gape. This bitch is crazy. Full-blown fucking crazy.

Casimir, tell me you are getting this. Because if what she is saying is true. How the fuck do we fight a blood-witch?

On it. Is the only thing he responds but I feel the pain and anger through our bond.

Now I was fighting against whether to use the knife on this bitch or my grandfather, but someone was definitely getting fucking stabbed.

"You can try and sever the bond, but it won't work." I hiss at her.

"Charming," Kathleen says drolly. "Let's get this shit done with, I have plans." She runs a finger down Duncan's back, and I don't bother to hide my gag. A loud bang echoes around the pack house, and our gazes turn towards the door just as a horse comes galloping in before rearing on its back legs, kicking its front hooves into the air. *Fucking, Storm.*

Casimir

THE FACES of the Council members may as well be carved out of stone as quiet fury flows through them. I watch as Adaline, Letty, Maddison, and Jo weave a spell to counter whatever magic Kathleen is working with. To kill shifters for the chance to be a little more powerful or to get drugs is absolutely mind-boggling. But the fact that all of this corruption was happening and no one was aware? Incompetence. What happened here tonight will stay here. But if the Council didn't start implementing better policies, we may as well give ourselves to humans for experimentation. We are only as strong as our weakest link, and right now, we are pretty damn weak.

I am itching to move forward, to rip out the throat of whoever participated in the murder of my pack. Casemiro paid for his sins; it is time for others to pay up too.

"How much fucking longer? The bad-guy speeches should be done. We have our evidence. If this bitch starts singing Bad Guy, she will ruin everything. I have a plan of action for when we bust in that joint, and I have to time it perfectly, or it will look lame," Storm scowls.

I roll my eyes and, despite the circumstance, bite back a laugh. The anger thrumming through her is evident, but even more plain is the disappointment and pain radiating from Calian. She is a perfect distraction, and she plays the part well.

"Can we get this show on the road…" Kathleen's voice comes through, and my heart jumps.

"That's it! That is my cue. Time to get majestic up in this bitch," Storm strips off her clothes and runs out of the woods butt-ass naked before she shifts. The wolves on the property freeze in confusion, and at my signal, our party moves to attack. Ralph whoops as he tears into the first wolf he sees while Calian sighs as he runs after Storm, the Council, Tristan, and I following suit.

We get there just in time to see Storm's majestic,' entrance, and I have to admit, it was undoubtedly a 10 out of 10 as far as dramatic entrances into an evil villain lair go.

CHAPTER 31
ANEIRA

My Grandfather hisses, and Kathleen's face goes pale as the council files in behind Storm. *Looking a little grey there bitch.*

Storm runs towards the dinner table. One of the pack wolves from earlier tries to stand in her way before she rears up and puts her hoof through his head.

Fuck, that was a way better brain splatter than mine. I smile as she looks at me, giving me a look that I'm sure is her mare version of 'Did you see that? fucking awesome, right?' She turns around to throw off a wolf that was about to attack her, and she neighs with, what I can only assume, was a blood-thirsty cry to war. *Go bestfriend, thats' my bestfriend.*

Behind her, Casimir and Tristan shift, cutting a path through the wolves pouring in from all sides of the pack house.

From the corner of my eye, I see Kathleen and my grandfather trying to escape. *Oh no, you fucking don't.*

Leaping onto the table to avoid the clattered chairs, I let my claws out as I put a burst of speed and head them off before they get to whatever secret villain back door I am sure my grandfather has somewhere here.

I jump in front of them, "Oh no, you murdering little bitches. There are only two ways either of you leave here tonight. In death or with the fucking Council. I prefer death, myself. So let's fucking choose." I growl.

Duncan goes to open his mouth, but my mother cuts him off, "Oh no. Not the Council. My father has a lot of sins, but his greatest one? Betraying his blood, and his duty, to suit his own needs. As the closest blood relative to the current Alpha, as is my right, I will take what is owed to me by taking your life," my mother shoves her hand through my grandfather's back and pulls out his still beating heart.

Kathleen screams as he falls to the floor. "You bitch! What have you done?!" Kathleen's eyes go black, and her mouth falls open, but before she can utter whatever bullshit D- Grade Avada Kedavra spell, I swipe my claws through her neck before giving her the same send-off my mother gave her father. Beating hearts, 8 out 10 do not recommend. The other 2 points are because it totally looks cool.

"Your throat for your lies and your heart because you're a spy," I sing-song as she falls to the floor in a heap.

As Kathleen stops twitching, my mom falls to the ground with a gasp.

"He's here," my mom murmurs, her face wet with tears.

"Who is here? Mom?"

"My mate, he is here," her voice turns frantic as she stands up and stumbles towards the very one-sided melee. Five minutes ago, they were barreling into the room. Now, they were limping out. I mean, honestly, my grandfather's wolves were just pitiful. What the fuck is the point of tactical gear if you couldn't even follow through?

I follow my mom, but when her eyes land on Hairalt, she chokes back a sob as she runs towards him at full speed. They crash, a meeting of lips, tears, and touches as they both try to figure out if either of the other is real.

I look away, letting them have this moment as I look for Casimir.

Everything suddenly makes sense, Kathleen working with the Council closer to Harailt, presumably to make sure the bond was actually severed. Then, my wolf recognizing him but not knowing how. Mic Drop.

Stay tuned for another episode of 'How I Met Your Wolf-Daddy.'

I shake my head as Storm stands with Calian, wrapped in one of the ugly tapestries that were laying in ruin around the room.

"Aneira, did you see my majestic as fuck entrance? Let Pixar top that shit!" She pumps her arms in the air, and I choke back a laugh while Calian sighs. The Council stands by the door, looking around with fascination. I am sure they helped, but I mean, I don't think they counted on the bloodthirsty Alpha Mates from Cabria.

"Another dress covered in blood? Am I going to have to worry about this becoming a kink?" Casimir laughs as he pulls me into his arms.

I shrug, "That depends. Are you into it?"

"At this point, I think I'll be into whatever keeps you off and away from planes, boats, tinted vans…"

"Let's not forget bathrooms...Lots of nefarious things can happen in a bathroom," I add with a smile.

"Well, before we go as far as me having to resort to being a *Une Dame Pipi,* how about we just get you home in our bed, where I'll keep you safe for several, several hours?"

I blink, "You just called yourself a bathroom attendant in French. Kinky and foreign? You can take me anywhere you want and do whatever the fuck you want to me."

He throws his head back and laughs, "I plan to, Mate. I plan to."

EPILOGUE

Aniera
About 8 months later

I bite back a scream as another contraction rocks my body and punches my uterus in the face.

"I swear to all the goddesses in the world, new and old, all cultures, that I am never having another baby by you," my face red, I squeeze his hand for dear life as my voice echoes throughout the birthing room that Storm had set up at our pack house. Even with commuting to the bookstore daily, for the most part, and to Calians displeasure, Storm was often over on our lands directing the builders to make sure Casimir's and I's house was built to *her* specifications. Apparently, having ultra-wide and tall doors was necessary in case she needed to shift while she was indoors as well as be able to make 'majestic' entrances. I was too tired growing uterine invaders to even argue. And considering she crushed a few skulls in my honor, she could totally get dibs on the build for the sheer amount of laughs that memory brought me.

Casimir winced and looked at Calian, who was on my other side, holding my other hand while Storm filled the birthing pool with water.

"You tell him Aneira, no more coochie snuggles because your vagina is about to be ripped open and become a permanent portal to the uterine underworld!" She cackles, and I blow out a breath, the tightening in my lower belly subsiding momentarily.

"That is officially two minutes apart. It would be best if you started getting into the water now, Aneira," Tristan clicks his old fashion timer with a grin on his face. It turns out that Tristan was not only the pack second, but the pack doctor. Color me surprised when he walked into the clinic on the pack lands asking me to remove my clothes and open my legs. After Casimir stopped laughing,when he ran in to find Tristan bleeding from his mouth after I punched him, he explained everything. I would have apologized but that was totally something that should have been shared with the class, I.e. *Me.*

"Explain to me, again, why role-playing as Ariel will make this easier?" I push myself up from the ball with Casimir and Calians help and sigh in relief as the warm water eases the ache in my lower back slightly.

"This is your first baby, babe. The water will help blood circulation and will relax your muscles so you can handle the pain and give birth easily," Storm repeats for the fifth time that day, her face bright with excitement. She was bouncing on her heels since she trotted her ass here from her house. I barely hung up the phone to let her know I was in labor before she came bounding in through the front door, full stop. I was suddenly very grateful for the extra large, extra durable doors.

Casimir follows me into the water and kneels in front of my crouched body with a tender look on his face, his voice hitching, "I love you so much, my little wolf."

I open my mouth to say the same, but instead an inhuman wail comes out as another contraction hits me, this one a lot closer than the ones before. "OOWWW, FUCKINGSHIT-BALLSCUNTLICKINGASSHOLERIMMINGIMPREGNAT-INGMOTHERFUCKER."

Storm blinks and breaks out into peels of laughter, "ass-hole...rimming." She says breathlessly, "That's fucking classic. oh man, I wish you would have let me record this shit." Calian hides a smile and shakes his head in sympathy as he takes in Casimir's stricken expression. He knows I love him, but right now, I am firmly past the 'fated-mated' exit and quickly approaching the 'ripping out my vagina and never having sex again' exit on the highway of 'Take This Dick Like A Good Girl,' which I will be renaming, 'No.'

I glared at Storm, and my wolf nudged me. My eyes widened slightly, and maybe it was the excitement in the room or all the increased pheromones and scents, but Storm could laugh all she wanted; I had something for her ass too. But before I could say anything, Tristan reaches into the water to feel between my legs. Still the weirdest thing ever, in case you were wondering.

"Okay, Aneira, it's time to push on the next contraction. I can feel the head. Alpha," he looks at Casimir, "be ready to catch." Fucking catch. I am now also, a baseball portal.

I feel another contraction come on, but this time I do as

Tristan asks and push. "Ahhhh, fuckingshitthisbetterbethe-cutestlittlewolfbabyinexistence," I cry.

It is an interesting feeling, giving birth, almost like being ripped open and feeling a massive rush of relief at the same time.

Casimir reaches down and 'catches' the slippery, slightly discolored, mostly bright red, mushed-looking ball that comes out of me with a proud smile. I sigh in relief as he cradles the... baby...his eyes watering. Tristan quickly clamps the umbilical cord while Calian and Storm crowd around him and exclaim an emotional, 'Aww.'

"It's a boy!" Casimir cries, giving the baby a slight tap on the buttocks, causing him to let out a keen wail of anger. I feel my breast tighten at his cry, and my breath catches. Tristan runs to the room's window and yells, "It's a boy!" I choke back a sobbed laugh as a chorus of loud cheers, howls, and neighs echo around the pack lands as our packs celebrate.

The sound startles our son, who starts to scream again, and as I reach for him, I feel another contraction take over my body.

"Aneira! What's wrong?" Casimir panics as he hears my low moan. He looks helplessly at Tristan, who reaches back into the water.

I feel my strength depleting, and I let out a low cry. Tristan meets my gaze, his expression tender but stern, "Aneira, I know you're tired. You're doing great, but you'll have to push again. Do you understand me? This is not over. We never saw another baby on the ultrasound. This will be easier. Are you ready?"

My wolf nudges me, and I take a deep breath and nod, feeling another contraction pulse through me.

"Atta girl, now PUSH!"

Seconds later, I'm holding another wrinkly mess in my arms as Tristan catches and passes me my...daughter. My eyes fill as her cry echoes around the room. Ignoring the second round of cheers as Tristan makes another announcement, Casimir moves to my side, and the babies reach for each other, instantly calming. We are speechless as both of them open their eyes and see their wolves peaking out, making our eyes glow in response.

"What should we name them, my beautiful mate?" his voice soft, tears streaming down his face.

"How about," I look towards Calian and Storm, who look beside themself with emotions. "Tempest and Calan?"

Calian rubs Storm's back as Storm bursts into tears, "I'm an auntie. I'm an auntie."

Tristan smiles brightly, "Let's get those beautiful wolf pups to latch on, Mom and Dad." He chuckles. "Wow, Alpha to a newly established pack, a husband, and a dad all in less than a year."

As we maneuver both babies on each breast, I smile brightly, "Oh, this is just the start."

The End.

*Can't get enough of Cabria Falls? The fun doesn't end here! Stay tuned for Storm and Calians Story next. *

Acknowledgments

Readers- I love you dearly, without you my dream to spread written magic wouldn't be possible.

Of Course, a big thank you to all my fantastic alpha and beta readers, ya'll are the real MVPS and will forever have a special place in a dark, comedic heart.

Deadass, though, shout out to the KeyBoard Wh0res. We may bang our keyboards harder than a horny jackrabbit bangs his next-door rabbit mistress, but we get the fucking job done.

Mads and *Jo*, you put all the beef in my taco, and I love y'all long time for it. You guys are the guac to my taco. (Bitch I know the GUAC IS EXTRA! & so are we)

Husband/Soulmate- Because of you, I will forever have inspiration. Every facet of you is more than I can ever possibly contain in one book. You are my true and forever soulmate.

Also, *thanks kids* for going to your dad instead of me when I'm deep in my cave.

About Ruby

Ruby curses a bit too much, moms a bit too hard, and loves her husband with everything she is. Even more so, she loves all her characters because, in some aspects, they are a small representation of who Ruby is; bold, unapologetic, and downright inappropriately hilarious. She has never been able to do anything without being considered a bit TOO MUCH. But that is okay because there is never such a thing as too much love (for oneself or others), too much sex, or too much support for her friends and family.

Oh, Ruby is also a bit of a smut enthusiast and proud of it.

ALSO BY RUBY SMOKE

Veiled (Concealed in Myths Why Choose Romance)

Femme Fatale (Erotic Collection F/F Menage Monster Romance)

Infiltrated (Concealed in Shadows Book 1 Why Choose Romance)

Ours to Keep (Anthology)

Petty Betty

Ruby's Nut House: A Ruby Smoke Reader Group

Within the Veil (Concealed in Myths 2 Why Choose Romance)

Insurrection (Concealed in Shadows 2 Why Choose Romance)

The Art Of Roleplay (Erotic Encounters Why Choose Romance *EROTICA*)

Love at First Neigh (Cabria Falls 2 Horse Shifter Novel) *(Storm & Calian)*

Petty in Paradise (Petty Betty Book 2) *(Maeve and Ivor)*

Cat Got Your Tong's? (Cabria Falls 3 Cougar Shifter Novel) *(Ralph & Hazel)*

Petty Much In Love (Petty Betty 3) *(Lia and Oskar)*

'Un Poquito' Petty (Petty Betty Book 4) *(Kati & Lawrence)*